Murder in Bloody Weald

A Redmond and Haze Mystery

Book 16

By Irina Shapiro

Copyright

© 2025 by Irina Shapiro

All rights reserved. No part of this book may be reproduced in any form, except for quotations in printed reviews, without permission in writing from the author.

All characters are fictional. Any resemblances to actual people (except those who are actual historical figures) are purely coincidental.

Cover created by MiblArt

Table of Contents

Prologue 5
Chapter 1 8
Chapter 2 13
Chapter 3 20
Chapter 4 26
Chapter 5 29
Chapter 6 34
Chapter 7 37
Chapter 8 47
Chapter 9 53
Chapter 10 62
Chapter 11 71
Chapter 12 78
Chapter 13 90
Chapter 14 93
Chapter 15 99
Chapter 16 111
Chapter 17 114
Chapter 18 117
Chapter 19 125
Chapter 20 138
Chapter 21 144
Chapter 22 151
Chapter 23 159
Chapter 24 162
Chapter 25 169
Chapter 26 173

Chapter 27 176
Chapter 28 181
Chapter 29 186
Chapter 30 197
Chapter 31 201
Chapter 32 211
Chapter 33 215
Chapter 34 221
Chapter 35 231
Chapter 36 238
Chapter 37 244
Chapter 38 248
Epilogue..255

Prologue

The late afternoon sun dappled the leaves of the massive trees, the shadowy spaces beneath the canopies pleasantly cool, and the ground upturned by gnarled roots and covered by thick bracken. Bloody cranesbill, the flowers that had given the ancient wood its name, were no longer in bloom, but Bloody Weald seemed frozen in time, the trees that had taken root a thousand years before witnesses to centuries of violent conflict and home to outlaws and the travelers who came by every year and camped in nearby Bloody Mead.

This afternoon there was nothing sinister about the medieval forest. The birds were singing, the sun was shining, and school wasn't due to start until next week. Micah wished he didn't have to go back to Westbridge Academy, but if he hoped to become a doctor, he had to get an education. He had thought he wanted to be a detective, like Daniel Haze, but had decided that he would rather save lives than try to unravel the deaths of those already lost. He hadn't told his guardian yet but knew Jason Redmond would be overjoyed to hear that Micah wanted to follow in his footsteps, and Jason would help him in any way he could. No orphaned child could be more blessed, and Micah thanked his lucky stars every day, secretly believing that his mam was looking out for him from heaven. He would make her proud, as well as the Captain—the name Micah still used for Jason Redmond, even though his days in the Union Army were far behind him.

Tom Marin walked next to Micah. He was chattering as usual, pointing out rare birds and deer tracks. Tom's father was a gamekeeper, so Tom spent most of his time outdoors, learning the ways of nature. He would take over for his father one day and raise his family in the tiny cottage that was tied to the Chadwick estate, which was some miles from Bloody Weald. Tom had no other aspirations, and Micah realized that this was probably the last occasion they would spend any considerable time together before life pulled them in different directions. Already they had grown apart, Micah looking to the future as Tom became more deeply rooted in village life. Still, it was nice to have this last summer.

Micah was tired and hungry and was looking forward to a cup of tea and a jam tart. Mrs. Dodson had promised to bake a batch today, and she always set aside a few extra tarts for Micah, who could easily eat four in one sitting. Micah was just about to invite Tom to share this bounty when Tom froze like a deer that had sensed a hunter's presence.

"What is it?" Micah asked. He stopped walking and turned to look at Tom, who was staring straight ahead, his eyes wide and his mouth hanging open.

Tom didn't say anything, just pointed toward something up ahead. Micah squinted, trying to see what had stopped his friend in his tracks. It took a moment, since the man's brown coat blended with his surroundings, and it was difficult to make out his face. The man was very still and appeared to be leaning against a tree, but there was something unnatural about his pose.

"Blimey," Tom said, his voice low. "What do you reckon that's all about?"

"I don't know, but something doesn't feel right," Micah said softly. "Let's tread carefully, yeah?"

Tom nodded, and they made their way forward, stopping every few paces to assess the situation. But by the time they got close enough to see the man clearly, they knew there was no need for stealth. He stood sagging against the tree, only a thick rope wound around his torso holding him up. A burlap sack loosely covered his head, and an arrow protruded from his chest. The front of his coat was soaked with dried blood, and a tall top hat lay upturned on the ground. His clothes were fashionable, the snowy cravat was expertly tied, and the tall leather boots shone with polish. A thick gold watch chain snaked from a button on his waistcoat toward his pocket.

Tom must have noticed it too because he said, "So not robbery, then."

"We have to get the Captain," Micah said. "He'll know what to do."

"Let's go," Tom said, and they took off at a run, their fishing poles slapping against their thighs and the fish Tom carried flapping as if it were still alive.

Micah had seen plenty of dead bodies when he had been a drummer boy during the American Civil War, but those men had been casualties of war who had died on a battlefield. This body was quite different. The man, whoever he was, had not been defending his country or following orders. He was a victim of cold-blooded murder.

Chapter 1

Monday, September 6, 1869

Jason Redmond set down his teacup and leaned against the back of the armchair, his gaze on his wife, who at nearly five months pregnant was the picture of blooming health. The only evidence of her condition was her slightly rounded face and fuller bosom, since her swelling abdomen was disguised by the voluminous skirts of her gown. Katherine planned to make her final public appearance next week, at Daniel Haze and Flora Tarrant's wedding, then she would follow Jason's orders, loosen her corset, and spend the remainder of the pregnancy in peace and comfort.

Not for the first time, Jason reflected on how fortunate they were to be able to leave London and spend the summer at Jason's ancestral estate at a time when so many in the city were ill with cholera. They hadn't resided at Redmond Hall in nearly two years, choosing instead to make their home in Knightsbridge, where Katherine could participate in charitable causes and help those in need, and Jason could volunteer at St. George's Hospital, and lend his services to Scotland Yard. The Yard had its own staff surgeon, but Jason took on the more challenging cases, conducting autopsies on victims whose deaths weren't straightforward and whose postmortem results could help build a picture not only of their lives but also their final moments, which was sometimes vital to solving a crime.

"Can I pour you more tea?" Jason asked when Katherine set her cup down next to his.

Katherine smiled at him indulgently. Men weren't supposed to pour out. That was the woman's job, but Katherine was used to Jason's unconventional ways and no longer tried to guide him when it came to social conventions. She liked the fact that he was different, and when she called him *Yank*, Jason saw the affection in her eyes and the quirking of her mouth. They were truly blessed, and Jason was thankful every day that he had been granted a second chance at life after he had nearly died in Georgia toward the end of the American Civil War.

"Please," Katherine said, and rested her hand on her stomach, her face glowing with contentment.

Jason refreshed Katherine's tea, added a splash of milk, and placed two fairy cakes on her saucer, then passed the tea back to her.

"I've already had two cakes," Katherine protested.

"Have two more. It's a long while until dinner, and you should eat something every few hours."

Katherine obediently took a bite of a dainty cake and set it down on the plate. "I'm absolutely fine, Jason. You needn't fuss."

"Spoken like a true Brit," Jason replied, and reached for the last fairy cake, which he popped into his mouth.

He knew Katherine was fine, but he still worried. So many things could go wrong, and a staggering number of women died either during or after childbirth. As did their children. The healthier and stronger Katherine was, the better chance that she would survive the delivery and recover normally in the weeks after. Jason tried not to think too much about their baby. He wanted to picture the infant and couldn't wait to hold it in his arms, but he had grown more superstitious than he liked to admit and didn't care to tempt fate. One day at a time, he reminded himself. One day at a time.

Jason was distracted from his thoughts by a commotion in the foyer and Dodson's reproachful tone. And then, Micah and Tom exploded into the drawing room, Dodson on their heels, his expression apologetic.

"I'm sorry, my lord," he began, but Jason waved his apology away, immediately recognizing that something was wrong.

The boys were pale, their breathing ragged as they looked from Jason to Katherine, as though uncertain if they should speak until Katherine left the room.

"What is it? What's wrong?" Jason asked, looking the boys over carefully to make certain no one was hurt.

They both looked fine, but something had clearly happened, and it had to be serious since neither boy was easily frightened.

"Let's talk in the library," Jason said, and shepherded the boys out of the drawing room. He didn't want Katherine upset and needed to hear their account on his own before he shared the news with her.

"There's a body. In the woods," Micah cried as soon as Jason shut the door behind them. Micah was no stranger to violent death, and it took much to rattle him to such a degree.

"Did you recognize the deceased?" Jason asked.

"We didn't see his face," Tom said. "He was tied to a tree, and someone put a sack over his head."

"You think this man was murdered?"

Jason fervently hoped this was some silly prank and the person wasn't really dead, but he instinctively knew that his hope was in vain. Micah and Tom knew a dead body when they saw one, and Jason was certain they would have checked before running all the way back to summon him.

The boys nodded in unison. "He was shot with an arrow, right through the heart," Tom exclaimed. "His coat was soaked with blood."

"Where did you find him?"

"We were walking back from our favorite fishing spot," Micah said. "We were hungry, so we took a shortcut through Bloody Weald."

Jason had passed through Bloody Weald only a handful of times, and mostly on horseback, since the road that cut through the wood wasn't wide enough for a carriage. The growth was dense, the silence almost menacing, especially after dark. Bloody Weald was part of both the Chadwick and Talbot estates but included public walking paths, since the people of Birch Hill and the surrounding villages had cut through the forest for centuries. It was a place of myth and legend, and there were some who claimed that King Arthur's Camelot had been located at Colchester and that Arthur and his knights had ridden frequently through the forest. Jason didn't really believe King Arthur had ever existed, but it was a nice story, and he could easily accept that the forest had seen its share of clashes and had offered shelter to people in search of a safe haven.

"Is there anything else you can tell me about the victim?" Jason asked as he studied the boys' anxious faces.

"He is dressed like a gentleman," Micah said. "And I think he is young."

"His watch was still in his waistcoat pocket, so he wasn't robbed," Tom added.

"How did he get there?" Jason asked. "Did you see a horse?" The boys shook their heads. "Was there anything near the victim?"

"No," Micah said. "We didn't see anything."

Jason nodded, his mind already weighing up the situation. The boys weren't skilled at assessing a crime scene, and they had been frightened by what they'd found. Whoever had killed the man could have left clues behind, but before Jason and Daniel searched the area, they had to identify the victim. There had to be a reason someone had put a bag over his head.

"Can you find your way back to where you saw this man?"

"Yes," Tom said. Micah nodded.

"Okay. Tom, fetch Inspector Haze and bring him to the woods. Micah, lead me to the body. Not a word to anyone," Jason warned the boys just before opening the library door.

Jason hurried upstairs and grabbed his medical bag, just in case, but he didn't think he'd have need of it. If the man had been shot through the heart, chances were he was long dead, and there was even less chance that the death had been the result of an accident. It seemed Jason didn't have to return to London to investigate a case. Murder had come to Birch Hill once again, and it was up to him and Daniel to see justice done, since there was no longer a parish constable in the village, and the Brentwood Police station was nearly an hour away.

"Lead the way," Jason said as he followed Micah outside. Micah nodded and took off at a trot.

Chapter 2

Daniel maneuvered the dogcart down the narrow path, then tied up the horse as close as he could to the place where Tom claimed he and Micah had found the body. By the time Tom led Daniel to the spot, Jason and Micah were already there, the two standing well back and staring at the corpse. Jason's medical bag was on the ground, near the tree, but Daniel could see right away that the victim was beyond earthly help. The head was covered with a burlap bag and tilted to the side, the hands hanging limp. The rope was wound twice around the man's chest, the knot behind the tree, where he couldn't have reached it even if he'd tried to free himself.

Tom had been accurate in his description. The man appeared to be young and fit, and well-to-do. The coat was made of fine broadcloth, and the boots must have cost more than Daniel earned in a month. The buttons of the waistcoat had the gleam of polished silver, and the watchchain could be goldplate, but Daniel suspected it was solid gold. The victim's silk top hat looked brand new and shone dully in the sunlight filtering through the trees.

"I came as quickly as I could," Daniel said when both Jason and Micah turned at the sound of him and Tom crashing through the forest. "Should we send for Inspector Pullman?"

As an inspector with Scotland Yard, Daniel did not have official jurisdiction in Essex since Essex had its own police service, and given that he was getting married in less than a week, the last thing he wanted was to become embroiled in what was clearly murder. Inspector Pullman, who had assisted Daniel many times while Daniel had served at the Brentwood Constabulary, was still green and needed time to gain experience, but he was competent enough. And if he needed help, he could always turn to his boss, Detective Inspector Coleridge, who had been something of a mentor to Daniel and had been happy to help when Jason and Daniel had found themselves on his patch.

Jason shook his head but didn't respond to Daniel's inquiry.

"What can you tell me?" Daniel asked, wondering why Jason was being so reticent.

"Rigor mortis has set in, and there is evidence of livor mortis in the fingers, since blood begins to pool in the lowest points of the body approximately six hours after death. I expect there's livor mortis in the feet as well, since the victim was left upright. I would put the time of death somewhere between ten a.m. and noon. The cause of death appears to be an arrow to the victim's heart. I think he was shot at fairly close range."

"Why do you think that?" Daniel asked.

"The forest is densely wooded, but the killer was able to aim straight for the heart. Had they been far away, a branch or a tree trunk might have got in the way."

"The killer had to be skilled with a bow and arrow," Daniel observed.

"Yes. I doubt this was a lucky shot. I searched the area before you arrived but saw nothing out of the ordinary. No other arrows, no broken branches or twigs."

"In other words, no evidence of someone crashing through the woods," Daniel surmised.

"Exactly. This wasn't someone who was in a panic, which would suggest that this was planned."

"So, you think the killer was lying in wait?" Daniel asked.

"It's possible, but they would have had to know that the victim would be coming this way."

"Or they might have followed him at a distance. Like a hunter stalking their prey," Tom suggested.

"Yes, they might have," Jason agreed, "but they would have to be stealthy to avoid detection."

"Maybe the victim realized he was being followed, and this is where the confrontation took place," Micah suggested.

Jason shook his head. "The killer would have to be a few yards away for the arrow to gain enough velocity to pierce skin and muscle. And since the victim was shot in the chest, he was likely walking toward the killer rather than away from them."

"Maybe they tied him first," Micah speculated, "and used him for target practice."

"The victim's hands are covered with blood, but his clothes are not in disarray, and there are no bruises on his hands or wrists. I think he clutched at the wound when he was shot but knew not to pull out the arrow because the tip would do more damage when extracted. I suspect the killer tied up the victim once he was already dead and put the bag on his head."

"To hide his identity?" Micah asked.

"Possibly. Or maybe to preserve his face for as long as possible before the birds and the animals got to him," Jason replied.

"Do you know who he is?" Daniel asked, his gaze going to the burlap sack.

He was surprised Jason had waited to remove the sack. It would have been the first thing Daniel would have done when arriving on the scene, and Jason's decision to wait made Daniel uneasy. Try as he might, he couldn't see anything through the dense weave, and the sack covered the man down to his cravat, so even his neck wasn't visible. Apprehension raced up Daniel's spine like a centipede and settled heavily beneath his breastbone. At this point, the need to know overrode every other instinct.

Jason turned to Micah and Tom, who were watching Jason intently, their eyes round with curiosity and shock. Daniel thought

Jason would send the boys away, but then Jason turned back to Daniel.

"I didn't take off the sack, but I know who the victim is."

"How?" Daniel asked.

"I recognize the watch, and I have seen him wear that waistcoat."

Unable to bear the suspense any longer, Daniel approached the body and pulled off the sack. His breath escaped in a loud whoosh when he came face to face with the victim. He'd seen that face before, knew that gleaming hair, and had looked into the eyes that had either twinkled with amusement or been narrowed in mockery or anger. The bright blue irises were frozen in a blank stare of death, but the eyes were still beautiful. The man's generous mouth was slack, the golden stubble on his cheeks glinting in the late afternoon sun. Even in death, the victim looked like the subject of a medieval painting, his modern clothes the only thing that distinguished him from a Biblical saint. St. Sebastian came to mind, writhing in agony as his body was pierced with arrows, but the man before them was no saint. In fact, he was more closely related to the devil.

"Tristan Carmichael," Daniel said quietly.

He wasn't all that surprised to find that someone had finally taken justice into their own hands, as the Carmichaels had many enemies, but he was shocked by the method of the murder. He would have thought that Carmichael would get shot with a gun or shanked in the back, but Daniel had never expected to find an arrow protruding from the man's chest. There had to be some hidden symbolism to Carmichael's death, even though the man before Daniel had been anything but a martyr, but at the moment, the only thing on Daniel's mind was his upcoming wedding and the wedding trip he and Flora planned to take. They were going to Scotland, where it was colder and the outbreak of cholera that had been raging in the South for months wasn't a threat.

Daniel had been looking forward to spending time with his bride, who had been tantalizingly close but just out of his reach these past few months. They would be truly alone for the first time, free to explore their feelings and bodies at leisure. Their wedding trip would be slow and luxurious, the weeks away devoid of the fear, pain, and never-ending ugliness that had punctuated Daniel's London life. Daniel thought of all the ways in which his precious happiness could be disrupted if he allowed himself to get involved in the investigation, and he unwittingly shook his head, desperate to push away a gnawing sense of inevitability.

"I think you and I need to take this one, Jason," Daniel said at last. "We have too much history with the Carmichaels to allow Inspector Pullman to head up the investigation."

Inspector Pullman, for all his good intentions, wasn't qualified to unpick the life and death of a man who'd been a viper in a nest that spanned both Essex and London and was expanding daily by means of opium, prostitution, smuggling, and intimidation.

More than anything, Daniel wanted to turn the investigation over to the Brentwood Constabulary and wash his hands of the Carmichaels, but this wasn't a case for the local police. This went much deeper and might lead to London, where Brentwood officers had no authority, and Scotland Yard would need to get involved.

"We owe him nothing," Jason said.

"No, we don't, but we owe it to the community. This murder happened on our patch. It's important to figure out what happened and if this was an isolated incident or part of a bigger conflict that could put Birch Hill at the center of a turf war."

Jason sighed heavily. "Well, when you put it that way."

"Let's get him down," Daniel said. "Where do you want to move the body?"

"Redmond Hall. There's a disused shed behind the stables. It's cool, so the body will keep for several days."

"I came in a dogcart, so I'll be able to deliver the body to you."

"Thank you." Jason walked behind the tree and began to untie the rope. "This is an unusual knot," he said.

"It almost looks medieval," Micah piped up.

"How so?" Jason asked.

Micah shrugged. "I've seen something like it in a drawing."

"A drawing of what?"

"I think it was of a ship. This might be a nautical knot," Micah said eagerly.

Jason seemed to file the information away, and the two men worked to untie the rope and lower the body to the ground.

"Shall we pull out the arrow?" Daniel asked. The arrowhead was embedded deep inside the body and would probably mangle the flesh if pulled backward.

"Let's leave it for now," Jason said. "I'll remove it surgically once I get him on the table. And let's put up the top of the cart to shield the body from view. We don't want anyone to see you with Tristan Carmichael's earthly remains. You know how gossip spreads around here."

Daniel nodded. Little of interest happened in Birch Hill, and the Carmichaels were both respected and feared since their influence stretched far and wide, as did the profits from their business dealings. There would be some who would jump to unwarranted conclusions that could result in Daniel arriving at church in a casket rather than his wedding finery.

Daniel nodded and bent down to grab the legs. Jason picked up Carmichael's torso, and together they carried the body to the cart. Rigor mortis prevented them from bending Tristan's legs, so they positioned the body against the seat and anchored it by planting Tristan's feet against the front panel. Then Daniel pulled up the leather top in case he should come across someone in the lane. The top did not conceal the body, but the shadow it cast made it more difficult to make out the passenger's face and upper body. Unless the driver of the oncoming vehicle slowed down and looked very closely, they would not notice the shaft of the arrow or make out the dried blood on Carmichael's brown coat.

Micah ran up behind them and handed Jason Tristan's top hat, which Jason plopped on Carmichael's head.

"See you at Redmond Hall," Daniel said once he had climbed in and taken up the reins.

Jason lifted a hand in farewell, and he and Micah headed back to collect his bag, the rope, and Tom.

Chapter 3

Once Daniel had brought the body and the boys had been dispatched to the kitchen to enjoy well-deserved tea and jam tarts, Jason and Daniel reconvened in the shed. Tristan Carmichael's body lay on the trestle table between them, and the late-afternoon light gilded his features, making him look as if he were merely asleep since Jason had shut the man's eyes. If not for the arrow protruding from Tristan's chest, Daniel would have expected him to awaken, sit up, and demand to know what he was doing in Jason's shed.

"Are you going to autopsy him?" Daniel asked once he'd managed to tear his gaze from Tristan's still face.

"The cause of death is obvious, and, in this case, I don't think I should open up the body without permission."

"Yes, I agree."

Tristan Carmichael was the only son of Lance Carmichael, who'd held Essex in a firm grip of vice for decades and wouldn't look kindly on Tristan's body undergoing an unauthorized postmortem in a shed by the stables. Such lack of respect might lead to repercussions neither Daniel nor Jason were prepared to risk, not because they were afraid for themselves, but because they feared for their loved ones.

Lance Carmichael's name elicited fear in everyone, from gentlemen, whose many sins Carmichael could divulge whenever he chose to, to working men, whose businesses and jobs could disappear on Carmichael's say-so, leaving their families to starve. Lance Carmichael was good to those who served him well and poured money into his many enterprises, but the threat was always there, and everyone knew of someone who'd stepped out of line and had paid the ultimate price in either reputation, fortune, or their very life.

The Carmichael network had grown exponentially since Tristan had been sent to London to oversee expansion into the city and had managed to quash or absorb several less-powerful gangs in order to take control of the East Side. Despite playing at being a gentleman and adopting the dress and manners of his betters, Tristan had been a remorseless thug. The promise of grievous bodily harm or financial ruin had usually been enough to get him what he'd wanted, and as he had explained to Jason when Jason had questioned him in connection with the abduction of Charlotte Haze, the gangs operated according to their own code of honor. For the most part, this meant they did not go after each other's wives or children and limited their vengeance to those directly involved, but that could always change, depending on the offense, and an entire family could be exterminated.

"We need to inform Lance Carmichael of his son's death," Daniel said. "I expect he will tell the rest of the family and send someone to collect the body."

"I would rather his men did not come to my home, but I don't care to keep the remains here any longer than necessary either. Perhaps I will deliver the body myself," Jason replied.

"What was Tristan doing here?" Daniel asked as he looked down at the corpse. "He was based in London, and even if he had come to visit his family, he wouldn't be anywhere near Bloody Weald."

"Perhaps he'd come to see someone else," Jason suggested.

"You mean Davy Brody?"

"Davy has a long history of working with the Carmichaels and sells their ale at the Red Stag. And at one time, Tristan was very fond of Moll Brody."

Tristan and Moll had enjoyed a brief courtship several years before, but their budding romance had come to an abrupt end when Lance had discovered that his son had been cozying up to a barmaid who was known to be generous with her affections. Moll wasn't the sort of woman Lance had wanted for his son, and shortly after the relationship had ended, Tristan had married a woman of his father's choosing. Last Daniel had heard, Tristan and his bride had welcomed a son, and by his own admission, Tristan also had an illegitimate son from a liaison he'd engaged in before his marriage. The boy would be about two or three now and lived with his mother, but Tristan had taken an interest in his son and made sure the child and his mother wanted for nothing.

"Moll would be a good place to start," Jason said.

"But Moll is married to Bruce Plimpton now," Daniel protested.

"I'm not suggesting that Moll and Tristan were still romantically involved, but Moll always knew everything that went on in the village and beyond. And she's married to a known associate of the Carmichaels. She might know what Tristan was doing in Birch Hill and whom he might have been meeting in the woods."

"You think he was meeting someone?" Daniel asked.

"Tristan Carmichael never struck me as someone who enjoyed nature. Why else would he go to Bloody Weald if not to meet with someone in secret?"

"Moll doesn't even live in Birch Hill anymore," Daniel reminded Jason.

"No, but she still has ties to the village and comes to visit her uncle on a regular basis."

"How do you know?" Daniel asked, genuinely curious.

Jason's interaction with the villagers was limited to the family's weekly outing to church and the occasional accident that required surgical intervention. He wasn't the sort to gossip with his patients, and Katherine Redmond wasn't one to engage in baseless tittle-tattle.

"Moll and Mary grew close while Mary lived with us in Birch Hill," Jason replied. "Moll still sees Mary from time to time. I believe they met several times over the summer."

Daniel nodded. That made perfect sense. Micah's sister, Mary, had never quite fit in in Birch Hill. Neither family nor a servant in Jason's home, Mary was the only Irish inhabitant in the village other than Micah, and her fiery nature as well as her illegitimate child had made her something of a pariah among the villagers. Moll, who had a reputation of her own to contend with, had befriended Mary, and the two young women had probably confided in each other, knowing they wouldn't be harshly judged. Daniel hadn't known that they had renewed their friendship since Mary had returned from America, but it made perfect sense that they would find comfort in each other's company once again.

"Do you think Mary might know something?" Daniel asked.

"I doubt it, but I will ask," Jason promised. "But first, I need to learn as much as possible from the body and the method of murder without conducting a postmortem."

"Is there anything unique about the arrow?" Daniel asked.

"I don't know very much about archery, but it looks fairly standard to me. The fletching is made of brownish feathers. Maybe pheasant or wild turkey. What do you think?"

Daniel ran his fingers over the fletching. "I expect some noblemen prefer to use distinctive fletching, but they would use arrows only when bow hunting on their own land, which is rare these days. I've never been invited to join a hunt, but I believe rifles are the weapons of choice."

"And what would they use for fletching if they did hunt with a bow?"

"Probably feathers from birds found on their estate, but they wouldn't make the arrows themselves."

"So, who would make the arrows for them?"

Daniel shrugged. "Perhaps their gamekeepers, or they would have the arrows custom made."

"Do you know of anyone in or around Birch Hill who hunts with a bow?" Jason asked.

"Bloody Weald lies at the edge of the Chadwick and Talbot estates, but there hasn't been a hunt organized by the Chadwicks since Colonel Chadwick died, and Tom would recognize the arrow if it was made by his father."

"What about Squire Talbot?"

"The squire used to join hunts organized by Colonel Chadwick, but the Talbots are still in half mourning for their daughter. According to my mother-in-law, they occasionally dine in company but don't accept invitations to any other social events. And Squire Talbot is not someone who has ever hunted for the pleasure of it."

"Would a bow and arrow be used for anything else?" Jason asked.

"Archery competitions."

"What about poaching?"

Daniel considered the question. "I suppose it's possible, but poachers usually come out at night, which would make it difficult to hunt with a bow, especially since most animals go to ground after sunset. Poachers are more likely to use traps, but I don't believe anyone in the area has reported an ongoing problem with poachers in recent years."

"I see," Jason said resignedly. "There isn't much to go on."

"No."

The light that streamed through the open door of the shed had softened, the rays slanting as the autumn sun began its descent toward the horizon. It was too late in the day to do anything but wish each other a good evening and return to their respective homes.

"I will call on Lance Carmichael first thing tomorrow," Daniel said as he moved toward the door.

"And I will have a word with Moll."

"She always did have a soft spot for you, but then Moll had a soft spot for anything in trousers," Daniel said.

"People are quick to jump to conclusions," Jason replied sternly. "I don't know that Moll ever indulged her passions, but her flirtatious nature made her an easy mark. I'm glad she's finally settled, although I do wish she'd picked a man who's not affiliated with the Carmichaels, even peripherally."

He reached for a padlock that rested on a dusty shelf and turned the key experimentally to make sure it worked. Then the two men stepped outside, and Jason locked the shed behind them, putting the key in his pocket before they walked companionably toward the house in the gathering twilight.

Chapter 4

When Daniel returned to his mother-in-law's house, where he was staying until the wedding, he wished he could go up to his room, but it would have been rude not to join Mrs. Elderman for dinner, since it was just the two of them. Charlotte had eaten a nursery supper and was already in bed, and Tilda was ready to serve the first course as soon as Daniel washed up and presented himself in the dining room. Daniel thought he smelled roast chicken and hoped his mind wasn't playing tricks on him since Mrs. Elderman had been subsisting on a diet of mostly clear soup and steamed fish due to frequent indigestion. Daniel was ready for something more substantial, but even if Tilda had made mutton chops, which were a favorite, he would still have misgivings about dining with Mrs. Elderman.

Daniel had always liked his mother-in-law and had leaned on her after Sarah had died, but now, being in the house where he and Sarah had lived, where Felix and Charlotte had been born, and where Sarah had been laid out before her funeral, Daniel felt like he couldn't breathe. Harriet must have felt the strain too because when Daniel joined her at the table, her shoulders were slumped, and her gaze was fixed on her empty plate. She still wore unrelieved black in honor of the daughter she had lost, and her face and hair had become grayer, the strands of dark brown now overwhelmed by silver.

Daniel suddenly realized how much older she looked and how melancholy she had become since he had taken Charlotte back to London after leaving her with her grandmother for several months following Charlotte's terrifying abduction. Harriet had been happy to have Charlotte and had offered to keep her indefinitely, but Daniel had refused. Charlotte was his daughter, and she belonged with him, and now she was to have a new mother, a circumstance Harriet accepted but was understandably distressed about, even though she knew and liked Flora.

"I'm sorry," Daniel said once Tilda served the soup and left them on their own.

He wasn't sure what he was apologizing for, probably all of it, but he felt it needed to be said, and the tension and simmering resentment between him and Harriet acknowledged.

"I know, Daniel," Harriet said, and lifted her gaze to look at him.

"You will still see Charlotte all the time," Daniel promised, but he wondered if that was true.

They would have to visit Flora's parents from time to time, but Ardith Hall was miles from Birch Hill, and it would be awkward to visit his ex-mother-in-law. Harriet liked Flora just fine as Charlotte's nanny and thought her calm, self-assured manner was good for the child, but now Flora was to be Charlotte's mother, so the balance of power between the two women would change. Flora would no longer have to defer to Harriet, and Harriet would have to court Flora's favor if she hoped to remain part of her granddaughter's life. Daniel would never intentionally exclude Harriet, but he couldn't promise that after the marriage she would remain as big a part of his and Charlotte's lives as she had been.

"I don't think I am going to attend the wedding, Daniel," Harriet said.

She seemed to fold in on herself as she said this, as if bracing for his anger, but Daniel understood. How could Harriet watch him marry someone else when her daughter was buried in the church graveyard, next to the grandson who'd never grow into a man? How could she encourage Charlotte to hold the hand of the woman who would from that day on be her mother and replace Sarah in all the ways that mattered? And how could she let go of the life she'd had when there was nothing to fill the hours until a permanent night descended, and she joined her loved ones in the afterlife?

To die young was cruel, but to outlive everyone you loved was sometimes even crueler. It was a punishment for being strong and resilient, and for holding on when there was nothing left to live for. Daniel wished he could tell Harriet that she would be a part of his new family, but that would be unkind, since he couldn't really deliver on such a promise. Flora wanted to live in London, as far away from Birch Hill as possible, and Daniel was in no rush to return to the place where he'd known so much loss and pain.

"I wish you nothing but joy, Daniel. You deserve it, and Flora will be a good wife to you, but I can't bear to watch you start a new life when Sarah's life is done."

"I quite understand, Mrs. Elderman," Daniel said, and swallowed hard.

"How did it all go so wrong for us?" Harriet asked mournfully.

Daniel didn't think she expected a reply and didn't make one because he didn't know. The obvious answer was that Felix's death had crushed Sarah in a way she had never been able to fully recover from, but looking back, Daniel thought that perhaps the signs had always been there. Sarah had been given to melancholia even before they had married and had never quite got over her father's death. Her emotional fragility combined with the guilt she had felt after Felix's accident had been too much for her to bear, even though she'd still had a loving husband and a new baby to live for. Daniel no longer blamed Sarah for taking her own life. Shattered as he had been after her death, he was ready to move on and refused to feel guilty. He might not have swallowed a bottle of laudanum to numb his pain, but he had hurt, and he didn't want to hurt anymore. It was time to move forward.

The remainder of the meal passed in silence, and when Daniel wished Harriet a good night and trudged upstairs to the bedroom he'd shared with Sarah, he knew that he would never return to this house, at least not to stay for any length of time. He couldn't wait for his family to return to their little house in London, but before he got married and went home, he had a murder to solve.

Chapter 5

Jason had no choice but to tell Katherine what had happened to Tristan Carmichael and allow her to speculate at length over dinner. She'd find out soon enough anyway, since news traveled fast in these sleepy hamlets, the villagers eager to share even the most mundane tidbits out of sheer boredom and boundless curiosity. Micah was only too happy to join in with his own theories, but by the time dinner came to an end, they were no closer to a plausible scenario and had come up with more questions than answers. Jason had hoped to speak to Mary, but she had asked for a tray in her room and had retired after putting the children to sleep.

Once Katherine had retreated to the drawing room to read for a while before going up to bed, Jason made his way upstairs and knocked on Mary's door.

"Come in," Mary called.

Her voice sounded weak, and she looked tired and drawn when Jason entered the room. Mary was sitting in an armchair by the window, her gaze fixed on the lush parkland beyond. She was still fully dressed, but the top two buttons of her collar were undone to reveal the pale column of her neck, and the fiery red hair that she had pinned up first thing in the morning tumbled about her shoulders, the waves rippling about her face like leaping flames.

"Mary, are you all right?" Jason asked. "I had hoped you would join us for dinner."

"I'm sorry, Captain, but I heard what happened from Micah and couldn't bear to hear talk of death."

"I can understand that," Jason said.

Mary didn't often mention her late husband, who had been murdered not long after they had been married. His death had been retribution for skimming proceeds from his Boston gang bosses and a warning to Mary to return the stolen funds. In fear for her life, Mary had been forced to flee and had found her way to the only safe harbor she could think of—the Redmonds—but her infant daughter had died during the crossing, a tragedy that had left a deep, jagged scar on Mary's heart that would likely never fully heal.

Catriona was the most recent name in a long list of people Mary had lost and had been unable to bury or mourn properly. Her father's and older brother's bodies had been consigned to a mass grave in Georgia. Her son Liam's father had died on some unnamed battlefield, and she'd had no time to see to her husband's remains. It wasn't hard to see that the losses she'd suffered weighed heavily on Mary, and although she was one of the most resilient people Jason had ever met, no twenty-year-old could suffer that much and not be profoundly changed. Jason desperately wished he could help, as he had helped Micah over the years, but Mary wasn't like her little brother and would not freely accept what Jason offered, her pride preventing her from relying on him so completely.

"I'm tired, Captain. Tired of this life," Mary said softly, her gaze fixed on some distant point. Her Irish lilt was more pronounced when she was angry or sad, and Jason heard it now, a cry for help from her wounded soul.

"Please don't say that," Jason implored as he drew closer.

He wanted to pull Mary into his arms and hold her, but that would be inappropriate and might be taken the wrong way. Instead, he stood awkwardly in the middle of the room, his gaze trained on the lonely girl by the window.

"I don't know where I belong," Mary said quietly. "When I was in America, I longed for England, and now that I'm here, I long for home."

"I know just how you feel, Mary," Jason said. "I felt much the same after I was freed from the prison camp. I had dreamed of coming home, but when I got there, my parents were gone, my fiancée was married to another man, and I wasn't the same person who'd gone off to fight only a few years before. It took time for me to come to terms with everything that had happened and begin to build a new life."

Mary nodded, and Jason could see what she wanted to say but intentionally held back for fear of offending him. He hadn't lost two lovers in only a few years, nor had he lost a child. His daughter slept upstairs in the lovely nursery that was big enough for half a dozen children. His wife was downstairs, happy, healthy, and awaiting the birth of a new baby. And he had a grand home in the country and another in London with a staff to look after his every need.

He also had a profession to fall back on and the admiration and respect of his colleagues, both at the hospital and at Scotland Yard. Jason wasn't an Irish orphan who didn't have two shillings to rub together or any family to rely on save Micah, who although a clever, capable young man was still hardly more than a child in all the ways that mattered.

"Mary, is there anything I can do? You know I only want to help."

"I'm suffocating here, Captain. I want to go back to London, where at least there are others like me. I need to go to Mass and light a candle for my girl. And I must earn a living."

"We will be back in London in a matter of weeks. I will be happy to come with you to Mass, if you will permit me, and I will gladly assist you in finding employment."

Mary cocked her head and fixed him with a blue stare. Jason could see that there was something she had settled on but was wary of asking.

"What is it, Mary? What can I do?" he asked gently.

Mary sighed. "I would like to go to Florence Nightingale's school of nursing at St. Thomas's Hospital, but there are impediments," she said quietly.

Jason nodded. He knew what those impediments were. Given her personal and cultural background, Mary might not be accepted, and if she was, she would have to live at the dormitory until she completed the program, which typically lasted a year. Once finished, the nurses were immediately placed in private homes or institutions, a situation Mary would not qualify for because she had a child.

"And if there were no impediments, would becoming a nurse make you happy?"

"I enjoy caring for people, and I need to know that I can earn a fair wage that will allow me to support myself and Liam until he comes of age. I cannot rely on your help for the rest of my days, Captain. It's not fair to you or me."

"I agree, so here's what I propose," Jason said. He had to think on his feet, but all he needed was an outline of a plan. The rest could be worked out later. "I will ensure you are accepted into the program. The head of surgery at St. Thomas's owes me a favor and can put in a good word with the committee. Liam will remain with us until you complete the course. Once you have qualified as a nurse, I will help you find a live-out position so that you can come home at the end of the day. And if you choose to accept a live-in situation, then we will reassess and decide what's best for Liam. How does that sound?"

Mary blessed Jason with a tearful smile and nodded. "You are too good to me, Captain, and love me way more than I deserve."

"Mary, you are a member of my family, and Liam will always have a place with us, as one of our children. You need never worry about him."

"You owe us nothing," Mary cried.

"I owe you everything," Jason replied without a moment's hesitation. "If not for Micah, I don't think I would have survived Andersonville Prison. I would have died like so many others because they could no longer find a reason to hold on. I had a little boy to care for, so I forced myself to wake every day and put one foot in front of the other so that he would have someone to hold him when he cried at night. You and Micah are mine not by blood but by choice, and that's just as precious. Stop tearing yourself up, Mary, and let us love you."

Mary nodded as tears slid down her face. "God really does work in mysterious ways, doesn't he, Captain?"

"So I'm told. Do we have an agreement?"

"Yes," Mary whispered. "And thank you. I feel so much more hopeful."

Mary stood and flew into Jason's arms, allowing him to hold her at last. It was only after he had left her to make her plans that he realized he'd never asked her about Moll.

Chapter 6

Tuesday, September 7

Jason was up well before dawn. He'd slept badly, his slumber plagued by disturbing dreams in which Tristan Carmichael had begged him to find his killer and avenge his death. Jason had never imagined he would take up Tristan Carmichael's cause, and although vengeance was never part of his purpose, he intended to discover what had happened and why. Unless Tristan's death had been the result of a horrible accident, which didn't seem likely, someone had set out to kill him in a strange and primitive way. Had the blindfold been meant to mirror an execution, or had the killer pulled the sack over Tristan's head once he had already been dead?

Whoever had shot Tristan Carmichal had come prepared with a weapon, rope, and a sack, which could speak to premeditation, but Jason supposed a hunter might have those things to hand as well. The sack could hold small animals or bait for traps, and the rope might be used to hoist a larger kill, such as a deer, while the hunter disemboweled and exsanguinated the carcass. Perhaps someone had shot Carmichael by accident, and instead of alerting the proper authorities, they had panicked and decided to make the death look like murder. That didn't strike Jason as a very reasonable plan, but people did illogical things when in the grip of fear. Jason didn't think it was likely, though. His gut instinct, which had been honed during previous investigations, told him they were looking for someone with intent.

It was difficult enough to discern the motive when the victim had led a relatively blameless life, but Tristan Carmichael must have made dozens of enemies who would be only too happy to dispatch him, especially if they could find a way to get away with it. The method of murder was key, Jason decided as he faced himself in the mirror and scraped a razor across his jaw. If Carmichael had been murdered by a rival, why would they kill him in such an unusual way? The gangs were known for stabbing, clubbing, and gunning down their enemies, so why would anyone decide on a weapon more appropriate to the Middle Ages? And if the killing had been personal in nature, the method still made little sense.

And why kill him in a forest in Essex? Tristan spent most of his time in London. The Carmichaels received shipments by boat and kept several warehouses near the docks. What better way to dispose of a body than to toss it into the Thames? The river was the dumping ground for all sorts of refuse, much of it organic in nature. Dead animals, bodies of suicides, and unidentified victims of crime floated down the river in an endless procession. Jason couldn't help but think that there was symbolism in the way Tristan had been killed, but until he learned more about Tristan's life, he could hardly understand the significance of his death.

Jason finished shaving, splashed some water on his face, and dried it with a fresh towel, then headed to his dressing room. Henley usually laid out his clothes the night before, since Jason was frequently up early and didn't require the valet's assistance when getting dressed. He was perfectly capable of tying his own cravat and putting on his coat. He picked up his brush and was surprised to notice several silver strands running through the black hair at his temples when he looked in the mirror. More and more, he resembled his father at the same age, and he recalled quite clearly that he'd thought his dad old when he had only been around thirty-five.

Would Lily and the new child think Jason old when they became adolescents? Probably, but that was the way of parents and children, and by the time the children got to the same age, they realized they weren't old at all but radiated maturity rather than decrepitude. Jason smiled at himself in the mirror. He still had a few good years left to him, and the gray hair made him look distinguished, he decided as he ran a hand through his still-thick locks and headed downstairs.

Mrs. Dodson was already in the kitchen and was happy to make Jason breakfast before he set off. Moll Plimpton, née Brody, lived in a village near Epping. With any luck, her husband Bruce would be at home, so Jason could speak to him as well. Bruce Plimpton's father, Conrad, known to his cronies as Limpy, was a known associate of Lance Carmichael, and their interests tended to overlap more often than not. The relationship between the families went back decades, to when Lance and Limpy had been nothing more than teenage foot soldiers in a gang that had operated near Hullsbridge. Bruce was bound to know something of Tristan's business dealings, but whether he would be willing to help Jason was another matter entirely.

When Jason finished his breakfast and stepped outside into the lovely September morning, Joe was already waiting for him with the brougham. The air was wonderfully crisp, and the sun was shining, and for one mad moment, Jason wished he could ride with Joe on the bench, but that would be unseemly and probably make Joe uncomfortable. Sighing with resignation, he climbed into the carriage and settled in. If he knew country roads, it would be a bumpy ride.

Chapter 7

Daniel was ready to set off for Brentwood immediately after his solitary breakfast. Harriet rarely came downstairs before nine o'clock, and Charlotte had her breakfast in the kitchen, where Tilda could go about her work and keep an eye on the child at the same time. Daniel did pop in to say good morning and wish them both a good day. Charlotte sat at the scrubbed pine table, a half-eaten slice of bread and jam on her plate and an untouched cup of milk at her elbow. Charlotte hated milk, especially if it was warm. Tilda was kneading dough, a smudge of flour on her cheek and a lock of hair falling into her flushed face. It was warm, and the smell of yeast hung in the air, along with the earthy scent of root vegetables that a neighbor had brought by that morning on his way to the market.

"Where are you going, Papa?" Charlotte demanded, her little face set in lines of indignation.

"I'm going to see an old acquaintance."

"Is it about the wedding?"

"No, darling. This is work."

"But you work in London," Charlotte protested. "Why are you working here?"

She was now old enough to make connections and voice her objections, and although Daniel loved this new stage in her development, he also realized he would need to explain himself much more frequently and in a way that was believable because Charlotte could spot a fib from a mile away.

"This is connected to my work in London," Daniel said, which was partially true.

Charlotte looked dubious but accepted his explanation. "When will I see Flora? I miss her."

"Not until the wedding," Daniel said. "It's only a few more days."

Charlotte's eyes filled with tears. "Can't I go to Ardith Hall?"

"I'm afraid you will have to remain here, with your grandmama."

"But I don't want to stay with Grandmama. She doesn't play with me," Charlotte moaned.

"Then you can play by yourself. You have your doll and picture books you can look at."

"Can I go play with Lily and Liam? Tilda can take me."

"Charlotte, Tilda is busy, and you can't go to someone's home uninvited. It's bad manners," Daniel admonished.

"But you go to Redmond Hall uninvited all the time."

He couldn't argue with that. "Maybe you can go play with Lily and Liam tomorrow. Would that be all right?"

"I suppose," Charlotte replied sulkily. "But I'd still rather go see Flora."

"I'm sure you would," Daniel grumbled. He kissed Charlotte's dark curls and patted her gently on the head. "Have a good day, darling, and behave for Grandmama."

Charlotte sighed like a woman who'd known hardship, and Daniel beat a hasty retreat before she thought of something else she needed to tell him.

As he climbed into the dogcart, he inwardly admitted that he was nervous about the upcoming meeting with Lance Carmichael. The elder Carmichael was unforgiving and fierce, and unlike his son, who had been young and cocky and had at times relied on his good looks and charm to achieve his goals, Lance tended to resort to intimidation and didn't see the point of bothering with social niceties. And he wasn't likely to thank the man who delivered news of his son's death.

If ever there was an occasion to kill the messenger, this was it. Not for the first time since discovering the body, Daniel wished he hadn't involved himself in this case, but now that Tristan's remains reposed in Jason's shed, it was too late to change his mind. Lance Carmichael would be made aware of the circumstances in which Tristan had been discovered and demand to know where his body was being kept.

When Daniel pulled up to the Carmichaels' palatial home on the outskirts of Brentwood and passed through the tall wrought-iron gates that led to a curving, tree-lined drive, he reflected that the family had risen even further than he had realized. The house was immense, and the grounds and parkland were extensive and beautifully upkept. Carmichael had either purchased the house from some down-on-their-luck noble family or had taken it by force as payment or punishment for some transgression. Lance was the sovereign of his own kingdom, and he was about to learn that the heir apparent would not inherit the world his father had created for him.

An adolescent boy came running from the stables to greet Daniel as soon as he approached the grand entrance. The portico was supported by eight soaring Corinthian columns, and the steps were so wide that at least ten people could walk shoulder to shoulder without actually touching. Stone urns large enough for Daniel to hide in flanked the lower steps and contained a profusion of flowers that added a spot of color to the gray stone façade. The boy took hold of the bridle and would look after the horse and cart while Daniel was inside and bring them around once he was ready to leave, but that was only if Daniel was admitted.

Four men came through the front door and made their way down the steps toward Daniel, their hands on pistols that were worn in leather holsters for easy reach. Three of the four were strapping young lads, but it was obvious that the older man was in charge. He was of middling height but had the thick neck, powerful shoulders, and well-muscled arms of someone who frequently engaged in physical activity, most likely boxing, or bare-knuckle fighting. His carefully oiled black hair was parted in the center, he had deep-set dark eyes and heavy brows, and his nose looked to have been broken, since it wasn't perfectly straight and had a noticeable bump at the bridge. The man wore his tweed cap at a rakish angle, and unlike the other three, he wore a satin waistcoat and a tie.

"Who are you, and what's your business here?" he asked as he openly sized up Daniel.

"I am Inspector Haze of Scotland Yard, and I must see Mr. Carmichael."

"Mr. Carmichael doesn't see coppers," the man sniggered. The other three chuckled as if he'd said something very amusing.

"It's urgent that I speak to him. I'm afraid I have news of the worst kind."

"And what news might that be, Inspector?"

Daniel didn't think he should share the news with Carmichael's flunkies, but if he didn't, he would be sent packing. "Mr. Carmichael's son, Tristan, is dead. His body was discovered in Bloody Weald."

The men exchanged stunned looks, as if silently asking if Daniel might be making this up in order to gain access to Lance Carmichael. Daniel took advantage of their momentary indecision and continued.

"The body is currently at Redmond Hall in Birch Hill. Lord Redmond, who's a well-respected surgeon, is keeping the remains safe. He has assessed the manner of death and is of the opinion that Tristan Carmichael was murdered."

"You do understand what will happen if this is some sort of trick?" the leader asked.

"I do."

"Frisk him," he said to the man standing next to him.

"Right away, Mr. Roy," the man replied.

"I am not armed," Daniel said, but the man frisked him anyway.

"He's telling the truth. He's not armed."

"I will take you inside, Inspector," Roy said. "You lot keep an eye out in case there are more of them coming."

"Yes, boss," the fellow who had frisked Daniel replied.

Roy led Daniel up the stairs and through the main door, past the butler, who noted their progress but didn't offer to take Daniel's things. He didn't appear surprised by the earliness of Daniel's visit. No self-respecting gentleman would see anyone before noon, but Lance Carmichael was no gentleman, and from what Daniel had heard of the man, he still kept working-man hours and was usually up at dawn.

Roy directed Daniel to a room just off the foyer. "Wait in the receiving room. Someone will be with you shortly."

Roy shut the door behind him as soon as Daniel was inside, and Daniel heard his receding footsteps on the tiled floor. With nothing left to do but wait, Daniel took off his hat, unbuttoned his coat, and settled in a chair that faced the door, the hat resting on his thigh. Looking around, he imagined that there had to be a similar receiving room at Buckingham Palace where visitors were left to wait, or stew.

The top half of the room was covered in pale green wallpaper with a delicate silver pattern, while the lower half was paneled in light-colored wood. The ceiling and window frames were dazzling white, which gave the room a bright, airy feel that was decidedly modern. There were six upholstered armchairs grouped around a low table where refreshments could be served, and a walnut sideboard held several decanters and a dozen cut crystal glasses arranged on a silver tray. A painting of a pastoral scene hung over the mantel, and there were lovely, frosted glass lamps affixed to the walls. Thick moss-green velvet drapes were held back with silver-colored tassels and could be drawn to keep out both the light and prying eyes.

Lance Carmichael probably received a wide range of visitors: business associates, rivals, politicians, and soldiers in his army. He wouldn't want to entertain these men in the drawing room, where he spent time with his family, or in his study, where he was bound to keep confidential papers. He also wouldn't want these men anywhere near his womenfolk, which as far as Daniel knew consisted of his current mistress and Tristan's young wife. Carmichael's two daughters were both married and no longer lived with their father.

Daniel waited for what was probably no more than ten minutes but seemed like an inordinately long time. His anxiety at finding himself alone in Carmichael's lair made him feel trapped, and although the room had seemed airy before, it now felt stuffy and oppressive. Daniel wished Jason had come with him and silently berated himself for his cowardice and unhealthy dependency on Jason Redmond. He was a grown man and an inspector with the greatest police service in the world. He did not need anyone to hold his hand, but he'd be lying if he couldn't admit to himself that he felt as frustrated and fretful as Charlotte when she was forced to confront something she dreaded.

It was a relief of sorts when the door finally opened and the man who'd questioned Daniel walked in, followed by Lance Carmichael. Daniel hadn't seen Lance Carmichael in person in years, and even then he'd only glimpsed him from a distance when Carmichael had come to Birch Hill and had disappeared into the Red Stag, presumably to speak to Davy Brody. Daniel was surprised by how little Carmichael had aged since then. He was of middling height, but he was broad, which gave the impression of strength. His hair, which had once been fair like his son's, was gently silvered but still thick, and his brows, moustache, and beard were more silver than blond. There were faint wrinkles around his eyes, and his forehead bore several horizontal lines that had deepened, but overall Lance Carmichael looked strong and imposing.

Daniel sprang to his feet and bowed from the neck. He wasn't sure of the proper greeting for a crime boss so decided to err on the side of caution and show deference and respect. He didn't hold Lance Carmichael in high esteem, but just then, Daniel's only goal was to deliver his news, ask the man a few questions, and leave in one piece, which meant he had to keep his opinions and his face under stringent control.

"Sit down, Inspector Haze," Lance Carmichael said, and lowered himself into the armchair directly opposite. "Leave us," he said to his bodyguard. "And shut the door." Carmichael waited until the man had gone, then said, "Why are you here?"

Daniel was taken aback by the question. He had assumed Carmichael would already know, given that Daniel had explained the reason for his visit to Carmichael's men, but it seemed the bodyguard hadn't cared to be the messenger either and had probably told his boss that Daniel had something important to discuss with him without going into details. *That was smart*, Daniel thought, *and telling*. If Carmichael's own man was afraid to tell him the truth, then Daniel had to tread very carefully indeed.

Daniel didn't think Lance Carmichael would appreciate dissembling, so he braced himself and came straight to the point. "Mr. Carmichael, the body of a man was discovered in Bloody Weald yesterday afternoon. He was tied to a tree, an arrow protruding from his chest. Lord Redmond and I were able to positively identify the victim as your son, Tristan Carmichael."

A strangled cry tore from Lance Carmichael. He turned a sickly shade of white, and his right hand clutched at his heart. His breathing grew ragged, and he slumped in his chair, his head drooping to the side as his chest heaved as if he were struggling to get enough air. Daniel thought Carmichael might have suffered a cardiac infarction and be in need of immediate medical assistance, but when Daniel half-rose, ready to call for help, Carmichael raised his hand to forestall him. Even at his lowest, it seemed he didn't want to show any sign of weakness to his men.

They sat in silence for a few minutes while Lance Carmichael stared out the window. His eyes glittered with tears, his neck pulled into his hunched shoulders. Gradually, his color and breathing returned to normal, and he straightened his spine, sucked in a quavering breath, and faced Daniel head on.

"First, I thank you for bringing the news in person. That took courage. And second, I want to know what happened to my son. What was Tristan doing in Bloody Weald?"

"I don't know," Daniel said.

"What do you know?"

"I know that someone killed him," Daniel said. "Neither Lord Redmond nor I believe Tristan's death was the result of an accident. We also think the method of murder might have been intended to make a statement."

Carmichael nodded. He understood all about making statements and instilling fear. "You think someone did this to send me a message?"

"I think that's very possible."

"And do you intend to find my son's killer?" Lance Carmichael asked.

His grief had morphed into anger and a need for vengeance. All he needed was a name, and then the killer would no doubt suffer a prolonged, excruciating death that would give Carmichael some small measure of peace in the face of shattering loss.

"At this stage, I have nothing to go on," Daniel admitted.

"Tell me everything you know. Spare no detail, no matter how small."

Daniel relayed only the facts, choosing to leave out anything he and Jason had spoken about in the privacy of the shed.

"Who discovered the body?" Carmichael asked.

"Tom Marin and Lord Redmond's ward, Michael Donovan. They were walking through the woods and had nothing to do with your son's death."

Carmichael nodded. "I didn't think they did."

"Do you know of anyone who was murdered in a similar manner?"

Daniel could hardly come out and ask if this was some form of gang justice or might be something rivals did to each other, but Lance Carmichael took his meaning.

"I do not," he replied. "This cowardly act appears to be completely unique in its execution."

Daniel noted the choice of word—*execution*—and hoped Carmichael would elaborate, but he went quiet, his pale blue gaze fixed on Daniel as if he expected him to offer something more.

"Would you be willing to answer a few questions, Mr. Carmichael?" Daniel asked carefully.

Lance Carmichael cocked his head to the side and studied Daniel. He was clearly weighing his options, and his decision was final and swift. "I will conduct my own investigation, and mete out my own justice, Inspector. My son's death will not go unavenged. And I want his body returned. He will be buried as God made him. Tell your surgeon that. He is not to be cut open. Is that understood?"

"Yes, sir. I will ask Lord Redmond to make the necessary arrangements."

"I can send my own people," Carmichael said gruffly.

"There's no need. Your son's remains will be delivered to you this week. May I speak to Mrs. Carmichael, sir?" Daniel asked when he realized he was about to be shown the door.

"My wife is long gone. God rest her soul."

"I meant Mrs. Tristan Carmichael," Daniel amended.

The older man looked conflicted, then gave a brief nod. "I suppose Cecily deserves to hear the news from you. Wait here."

Daniel wondered why Lance Carmichael had agreed to let him speak to Tristan's wife if he intended to conduct his own investigation, but then he thought he understood. Lance couldn't bring himself to tell her the news. It was a minute show of weakness, but no one would know it except him. And Daniel. One of the hardest things Daniel had had to do was tell Harriet that Sarah was dead and that she had killed herself. He would have given anything to have someone else break the news and allow him to speak to Harriet once enough time had passed for the shock to abate and her grief to solidify into stoic acceptance. Lance Carmichael couldn't bear to describe his son's murder to the only other person who was meant to love Tristan and to inform his wife that her son no longer had a father.

"Thank you, sir," Daniel said.

Carmichael left the room and pulled the door shut behind him, so Daniel couldn't see or hear what went on outside. For a while, it was ominously quiet, and he wondered if Carmichael had forgotten about him and gone upstairs, where he could be alone with his grief and give vent to his emotions without being seen, but then he heard the clicking of heels on the floor and knew that he was about to come face to face with Tristan's widow.

Chapter 8

Daniel had never seen Cecily Carmichael, not even from a distance, and was curious about the woman Lance had chosen for his son. She looked incredibly young, and her skin was very pale in the bright light of the autumn morning. Despite her ghostly pallor and subdued demeanor, Cecily was still exceptionally lovely. She had rich chestnut hair, pale green eyes, and a pouty mouth that was as pink as a rosebud. Her voluptuous figure was draped in a gown of apple green muslin, and the cream lace fichu and lace cuffs complemented her coloring. Cecily pushed down the bell-like crinolines in order to fit into the chair her father-in-law had just vacated and sat down, her fearful gaze fixed on Daniel as if she expected him to lunge at her.

"Mr. Roy just told me what happened to Tristan," she said. Her voice was faint, and Daniel wished he was in possession of smelling salts in case she fainted. The best thing to do was to keep her talking.

"I'm very sorry for your loss, Mrs. Carmichael," Daniel said, and meant it. No woman should lose her husband to murder, but it happened all too often in Daniel's line of work.

"Thank you," Cecily muttered.

"What precisely is Mr. Roy's position?" Daniel asked. He wondered if Roy was more than the guard dog he appeared to be.

"My father-in-law's head protector."

Daniel saw a flash of resentment in Cecily's eyes and decided that she wasn't going to faint dead away after all. She was shocked and scared, but also angry and defiant.

"Does Mr. Roy not protect you as well?"

"Oh, yes. He keeps me prisoner in this house. I'm not allowed to go further than the garden wall unless my father-in-law gives express permission and assigns me a guard or accompanies me himself. I expect I will never be allowed out again now that Tristan is dead. Or maybe I will have more freedom, since I'm no longer of any use to Lance," she mused. "I'm not leaving, though. Not without my son."

They both knew Tristan's son wasn't going anywhere. He was Lance Carmichael's heir, and whether Cecily stayed or not, the boy would remain with his grandfather.

"What happened to Tristan?" Cecily asked. "Roy didn't share any details. Just said he was found dead."

"We don't know what happened, but we will do everything in our power to find out," Daniel said, deftly avoiding having to describe the scene to Cecily Carmichael.

"Who's we?"

"Myself and Lord Redmond."

"What about the Brentwood Police?"

"I haven't alerted them to the situation."

Cecily's face twisted into a mask of hatred. "I don't expect they'll care or bother to investigate anyway. Coleridge will be glad to hear Tristan is dead. He'd like to see my father-in-law in his grave too. It would reflect well on Coleridge and his flunkies."

Daniel didn't bother to reply. Cecily was probably right, at least in part. He didn't think the constables at the Brentwood station were anyone's flunkies, but DI Coleridge would likely be glad to hear that Tristan Carmichael was dead, and he would like to see Lance Carmichael go the way of his son. The Carmichaels had been a thorn in his side for years, and their demise would grant him the opportunity to clean up Brentwood before Lance Carmichael's heir tried to make his mark.

"Mrs. Carmichael, what was your husband doing in Essex?"

"He came to Essex to wait out the cholera epidemic. He had been planning to return to London by the end of the month."

"Did he say anything to you that would help me to find his murderer? Was he in dispute with someone? Had someone threatened him?"

"Tristan never spoke to me in that way," Cecily said. "He didn't want to involve me in his affairs and tried to spare me the ugliness that so often accompanied his work. At least that was what he said. I don't think he trusted me or was interested in my opinion. My one purpose was to provide Tristan with an heir."

Daniel could believe that, but what Cecily had said about the Brentwood police and her use of the detective inspector's name proved that she knew more than she was prepared to admit.

"How do you know about DI Coleridge and his attitude toward your family?"

"My father-in-law treats me like a piece of furniture, Inspector," Cecily said. "He doesn't care what I overhear. And I do listen. Otherwise I won't know anything at all."

"Did you happen to overhear something that might help me?"

Cecily nodded. "I heard Tristan and Lance talking about someone named Nathaniel Cavey. They said he's been making inroads in Essex and has managed to get many men behind him."

"Who is he?"

"From the way they were talking, I assumed he was a rival," Cecily said. "And with Tristan out of the way, it will be much easier for him to move into London."

"Do you know where I might find Mr. Cavey?"

"I heard Tristan say that he lives on a houseboat and sometimes docks at Foulness Island."

"Did your husband have any other enemies, someone who would want to murder him in a way that garnered attention?"

"I expect Tristan had many enemies. Such is the lot of powerful men."

An odd expression passed over Cecily's face, and Daniel was quick to exploit her moment of doubt.

"Anything you tell me could be helpful, Mrs. Carmichael. No matter how trivial."

"It's just something I have been thinking lately."

"Tell me," Daniel invited.

"My father-in-law has given more responsibility to Harvey Boswell since Tristan went to London. With Tristan gone…"

"I see. And where would I find Mr. Boswell?"

"He's taken over Tristan's rooms above the Red Lantern."

The Red Lantern was an opium den in the heart of Brentwood, so Daniel wouldn't have far to go to find the man.

"What about Mr. Roy? Does he have aspirations of moving up the ranks?"

Cecily scoffed. "Roy is a trained monkey. All he knows how to do is to grind his organ."

"Meaning?" Daniel asked. He could think of more than one way to interpret what Cecily had said.

"Meaning he knows how to use his gun and his fists. There's not much between the ears, and my father-in-law appreciates intelligence above all else. It's easy to find men of violence. It's much more difficult to find men who can analyze and strategize."

Daniel didn't think Cecily had arrived at that theory on her own. She was repeating something she'd overheard, but the information was still useful. Tristan Carmichael had not feared Roy, but he had been worried about Cavey. That didn't mean that one of Lance Carmichael's men hadn't had reason to take him out, but as Daniel's mother used to say, there was no smoke without fire, and Daniel had to follow the smell of ashes.

"Are we done, Inspector?" Cecily asked.

She now seemed eager to leave, as if she had something more important to do, and Daniel suddenly realized that she had yet to show any grief for the husband she would never see again. Perhaps she would give vent to her emotions later, in private, or perhaps she was shocked but not overly heartbroken to be rid of a man who'd spent little time with her and had left her to live with his father, who censored her every move. Having met Cecily, Daniel thought she would have been much happier in London, managing her own home and enjoying the diversions the city had to offer.

"How old is your son, Mrs. Carmichael?" Daniel asked.

"Samuel is two." Cecily went white to the roots of her hair. "Do you think Sam is in danger?"

"I can't imagine anyone would wish to harm a two-year-old, but I suggest you keep a close watch on him in the coming days."

That really was pointless advice since Lance Carmichael would probably guard the boy around the clock, but Daniel still felt it needed to be said.

Cecily nodded, then sprang to her feet and hurried toward the door. She threw it open and ran outside, screaming, "Simpson, bring Samuel to me this instant. He is not to go for his walk today."

"Cecily, control yourself," came Lance Carmichael's deep voice. "Samuel is quite safe, and he needs fresh air and exercise."

Carmichael paused in the doorway to the receiving room. "I think it's time you were on your way, Inspector."

Daniel didn't need to be told twice and strode toward the door. He put on his hat and buttoned his coat while he waited for the boy he'd seen earlier to bring the cart around. Carmichael's guards had gone back inside, but he knew he was being watched. Daniel was glad the visit was out of the way and pleased to have two new names to investigate. He was also relieved that Lance Carmichael hadn't made any demands. If he wished to conduct his own inquiry, that was just fine with Daniel. He was duty bound to pursue the case, but he was in no way sorry Tristan Carmichael was dead, nor did he feel any particular sympathy toward the Carmichael family. The only one who deserved consideration was Samuel, but it would be a long time yet until the boy was of an age to understand how his family made their money and to formulate opinions of his own.

Chapter 9

Jason had made sure to leave the house before Micah was up, which hadn't been difficult since he liked to sleep in during the school holidays. Since he and Tom had discovered the body, Micah felt involved and wanted to help out with the investigation, but until Jason knew what, or more accurately, who they were dealing with, he didn't want Micah or Tom anywhere near the case. He couldn't blame the boys for taking an interest. Any adolescent would, especially after months of doing nothing but fishing, playing chess, and wandering about the countryside in search of diversion.

At fifteen, Micah and Tom were too old to be considered children but not old enough to be treated as men. It was an awkward phase in a young man's life, and Jason recalled all too well how he had butted heads with his father, sometimes just for the sake of arguing, because he'd felt frustrated at not being invited to give his opinion on matters that concerned him. Jason made certain to consult Micah on all things that pertained to him, but Micah could still be argumentative and stubborn, mostly due to the urges that were surging through his young body and the feelings they facilitated. All perfectly normal but not helpful when investigating a murder.

Settling more comfortably against the padded seat of the brougham, Jason looked out the window. It was a lovely morning, still pleasantly warm but with enough bite to remind one that winter was on its way. The sky was a pale blue, the clouds as fluffy as grazing sheep, and the grass still lush and green. Jason wished he could open the window and smell the air that was fragrant with earth, hay, and that special scent that brought him right back to autumn in New York. But the windows of the brougham did not open, so he had to content himself with the view and the making of plans.

After two months in Birch Hill, he was more than ready to return to London and his work at the hospital, but even once Micah returned to school next week, Jason had the cholera epidemic to consider and thought it too soon to expose his family to the teeming metropolis. Even if Katherine and the children never went further than their tiny garden, there were still tradesmen who came to the house and the patients Jason saw. All it took was for one person to get exposed and then the entire household might become infected. It was safer to wait until the colder weather set in. But perhaps he could go on ahead, and the others could follow in a few weeks. Jason didn't need much looking after and could easily manage on his own. He'd discuss his idea with Katherine tonight, but for the moment, he had to focus on the investigation. Daniel and Flora were getting married on Saturday, and Jason would not allow this gruesome case to interfere with their well-deserved happiness. If it came to it, he would investigate Tristan Carmichael's murder on his own, as long as Daniel and Flora didn't have to alter their plans and would set off on their honeymoon on Monday, as planned.

It didn't take too long to reach the village of Upper Harlow. A helpful farmer directed Joe to Moll's cottage, which was close enough to the center of the village to be a desirable location, but not so close that the residents had to worry about noise and constant dust from passing horses and wagons. Rose bushes dotted with pink blooms climbed the arbor in front of the cottage, and the narrow lawn was neat and lush. The polished brass knocker gleamed in the sun, the windowpanes appeared to be freshly painted, and the roof looked to have been recently thatched. Moll and Bruce Plimpton were obviously house-proud, and Jason was glad that Moll was the mistress of such a charming home after living with her uncle above the Red Stag since she was a small child.

After Jason knocked, he was admitted by a young maid, who although dewy by virtue of her age was, nevertheless, quite homely. Probably a wise decision on Moll's part since she understood all too well the allure of pretty young women and didn't care for Bruce to be faced with daily temptation. Either Moll was unsure of her husband or simply thinking ahead to a time when the honeymoon phase of the marriage had passed and Bruce began to take his wife for granted, as most men tended to do.

The maidservant directed Jason to the garden, where Moll sat on a bench beneath a leafy tree, a child tucked up in a cozy blanket sleeping peacefully in a basket at her feet. She smiled warmly when she saw Jason and came forward to greet him.

"As I live and breathe," Moll gushed as she looked up at Jason, a small smile playing about her generous mouth.

She hadn't changed a bit. If anything, marriage and motherhood had made her even lovelier. Moll eschewed a cap and wore her dark hair in a loose knot atop her head, and her dark eyes sparkled merrily. Her skin glowed golden after months of gentle sunshine, and her figure, which had always been buxom, was swathed in a ruffled morning gown the color of dusty rose.

"I'm happy to see you looking so well, Moll," Jason said.

"Ye don't look so bad yerself, yer lordship," Moll replied, and gave him an appreciative once-over. It seems some things never changed.

"Congratulations on your marriage and the birth of your baby."

Jason knew the child was a boy but didn't know his name, since his path hadn't crossed with Moll's since before her marriage. Moll had no call to visit Redmond Hall, and Jason had little reason to go to the Red Stag when Moll was there. The few times Moll and Mary had met up, they had walked in the woods or through the fields, where they were able to spend time together unobserved since they were a source of gossip for people who didn't have enough to occupy their minds.

Moll smiled proudly. "Thank ye, yer lordship. Lucas is 'is name. 'E's four months."

Jason peered into the basket, where the child was now awake and looking around with wide blue eyes. Golden strands peeked from beneath a frilly bonnet, and the child's cheeks were round and rosy with good health.

"Lucas likes to sleep outside," Moll explained. "Loves the fresh air."

"He is beautiful, Moll."

"'E is, isn't 'e?" Moll agreed, and beamed at the baby.

"Is your husband at home? I would love to meet him."

Moll scoffed. "'E's still abed, the lazy oaf," she said with obvious affection. "'E should be up and about soon. What brings ye to see us, my lord?"

Jason heard the discordant note of anxiety beneath Moll's friendly tone. She was astute enough to know that this wasn't a social call and Jason had to have a good reason for turning up at her door and asking after her husband.

"I need a word, Moll," Jason said. "Preferably in private."

Moll's gaze was troubled as she opened the back door, called out to the maidservant to take Lucas, and drew Jason away from the house and toward a narrow lane that ran behind the garden. In the past, Moll would have slid her arm through his and made some coy remark about going for a romantic stroll in the countryside, but today she was tense, her dark gaze searching his face for an explanation.

"Just tell me," she said as soon as they moved away from the cottage.

Moll wasn't one to beat around the bush, and Jason could see that whatever the news, she'd rather know what she was up against and outline her options than remain in the dark.

"Tristan Carmichael was murdered yesterday. Micah and Tom found him while walking through Bloody Weald."

Moll's hand flew to her mouth, and her eyes shone with tears. She had loved Tristan and had thought they would build a life together. She might have married Bruce in the end, but the loss of Tristan pained her, and she didn't bother to try to hide her feelings from Jason. The odd thing was that Tristan had seemed to love her too. Perhaps Moll had brought out some protective instinct in him, or maybe with Moll he had felt he could be entirely himself and not have to pretend. The two had shared a close bond, and possibly more than that, and would have married had Lance Carmichael not put an end to their courtship, most likely by threatening to hurt Moll if Tristan refused to obey his father's decree.

"Did 'e suffer?" Moll asked, her voice hoarse with emotion.

"I don't know," Jason replied truthfully.

He couldn't say with any accuracy how long it had taken Tristan to die, since he hadn't opened the body and hadn't been able to assess the damage the arrowhead had done to the heart. Tristan might have died very quickly, or the arrow could have nicked one of the ventricles and caused a slow hemorrhage, which would have taken considerably longer.

"So, why 'ave ye come to us, my lord? Do ye think we killed 'im?"

Moll tried to scoff, but Jason could see the fear in her eyes and was sure she knew more than she was letting on.

"I'm not accusing you of anything, but you've always had your ear to the ground, and your husband was Tristan's associate. Have you heard anything?"

Moll shook her head. "Bruce 'ardly ever saw Tristan. Tristan were always in London, running things from 'is posh new 'ouse."

"How do you know his house is posh?" Jason asked.

"Bruce went there once, to deliver something for Limpy. 'E told me."

"Tristan must have come to Essex quite frequently. His father, and his wife and son are here."

Moll's gaze slid away from Jason, and she shrugged, the gesture meant to imply that she was no longer familiar with Tristan's comings and goings and hadn't wanted to hear about his family. Clearly, his desertion still rankled, despite the positive change in her own circumstances.

"Did Bruce tell you if Tristan had any enemies or mention someone who might have held a grudge against him?"

"A man like Tristan Carmichael will always 'ave enemies, but I don't know of any by name," Moll replied.

"Is there anyone you can think of who is proficient with a bow and arrow?" Jason asked.

"A what?"

"Tristan was killed with an arrow."

Moll's eyes widened in shock. "Why would anyone…?" Her voice trailed off, and Jason thought she was probably imagining Tristan's final moments. "Even 'e didn't deserve that," she said at last.

"So, is there anyone that's skilled with a bow?" Jason asked again.

Moll looked thoughtful. "There's Evan Jones."

"Who's he?"

"Squire Talbot's gamekeeper. 'E likes to 'unt with a bow. Evan used to bring it to the Stag. Uncle Davy let him bring in the bow, but 'e drew the line at Evan's kill. 'E 'ad to leave 'is bag outside, in the yard, far from the livery, so the 'orses wouldn't smell fresh blood."

Moll wrinkled her nose in disgust. She was used to dealing with drunk, rowdy men, but she'd never had to handle the spoils of a hunt. Davy got his meat already butchered, and from what Jason had heard of Bruce Plimpton, he wasn't one for primitive pursuits.

"Did Evan Jones know Tristan?" Jason asked.

"'Course," Moll replied. "Everyone knew 'im. If not in person, then by reputation."

"Might this Evan Jones have had a grievance against Tristan Carmichael?"

"Ye'll 'ave to ask Evan that. I 'aven't spoken to the man since I quit working at the Stag," Moll replied defensively.

"When was the last time you saw Tristan?"

Moll shrugged, as if she couldn't remember, but Jason was sure she recalled the exact day, time, and what had been said as if it had happened yesterday. Moll was not only observant, but she also knew when to keep her mouth shut. Jason couldn't blame her if she didn't want to get embroiled in the investigation. Her involvement could put a strain on her marriage and possibly also bring Lance Carmichael to her door. Such a visit wouldn't end well if the older Carmichael thought Moll had information that would help him to flush out his son's killer. He would happily do whatever it took to get what he'd come for.

"I'd like to speak to your husband," Jason said again, and thought he saw Moll wince. But then she nodded and sighed deeply.

"Let's get back, and I'll wake 'im."

They retraced their steps and entered the house by the back door. The maidservant was in the kitchen, kneading dough on a large pine table. She cooed to the baby, who smiled at her from his basket, which was on the floor near the wall furthest from the hearth. A dark-haired man, presumably Bruce Plimpton, sat at the other end of the table, a plate of fried eggs and kippers before him. Bruce had heavy black brows and wore a moustache and long side whiskers, but the rest of his face was clean-shaven. Jason put him at around twenty-eight.

"Where've you been, Molly?" Bruce asked cheerily, then caught sight of Jason and drew himself up, his chin sticking out defiantly. "Who's this, then?"

"My apologies for disturbing you, Mr. Plimpton. I'm Jason Redmond. Moll and I know each other from Birch Hill."

"It's Lord Redmond, Bruce. I told you about him. Remember?" Moll said, and gave her husband a teasing smile.

Bruce's suspicious gaze settled on Jason, but then he seemed to relax and pushed to his feet, his head dipping in acknowledgment of Jason's rank. "I do apologize, your lordship. I didn't mean to be rude. Please, won't you step into the parlor?"

"Agnes, fetch some refreshments," Moll instructed the maidservant and went to pick up the baby.

"Thank you. I won't be staying long. I wanted a word, actually."

"With me?" Bruce's smile slid off his face, and his shoulders tensed.

"Yes, if you wouldn't mind. I will be happy to wait for you to finish your breakfast."

Jason made an effort to be as polite and non-threatening as possible. Bruce already had his hackles up, and Jason didn't want to make any trouble for Moll, who looked worried and tense as she held Lucas tightly, her chin resting atop his head.

"Erm, thank you," Bruce Plimpton said. "I'll join you in the parlor in a moment."

"Please don't rush," Jason said, and followed Moll to the parlor.

"Can't ye just leave us alone?" Moll hissed as soon as they were out of earshot of the kitchen. "I told ye, 'e doesn't know nothing."

"Then it will be a very short conversation," Jason replied.

Moll shot him an angry look, then sighed dramatically. "All right then, but I 'ave to feed the baby."

"See to your son, Moll," Jason said softly. "I'm sure Bruce and I will get on just fine."

Chapter 10

Once Moll had gone, Jason settled in a comfortable chair and surveyed the room. The parlor was clean and bright, the furnishings new, and the colors of the rug so vivid, Jason wondered if anyone ever walked on it. This was Moll's first home and, by the looks of it, Bruce's too. They were a young couple, just starting out on their journey together, and Jason hoped that despite Bruce's unsavory affiliations, life would be kind to them.

Jason's gaze settled on the wedding portrait proudly displayed on the mantel. Moll looked directly into the camera, her dark gaze triumphant and her generous lips on the verge of a smile. Bruce looked at his bride adoringly, and Jason thought that at least for him it had been a love match. Lucas, however, was unusually fair for a child who had dark-haired, dark-eyed parents. Jason knew nothing of Bruce's heritage, but Moll's mother had been Davy Brody's sister, and Davy was also dark in his coloring. Moll's father was Romani, one of the many young men who'd come through Birch Hill and had camped out at Bloody Mead. Of course, to jump to unwarranted conclusions was entirely unfair to Moll. Many children were fair in babyhood, but their hair often turned darker as they grew older. The eyes, however, tended to stay the same, at least as far as Jason was aware.

Moll's son was as cherubic as the Holy infant so frequently depicted by the Italian masters whose paintings Jason and Katherine had admired in Italy, and Jason couldn't help but recall that on first meeting Tristan Carmichael, he had thought his features angelic, his appearance deceptively at odds with the man he really was. Of course, there had been an angel who fit the description perfectly—Lucifer, the fallen seraph whose name had become synonymous with evil. People tended to trust appearances and first impressions, which made it easier for men like Tristan Carmichael to move through the world. Tristan could charm and seduce, which had made it that much easier for him to manipulate those who fell under his spell. Was Moll still in his thrall, or had she finally found happiness with a man who wasn't nearly as handsome but who seemed to love her? And did Bruce value his bride for her wit and fiery spirit, or had he been tempted by her lush looks?

Jason had learned the hard way during the war years that physical beauty had nothing to do with purity of the spirit, and that sometimes the individuals who looked harmless were the ones to fear since a pleasant countenance was a mask worn to hide a person's more violent urges. Who had Tristan Carmichael deceived or threatened to such a degree that they would ambush him in the woods, and why had they chosen a bow and arrow as a means of execution? Were the location and method significant, or was there something else at play here that Jason and Daniel had yet to uncover?

Jason's musings were interrupted when Bruce Plimpton walked into the parlor with the air of a man who was about to engage in a highly unpleasant task. Now that Bruce was standing before him, Jason noted that he was tall and solidly built, and could easily hold his own if it came to fisticuffs, as it probably did in his line of work. Plimpton was simply dressed in black trousers, a white shirt, and a black waistcoat. His shirt was open at the collar, and he wore no tie. And why would he? He had just risen from his bed and come down to breakfast, only to find an unwelcome visitor in his home.

Plimpton's hand unwittingly went to his collar, as if he had just realized that his casual appearance might be taken as a sign of disrespect. Regard for the nobility was so deeply ingrained that even men like Bruce Plimpton, who sailed precariously close to the wind, didn't dare challenge someone they knew to be above them on the social scale and didn't deign to question their betters' presence, even at such a socially unfashionable hour of the morning.

"How can I help, your lordship?" Plimpton asked once he was seated. He had rearranged his face into an expression of bland civility and would no doubt answer Jason's questions in a manner that appeared to be helpful but didn't reveal too much.

"How well do you know Tristan Carmichael, Mr. Plimpton?" Jason asked.

Plimpton seemed surprised by the question and had clearly not expected Tristan Carmichael to be the subject of the conversation—unless he had and was simply playing a part.

"I've known Tristan since we were small boys. We were friends once, but we've seen little of each other these past few years. Why do you ask?"

"Tristan Carmichael was found dead yesterday. Murdered."

Plimpton stared at Jason, his mouth hanging open in shock. "Murdered? Who by?"

"That's what I'm trying to figure out. He was killed in the woods, with an arrow to the heart. His body was tied to a tree, a burlap sack pulled over his head."

"Is this some sort of joke?" His brows knitting in consternation, Plimpton looked at Jason intently, as if trying to comprehend what Jason's role in Tristan's murder was, and what conclusions he had to have drawn in order to connect Bruce to the inquiry.

"It's no joke, I assure you. I removed Tristan Carmichael's body to Redmond Hall for medical examination. By the looks of it, he did not die quickly or easily."

"Why would anyone shoot Tristan with an arrow?"

"I admit I'm at a loss, Mr. Plimpton. Do you have any theories?"

"Any what?"

"Theories? Ideas?"

Plimpton looked genuinely confounded but didn't seem upset by the death of a childhood friend. He shrugged, his eyebrows lifting in time with his shoulders as he considered Jason's question.

"Tristan was wily, and oft times cruel," Plimpton said at last, "but I can't see anyone shooting him with an arrow and pulling a bag over his head."

"How *do* you see someone killing him?" Jason asked conversationally.

"Well, if it was a hit by a rival gang—organization," Plimpton quickly amended, "then I suppose they would either gun him down or slit his throat. They might even bludgeon him to death, but these days, archery is the sport of the nobility."

"Can you think of anyone who's good with a bow and arrow?"

"Cupid," Bruce Plimpton replied, and smiled at his own joke. "Perhaps Tristan's death was the result of a love affair gone wrong."

"Do you know of a woman he might have scorned?"

Bruce Plimpton shook his head. "From what I've heard, Tristan had been on the straight and narrow since his marriage, which doesn't mean he didn't sample the new merchandise that came into his brothels. But that's not the same as having an affair of the heart, is it? You know how it is."

Jason did. Most men didn't see sex with prostitutes as adultery. They simply regarded it as satisfying a need, much like buying a pie from a street vendor when they were hungry. Neither the dictates of morality nor the staggeringly high number of syphilis cases were a deterrent when it came to the sex trade, and as the Carmichaels were knee-deep in prostitution, Tristan didn't have to go far to satisfy his lust. But Bruce's revelation didn't help when it came to Tristan's murder. Even if Tristan had abused some poor woman, either in London or in Brentwood, the chances of her arranging to meet him in an out-of-the-way forest and bringing along a bow and arrow, rope, and a burlap sack were slim.

"I can think of a different way to describe Tristan's death," Jason mused. "Some might say he was hunted."

"Well, the hunters sometimes become the hunted, don't they, my lord?" Plimpton replied.

"Especially men who choose a life of violence. You live by the sword, you die by the sword."

Bruce Plimpton shot Jason a derisive look. "It's easy to sit in judgment when one has never known deprivation, but the view is a bit different for people born to poverty. What's better, slowly starving in some cold, leaky hovel or assuming charge of one's life, and taking what one deserves?"

"Is that how people like Carmichael justify it?"

"Ever heard of Robin Hood, your lordship, or is he not known in America?"

"I've heard of Robin Hood," Jason replied. "But I don't know that I would equate Tristan Carmichael with a folk hero."

"It's all a matter of perception, though, isn't it?" Bruce asked. "One man's criminal is another man's hero. The Carmichaels might take the lion's share for themselves, but they do offer the people who work for them a chance at a better life." His gaze swept over the well-appointed parlor.

"How do they offer the prostitutes they exploit a better life?" Jason demanded, but he thought he knew what Bruce Plimpton would say.

"Have you ever been to one of their brothels?"

"Can't say that I have."

"You should visit sometime, if only to educate yourself," Plimpton said. "The girls are clean, well fed, and cared for by a doctor when they fall ill. To my mind, that's vastly preferable to working a fourteen-hour day in some mill or dying of consumption in a workhouse. And if the women have a child, the children are looked after."

"Until they're old enough to be exploited in turn," Jason snapped.

"We are all exploited in our own way, aren't we, unless we are blessed with inherited wealth."

That was a direct dig at Jason, but he chose not to engage in a rebuttal. Plimpton wasn't wrong. There weren't many choices for people who had no family money or skills that would help them to support themselves and their children. It was either underpaid menial labor in life-threatening conditions or a life of prostitution or petty crime. Both choices often led to an early death, but the road to the grave was somewhat different.

Bruce chuckled bitterly when Jason didn't respond. "My family was dirt poor until my grandfather gave up farming and turned to smuggling. There was a time when one could grow rich by bringing in illegal goods and wrecking ships for their valuable cargo, but those days are long gone. Now the poor must find new ways to redistribute the wealth."

"Is that how you see supplying opium and running prostitutes? Redistribution of wealth?"

Bruce grinned, revealing straight, white teeth. "It's all supply and demand, isn't it, your lordship? When there's a demand, someone is always willing to supply. And someone is always willing to pay a premium for quality goods. No one forces anyone to smoke an opium pipe, but if a rich cove craves a few hours of oblivion, why not offer him a safe, comfortable place to enjoy said pipe? His money goes to pay men who have families to support. And if a man craves more carnal pleasures, then he can satisfy his needs with women who are clean and beautiful, and looked after by men who don't allow them to be abused. It's all business, my lord, and everyone understands their role in the process."

"And does Moll understand your role in the process?" Jason asked. He could barely hide his disdain for Bruce's way of thinking, but he could understand how this sort of logic made what Bruce did justifiable in his mind.

"Everything I do is strictly above board," Bruce said, his face taking on a pious expression. "I have a family now. I don't take any risks."

"So, what is it that you do for the Carmichaels?"

"I am a debt collector. I simply visit the debtor and ask for the money."

"And if they fail to pay?"

"Then we renegotiate the terms," Plimpton said. "It's all friendly-like."

"So, what you're saying is that no one would have any reason to murder Tristan because they all understand their roles and feel no resentment?"

"Precisely."

"And did Tristan Carmichael not have rivals who might want him dead?"

"If he did, he did not share his concerns with me. As I said, I haven't seen him in years."

Jason didn't believe that for a second, but he wasn't going to argue. He'd got all he was going to get out of Bruce Plimpton.

"Thank you for your time, Mr. Plimpton."

"My pleasure."

"I'm sorry for the death of your friend," Jason added a tad sarcastically.

"Tristan wasn't my friend, but I'm sorry he met with such a bad end. Wouldn't wish that on anyone."

"Say goodbye to Moll for me. And you have a beautiful boy."

Bruce's face lit up with affection. "Lucas is the light of our lives."

Jason left the cottage and made his way to the brougham, which was some way down the lane. The horses were grazing while Joe sat on the bench, his hat off, his face turned toward the sun.

"Are we all done here, sir?" Joe asked.

"It would appear so. Do you know Evan Jones?"

Joe nodded. "I've met the man. Why do you ask?"

"His name came up in conversation."

"Jones is new to the village."

When English villagers said that someone was new, that could mean they had been around for two or two hundred years. People whose families had lived in the same spot for centuries saw anyone who had settled there later as a newcomer. Jason himself was viewed not only as a new arrival but also as a curiosity, even though his family had lived in Birch Hill for generations. Being born in America negated all previous history as far as they were concerned, and Jason's father was rarely mentioned, since he'd committed the ultimate betrayal by marrying an American and settling in New York. Perhaps Evan Jones's family had a unique history as well.

"How new is new?" Jason asked as he pulled open the door to the brougham.

"About two years, so very new."

"And does his family originally come from these parts?"

"Nah," was all Joe said before taking up the reins.

"Can you take me to him?"

Joe nodded. "You'll have to go the last mile on foot, sir. The path is not wide enough for a carriage."

"What happened to the old gamekeeper?" Jason asked.

"Got the sack."

"Why?"

"Turned a blind eye to poachers," Joe said with a shake of his head. "I reckon he fancied himself something of a Robin Hood. Took from the rich and gave to the poor."

There was that reference again, Jason noted as he climbed in and settled in for the ride. It seemed he was about to visit Sherwood Forest.

Chapter 11

The gamekeeper's cottage on the Talbot estate stood at the center of a small clearing and was hardly more than a one-room hut. Jason supposed a family could live in the tiny structure but saw no evidence of Mrs. Jones or small children. The clearing was quiet and still, the only sounds the rustling of leaves and the birdsong that filled the air. A large black dog was stretched out next to the door, but the animal didn't seem alarmed by Jason's presence. The dog opened one eye, then lazily got to its feet and barked a few times before resuming its position, having presumably done its job.

The door opened, and a man of about twenty-five emerged onto the doorstep. He was tall and lean and wore buckskins and a well-worn linen shirt that hung past his narrow hips. His feet were bare. Sunlight dappled his fair hair when he stepped from beneath the lintel, and his light gaze appeared welcoming rather than wary.

"Good morning," Jason said, and lifted his hand in greeting. "Mr. Jones, I presume?"

"At your service. Have you lost your way, your lordship?"

Evan Jones apparently knew who Jason was, which was beneficial since Jason's position was sure to inspire trust in a man who clearly preferred to keep himself to himself. Jason knew everyone who lived in and around Birch Hill, and he had never seen Evan Jones in church or in the village. Moll had said that he occasionally stopped into the Red Stag, but that seemed to be the extent of his social interaction.

"I'm sorry to come by unannounced, Mr. Jones, but I was wondering if I might have a word," Jason said as he slowly came forward.

"If you're looking for a gamekeeper, I must warn you that I'm happy with my current situation, my lord."

"I'm not in the market for a gamekeeper," Jason replied. The Redmond estate wasn't sprawling enough to require the services of a gamekeeper, nor did Jason care for the hunt. And if poachers found their way onto Redmond land and helped themselves to rabbits or pheasants, they were welcome to them as far as Jason was concerned. "I actually wanted to speak to you regarding a different matter."

Evan Jones seemed reluctant to invite Jason inside. He smiled awkwardly and gestured toward a bench that ran along the front wall of the house. "Would you care to sit down, sir?"

"Thank you."

Jason settled on the bench, while Jones went to a nearby chopping block and set aside the axe before sitting down, his elbows resting on his thighs. The smell of burned coffee wafted through the open door.

"Did I interrupt your breakfast, Mr. Jones?" Jason asked.

"I was just having a cup of coffee. It's part of my morning ritual."

"Mine as well," Jason said. "I'm afraid tea doesn't revive me in the same way."

Jones nodded, then asked, "How can I help you, my lord?"

He was visibly uncomfortable and eager for Jason to get on his way. Perhaps the gamekeeper had chores to attend to, or the more likely explanation was that Jones simply didn't want Jason there in his private domain.

"I was told you prefer to hunt with bow and arrow."

Jones's eyebrows lifted in surprise. "And who told you that?"

"Moll Brody. Sorry—Plimpton."

"Moll is a good sort. I no longer go into the Stag now she's gone."

"So, *do* you hunt with a bow?" Jason asked.

"Yes. I find I can get a more accurate aim than with a musket."

"With a bow? Really?"

Jones's smile was unguarded for the first time. "I'm Welsh, your lordship."

"I'm sorry, but I don't follow."

Evan Jones nodded, probably recalling that Jason was American and no doubt ignorant of certain home truths. "Welsh archers were the best in the world. Legendary," he said proudly. "They could hit a tiny mark from one hundred yards away."

Jason hated to admit that he knew next to nothing about Welsh history and hoped for more of an explanation.

"My ancestors were archers of Gwent," Jones said, beaming with pride. "They fought at the Battle of Agincourt," he added when Jason failed to react.

"Was that not a few hundred years ago?"

"1415," Jones said with a nod of his tawny head. He made it sound as if the battle had taken place in 1815, which would still have been a long time ago.

"Ah," was all Jason could manage.

The conversation seemed to border on the absurd, but the connection to the long-ago battle obviously meant a lot to Jones, and for some reason, he needed Jason to know this obscure fact about his family.

"The men in my family have kept the skill alive. Allow me to show you."

Evan Jones stood and strode toward a tiny shed, then returned with a longbow and a leather quiver filled with arrows. "I made the bow and the arrows myself. It's wych elm, which makes for the strongest longbows in the world."

"And the arrows?" Jason asked. The fletching on the arrows was pure white. "May I see?"

"Of course."

Jones took out an arrow and held it out to Jason, who examined it carefully. It didn't look like the arrow he had removed from Tristan's chest, but that didn't mean it hadn't been made or shot by the same person. Evan Jones would be very foolish to use an arrow to commit a murder when it could be used to identify him.

"What do you use for fletching?" Jason asked.

"Feathers from a white owl. Traditionally, a right-handed archer would use feathers from the right wing, and a left-handed one would use feathers from the left. It's also advisable to use a cock feather on the outside and two hen feathers as stabilizers."

Jason had no clue what the man was talking about, since he'd never handled a bow, but he could see that Jones was passionate about the craft and eager to discuss the details.

"How do you obtain the feathers? Do you search for them in the woods?"

Jones chuckled. "Of course not. I keep barn owls and pluck a few feathers whenever I'm in need of more arrows, which is not often. I reuse the arrows again and again."

"Do you ever use brown or gray feathers?" Jason asked.

"Never."

"Why not?"

"Because they're difficult to spot in a forest. That's not a problem if I hunt larger game and can see where the animal fell, but if I shoot a bird in flight, say, then I have to find it once it falls from the sky."

"Ever hunt humans?" Jason asked, taking Jones by surprise.

The gamekeeper stared at him as if he had taken leave of his senses, then laughed. "I thought you were serious for a moment there, my lord."

"I was. I presume Welsh archers weren't famous for hunting rabbits."

"No. They fired at the enemy, and they never missed."

"The body of Tristan Carmichael was found in Bloody Weald yesterday. He was killed with an arrow and tied to a tree. Did you know him, Mr. Jones?"

All the blood seemed to drain out of the gamekeeper's face, but he drew himself up to his full height and fixed Jason with a defiant stare. "Yes, I knew him. He was a right bastard, and I can't say I'm sorry he's dead, but I wasn't the one who shot him."

"What did he do to you, Mr. Jones?" Jason asked.

Jones glowered at him. "He seduced my sister, got her with child, then after I confronted him, he made sure I lost my place with my previous employer, Lord Stanhope. Lord Stanhope was one of Lance Carmichael's cronies," Jones explained. "He sacked me without a character and withheld my wages."

"Where's your sister now?"

"Last I heard, Brynn was working at one of Tristan Carmichael's brothels in London."

"And the child?"

"Stillborn."

"Is Squire Talbot aware of your history with the Carmichaels?"

"He is, and he wasn't put off by it." Evan Jones exhaled heavily. "If I wanted to murder Tristan Carmichael, I would have done it years ago, and not in a way that would point a finger squarely at my chest."

"Why didn't you kill him?" Jason asked. He got the feeling that Evan Jones wouldn't hesitate to murder the man if he had decided on such a course of action, and he would probably never be caught.

"Because my sister begged me not to. She loved him, you see, and thought the sun shone out of his arse."

"Even after Carmichael abandoned her?"

"He didn't abandon her, not entirely. He still saw her regularly and made her think she was special to him. Fool that she is, she believed him. I washed my hands of the whole affair years ago. We all make our own bed, don't we, my lord?"

"That we do," Jason agreed. "Where were you on Sunday night, Mr. Jones?"

"Here. Alone. Unless you count Dog and the owls."

"And Monday morning?"

"Hunting. The squire fancied venison for his dinner."

"Where's the deer you killed?"

"In Squire Talbot's kitchens, at least part of it."

"Where's the rest?"

"The smokehouse. Squire's cook promised to give me some smoked venison once it's ready. Do you like venison, my lord?"

"Not particularly."

Evan Jones cocked his head to the side and studied Jason. "You can check with the cook. The kitchen maid and the scullion were there as well. I delivered the carcass around noon, then stayed to help butcher it. I didn't leave until after three o'clock."

"You could have murdered Carmichael in the morning. He'd been dead for hours by the time his remains were discovered."

"I could have, but I didn't," Jones said. "As far as I'm concerned, my sister's troubles are her own. It's just me and Dog now, and that's the way I like it."

There didn't seem anything more to say, so Jason bid Evan Jones a good day and retraced his steps to the carriage. Jones had given him much to think about, and he looked forward to discussing his findings with Daniel.

Chapter 12

The Red Lantern was in Gresham Road, in Brentwood. The opium den had got its name from the red lantern mounted above the door, its glowing light used to guide the desperate and the depraved to their version of heaven. Daniel had visited the den before, during an investigation, and was better prepared this time, but the sight that greeted him once he was through the door was no less appalling.

It was barely noon, but at least a dozen people, most of them men, lay supine on mismatched couches and soiled pallets, their eyes closed, their mouths slack, and their cheeks and chins glistening with drool. Their clothes were in disarray, and the stench of unwashed bodies was overlaid by the ever-present reek of opium, it's cloying odor sticking in Daniel's throat and nostrils and making him want to gag.

He wished he could throw open the windows and shake awake the users, who clung to the pipes even in their stupor. If only they could see themselves as he saw them, these lost souls who'd given in to the basest sort of weaknesses while lining the pockets of men like the Carmichaels. The purveyors never touched the stuff themselves; they understood the risks, but they were all too eager to let anyone who wandered in sample a pipe for free, knowing that once they got a taste for the poppy, they would be sure to come back and pay any amount of money to return to the opium dream that never seemed to loosen its grip on the user.

The last time Daniel had visited the Red Lantern, a Carmichael heavy had manned the door and had questioned Daniel's purpose, but today there was no one, save a Chinese attendant who glided between the pallets on silent feet, his long braid swaying against the black fabric of his cotton pajamas, his face impassive. Daniel was certain the den hadn't changed hands since Tristan Carmichael had lived upstairs, but perhaps the new management didn't see a need for additional security. Everyone was welcome, and no one would hassle the clients unless they'd overstayed their welcome and it was time to pay up.

The attendant gave Daniel a deferential nod and gestured toward an empty pallet, but Daniel shook his head. He didn't bother to explain that he wasn't there to seek oblivion. Instead, he mounted the stairs, surprised not to encounter any opposition. The door to the apartment upstairs stood slightly ajar, and Daniel pushed it open, thinking he'd probably find it empty.

This time, he wasn't met by a well-trained retainer who guarded his master like a loyal dog. The sumptuous furnishings, beautiful paintings, and carpets were gone, probably moved to Tristan's London townhouse, and used to furnish its many rooms. In their place were serviceable pieces, bare floors, and unadorned walls. The curtains were still there, the fabric probably too permeated with the reek of opium to be of use to Tristan in his new home.

The parlor had been converted into an office, and a large desk that faced the door dominated the space, its surface covered with stacks of paper and leather-bound ledgers, and its sides damaged by numerous nicks and scratches. A man sat behind the desk, a glowing cheroot dangling from his mouth. He was around Daniel's age, and had neatly parted and liberally oiled dark hair and a pencil moustache that gave him a rakish appearance. He was in his shirtsleeves, and a gleaming watch chain snaked from a button on his waistcoat to his pocket. He had been studying a document but looked up when Daniel walked in, the man's wire-rimmed specs magnifying cold, dark eyes.

"And you are?" the man asked. He didn't seem intimidated or even annoyed, just mildly curious.

"Inspector Haze."

Daniel refrained from mentioning that he worked for Scotland Yard. The Yard had no power here, and Daniel wasn't officially employed by the Brentwood Constabulary, although by the looks of it, the Brentwood police weren't doing much to curtail this outrage. Not that Daniel blamed them. The station was underfunded and understaffed, and couldn't hope to take on the

Carmichaels, not when there were fewer than a dozen men at DI Coleridge's command.

"How can I help you, Inspector?" the man asked. He placed his smoking cheroot in a stone ashtray without taking his eyes off Daniel for a second.

"Whom do I have the pleasure of addressing?" Daniel asked politely.

Speaking to a manager of an opium den was hardly a pleasure, but Flora always said that one should start as one meant to go on, and Daniel thought it good advice. Things were highly likely to deteriorate from here, but he could at least make a pretense at civility and see where it got him.

"Harvey Boswell, at your service, Inspector." This was said with a measure of sarcasm, but Daniel pretended not to notice.

"I'd like a word, Mr. Boswell."

"What about?"

A young woman, a girl really, that Daniel hadn't realized was in the flat appeared in the doorway behind him. Fair curls framed her heart-shaped face, and she had the soft brown eyes of a woodland doe. The young woman wore a striped gown of lavender and navy satin, and pretty sapphire earbobs sparkled in her ears. She wasn't a servant, so probably Boswell's wife. This assumption was bolstered by Boswell's reaction. He smiled at her affectionately, his gaze warming by several degrees, and she grinned back, revealing deep dimples that bracketed her generous mouth. Daniel was touched by the devotion that shone in the young woman's face. She clearly idolized her husband.

"Would you care for some tea?" she asked the men.

Daniel would have loved a cup of tea, but he didn't trust these people and would not imbibe anything in their home, if this was what it was. Perhaps the flat now served as an office and the couple resided somewhere more pleasant.

"Thank you, no, Mrs. Boswell," Daniel said.

"Miss Boswell," the woman corrected him, giggling.

"My sister," Boswell explained. "It's all right, Annie. Leave us." It was a command, but Boswell's voice was gentle, and Annie didn't seem to mind the dismissal.

Boswell hadn't invited Daniel to sit, but Daniel wasn't about to stand before his desk like a boy who's been called on the carpet. He stepped forward and sat in the guest chair, then took off his hat and set it on his thigh. Boswell nodded, as if he admired Daniel's boldness.

"So, why are you here, Inspector? You're not with the Brentwood Constabulary. I know every man there, so don't bother to pretend otherwise. And where's your pet nobleman?"

So, Boswell knew who Daniel was, which could be a help or a hindrance. Daniel was certain he was about to find out which.

"I thought you might like to know that Tristan Carmichael was found dead. Murdered."

That shocked Boswell. He stared at Daniel as if he were waiting to be told this was some sort of joke, or perhaps he thought it was a test of his loyalty to the Carmichaels. When Daniel didn't say anything more, Boswell removed his spectacles and peered at Daniel, his expression inscrutable.

"How was he murdered? And when?" Boswell asked at last, having apparently decided that Daniel was on the level.

"Yesterday. An arrow to the heart."

"What? Are you serious?" Harvey Boswell gaped at Daniel but must have seen no subterfuge in his eyes.

"I am, and I have taken it upon myself to investigate the case."

"Why?" Boswell demanded. "Tristan Carmichael was hardly an upstanding citizen."

"That doesn't mean someone can kill him and walk away without consequences. Murder is murder, Mr. Boswell, even when the victim is someone as reprehensible as your boss."

Boswell nodded in acknowledgement of this truth. "What do you think happened?"

"I don't know yet, but your name's come up," Daniel replied evenly.

"In what context?" Boswell had clearly not expected that and reared back at the suggestion that someone suspected him of the crime.

"With Tristan out of the way, you can move up the ranks. All the way to the top, if Lance Carmichael suffers a similar fate."

"You think I shot Tristan Carmichael with an arrow and plan to take out his father?" Boswell seemed genuinely surprised and more than a little offended.

"It's a possibility."

"I didn't kill Tristan. And if I had, I would have chosen a different weapon."

"What sort of weapon?" Daniel inquired.

"I'm not going to answer that, but use your imagination. I'm sure you've seen your share of murder victims in London."

"I have, and I must admit, the method is unusual. But we are, after all, in the country."

"What does that matter?" Boswell snapped.

"Lots of old houses, full of ancient weapons."

"And you think what, that someone would take a bow off the wall, find a couple of arrows, and go hunting for a man they have condemned to death?"

"It would appear so."

Boswell shook his head. "The method speaks to a man's character, Inspector, and I don't know what sort of person would choose a bow to take out their enemy."

"A man who might be taken with its symbolism."

"You lost me," Boswell said, opening his hands in a gesture of surrender.

"A bow puts one in mind of a hunter stalking their prey. Can you think of anyone who might enjoy hunting Tristan Carmichael?"

"I can, actually," Boswell replied resignedly. "Tristan made a lot of enemies."

"Can you name a few?"

"No."

"Why not?"

"Because I'm not a rat," Boswell said. "And I don't know anything for certain."

"Would you know if someone decided that Tristan Carmichael had to die?" Daniel asked.

"There would be talk."

"What sort of talk?" Daniel pressed.

"People might not always share happy news, but they will gladly spew their grievances to those they think they can trust. Strong emotion has a way of loosening tongues."

"And what sort of grievances would someone have against Tristan Carmichael?" Daniel asked.

Boswell looked conflicted. He didn't want to help Daniel, that was obvious, but he was noticeably worried. If someone had mentioned his name in the same sentence as Tristan's murder and thought that Boswell might target Lance Carmichael next, it was in his interest that Daniel find the killer, and quickly.

Sighing heavily, Boswell said, "Tristan was always protected by his name. It made him think he was untouchable. See, the thing is, Inspector, that in any organization, there are rules. And those rules must be respected. Tristan didn't think the rules applied to him."

"In what sense?"

"In the sense that he thought whatever he wanted was his for the taking. Money, women, power. As my father used to say, don't shit where you eat."

Daniel thought this excellent advice. "And Tristan did that?" he asked, but refrained from utilizing the exact same verbiage.

Boswell nodded. "His father was growing tired of his antics, so he put me in charge of Tristan's business interests in Essex. And if you ask me, it wouldn't have been long before someone else took over London."

"Are you suggesting that Lance Carmichael would oust his own son?"

"I'm suggesting that he would do whatever was necessary to show Tristan who was in charge," Boswell replied.

"Surely he wouldn't murder his own son."

"I never said he would," Boswell said. "Lance loved Tristan, and forgave him way too much, but he was ready to take him in hand and show him that until he was ready to act like a man, someone else would hold the reins."

"That someone could be you," Daniel pointed out.

Boswell chuckled. "Do you really think Lance Carmichael would allow the person who killed his son to continue to draw breath? Even if I wanted Tristan out of the way and thought I could move to London, I'd never risk killing him. I don't have a death wish, Inspector. And I have Annie to think about."

"What's she to do with it?" Daniel asked.

"If Lance Carmichael thought I was in any way responsible for the death of his only son, he would kill me, but first, he'd make me suffer."

"By hurting your sister?"

Boswell nodded, and his gaze softened. "Annie is the only pure thing in my life. I would never do anything to endanger her."

Daniel decided not to point out that Boswell endangered his sister whether he meant to or not. If someone wanted to get to him, all they had to do was get to her first. But Boswell seemed to think they were both safe as long as he didn't voice his grievances to the wrong people, or step on anyone's toes. If Lance Carmichael was any judge of character, he would never make Boswell his number two, Daniel mused. The man lacked the killer instinct that Tristan had had in spades.

"Did Tristan Carmichael ever meet Annie?" Daniel asked.

Annie was a lovely girl, just the sort to draw Tristan's eye. She could have easily fallen prey to his charm and been seduced by him. If Tristan Carmichael had debauched Annie, Daniel could see how Boswell could be roused to murder.

"No," Boswell replied without pausing to think. "Annie boarded at an all-girls' school in Hertfordshire until June. Tristan Carmichael came to see me once, a fortnight ago, and I told Annie to keep out of sight. I didn't trust Tristan with an innocent young girl."

"Why did Tristan Carmichael come to see you?"

"To discuss business, and to ask if I might be interested in relocating to London. He said he was in need of men he could trust."

"And were you interested?" Daniel asked.

Boswell shook his head. "No, I wasn't."

"Why?"

"Because I would have to take Annie with me, and I don't want her exposed to all that filth." Boswell chuckled. "I know what you're thinking, Inspector. I can see it in your face. Yes, my office is above an opium den, and that's not ideal, but better Annie sees weak men in the haze of an opium dream than be surrounded by men of violence who might think she's fair game."

"Your devotion to your sister is admirable," Daniel said, not bothering to hide his sarcasm.

"We all have lines we won't cross, Inspector Haze."

"But it seems someone has crossed a line. Surely you must suspect someone, Mr. Boswell. You have my word that no one will ever know the name came from you."

Boswell shook his head. "I'm not naming names, but if I were in your shoes, I might check to see who won the archery competition at St. Peter's annual fête this year."

"Why don't you tell me, since you already know," Daniel invited.

"All right. I will. Cecily Carmichael. The woman is lethal with a bow."

"Cecily Carmichael?"

Boswell nodded. "Hell hath no fury like a woman scorned."

Daniel didn't need to ask if Cecily Carmichael had been scorned. Tristan loved women and had probably not stopped carousing when he'd got married. And Cecily had not seemed overly heartbroken at the news of her husband's death. She had also been the one to mention Harvey Boswell. Perhaps she really suspected him, or maybe she was trying to deflect suspicion from herself.

"Where were you on Monday morning, Mr. Boswell?"

"With Annie. She can vouch for me."

That meant little since Daniel was sure Annie Boswell would say whatever her brother told her to say. Boswell obviously saw that in Daniel's face too because he added, "Annie and I went to the coffeehouse on the corner for breakfast. The proprietor is Mr. York, and he will confirm that we arrived at nine o'clock."

"Thank you for your candor, Mr. Boswell," Daniel said as he stood to leave.

He thought he might have a word with DI Coleridge about the Carmichaels' Brentwood operation. It was a crying shame that the den was allowed to operate on this nice residential street, in full view of the neighbors. Surely there was something he could do.

Boswell fixed Daniel with a dark stare, and Daniel had the uncomfortable feeling that the man was able to read his thoughts. "What we do here is not illegal, Inspector."

"But it is, Mr. Boswell," Daniel countered. "The Pharmacy Act of 1868 limits the sale of dangerous substances, which includes opium."

"To pharmacists."

"The law applies to opium dens as well."

"Does it?" Boswell replied with a small smile. "You can't shut us down, Inspector Haze, so don't even bother."

"And why shouldn't I bother?" Daniel asked angrily.

"Because no one at the Brentwood Constabulary will do your bidding."

"Why is that?"

Boswell shook his head, as if he couldn't quite believe the extent of Daniel's naivete. "Lance Carmichael has DI Coleridge and the magistrate in his pocket, so it would be rather pointless to try, since no action would be taken in the end."

"DI Coleridge is a man of honor, Mr. Boswell," Daniel protested.

"Honor can be bought, or suppressed by other means."

"I certainly hope not," Daniel said, but he could see the pity in Boswell's eyes. The man thought him deluded, and perhaps he was.

Brentwood wasn't so vast that DI Coleridge wouldn't be aware of an opium den on his doorstep. Perhaps he was handsomely paid to turn a blind eye, but the more likely possibility was that Coleridge knew he was outmanned and outgunned, and feared for his family's safety. He had a young daughter, a miracle child born to the Coleridges in middle age, that he doted on and would do anything to protect. Daniel turned on his heel and walked out.

"Good day, Inspector," Boswell called after him, but Daniel didn't bother to reply.

He walked directly to the coffeehouse at the corner and asked for the proprietor, who confirmed that Mr. Boswell and his charming sister had indeed come for breakfast at nine o'clock, as they did most weekday mornings. Miss Boswell had had toast, a soft-boiled egg, and fruit compote, and Mr. Boswell had had fried eggs, ham, and two slices of fried bread. Daniel thanked the man and left. He wondered why Miss Boswell couldn't make breakfast at home, but then he didn't suppose it made much sense to light the range and go through the trouble of making breakfast if neither Boswell was to remain at home and would need to put out the flame before leaving.

The fact that Boswell had an alibi didn't necessarily mean that he couldn't have murdered Tristan Carmichael since the time of death was an estimate. Boswell could have enjoyed a hearty breakfast with his sister after putting an arrow through a man's heart, but Daniel's copper's instinct, which had been honed to a fine point since he'd joined Scotland Yard, told him Harvey Boswell wasn't his man.

Chapter 13

His business in Brentwood finished, Daniel was all set to return to Birch Hill. He needed to confer with Jason, and if he was to go out to Foulness Island to speak to Nathaniel Cavey, he didn't think he should go on his own. Foulness Island was a sparsely populated enclave that was beautiful in its desolation but could be treacherous for someone who didn't understand its natural idiosyncrasies. And it was the perfect place to hide for a man who didn't care to be found.

As Daniel climbed into the dogcart and took up the reins, he reflected that Boswell had given him much to think about and wondered if he'd gone off on a fool's errand when he'd decided to investigate the case. He wasn't convinced that Carmichael's death was the result of either an internal or an external power struggle, but one thing he did know for certain was that if the killing was gang related, Lance Carmichael would leave no stone unturned to flush out his son's killer. And perhaps the wisest thing to do would be to let him use his own intelligence and resources to see the thing done. Daniel didn't have the necessary knowledge, nor would he be granted access to the inner workings of the Carmichael organization.

On the other hand, as he had just told Boswell, a murder was a murder, and as someone who had sworn to uphold the law, he could hardly pick and choose whose death was worth investigating. The world was probably a better place without Tristan Carmichael in it, but that could be said of many people whose actions had led to their untimely deaths. Regardless of what Tristan Carmichael had done, someone had lured him to the forest and shot him through the heart, leaving him to die in a place he wasn't likely to be discovered for hours, maybe even days.

Until Daniel had come face to face with his first murder victim during his stint as a constable in Whitechapel, he had not given much thought to the aftermath of death. A person was dead; that was the end of it as far as the victim was concerned. It was those around them who were left to grieve and, in some cases, to demand justice. But now Daniel understood that death wasn't the end, not truly. There was also the postmortem period during which the deceased was prepared for burial, and that period mattered. He had seen enough rotting corpses in the deadhouses and the bloated remains of floaters fished from the Thames to know that it mattered what happened to him after he died. He didn't care for his remains to be left in some alley or tossed into the river, just as he would strenuously object to his body undergoing an autopsy, his organs removed and examined, and his bones sawed apart for the sake of science. He respected science and the people who dedicated their lives to the pursuit of knowledge, but he didn't want to be one of their subjects, and hoped that when his time came, his remains would be treated with care and respect, and he would have a Christian funeral and a peaceful resting place, preferably next to people he had loved in life.

Intellectually, he understood that the details didn't really matter since he'd never know what happened to his body. Emotionally, it made a difference to how he perceived his inevitable end, and even though he had detested Tristan Carmichael in life, he still believed that the man deserved better than to be left in the woods to be gnawed on by hungry animals and pecked at by pitiless birds. And since Daniel had recently received a message from beyond the grave in which Sarah had given him leave to move on, he couldn't help but wonder if a person might be aware of what happened to them in death after all and carry the trauma of their passing into the spirit realm.

Daniel's musings on life and death were probably part of his spiritual growth and the self-examination he tended to engage in more frequently since meeting Jason, but when he stopped the cart before St. Peter's Church, Daniel wasn't overly concerned with his mortal soul. He thought he should verify Boswell's claim that Cecily Carmichael had indeed won the archery contest at the fête. Boswell could have been toying with him and pointing the finger at the one person who had good reason to resent Tristan Carmichael. Which might explain why Cecily had complained so bitterly about being kept prisoner at the Carmichael mansion—to deflect suspicion from herself.

Would someone notice if Cecily sneaked out early in the morning? Would they look for her if she did? Could Cecily manage to stay out long enough to commit murder? Quite possibly. Her escape and Tristan's murder would require extensive planning since she would need to get to Bloody Weald, murder her husband, get back to Brentwood, then explain her absence in a way that didn't arouse anyone's suspicion. Not an easy feat by any means, but Cecily was a beautiful young woman who might have engaged in a dalliance of her own while her husband made his fortune in London. If she had found a devoted accomplice among Carmichael's men, killing Tristan would become that much easier and would establish a motive. Once the period of mourning was over, Cecily would be free to marry again, since she would presumably no longer be of use to Lance Carmichael, and this time, she just might have a say in her own future.

Chapter 14

Daniel tied the reins to a post and walked into the church. The Sext service had just finished, and the attendees filed into the nave and headed toward the door, probably eager to get home and enjoy their well-deserved luncheon. Daniel would have enjoyed a spot of lunch himself, but he didn't care to linger in Brentwood. In London, he would have simply grabbed a hot pie or a cup of soup from a street vendor, but Brentwood didn't have many vendors, and those who made their living by selling street food congregated in areas where they could do the most business, such as the train station and the post office. No one bothered to stand outside a church on a weekday.

When he approached the vicar, the man greeted Daniel with a small smile, his face assuming an expression of inquisitive politeness. He probably thought Daniel had a question about the sermon or intended to contest something the vicar had said. He was no older than thirty, young to have his own church. Daniel had imagined all vicars were like Reverend Talbot, who was beginning to resemble a Biblical prophet as he approached old age. Thoughts of Bible stories put Daniel in mind of Abraham, and he suddenly wondered if Lance Carmichael would ever sacrifice his own son, as Abraham had been prepared to do. To equate Lance Carmichael with Abraham in a house of worship was blasphemy of the highest order, so Daniel dragged his mind away from such unholy comparisons. Carmichael wasn't guided by God, only by his own greed, which was not to be dismissed since for some greed was a religion all its own.

"Good afternoon," the vicar said. "How can I help? Mr.—erm…?"

"Haze," Daniel supplied. He had never met the vicar of St. Peter's Church and didn't think the man would be aware of his connection to the Brentwood Constabulary. It didn't really matter if he was, but Daniel thought the vicar might be more forthcoming if he saw Daniel as just another parishioner and not someone who might compromise a member of his flock.

"My wife and I recently moved to Brentwood," Daniel added.

"Oh, really? Where from?"

"London."

"A veritable den of vice," the vicar said solemnly.

"Quite," Daniel agreed.

"Do you have children, Mr. Haze?"

"Yes, a daughter. She's three years old."

The vicar nodded approvingly. "This is a wholesome place to raise a child. And once she'd older, perhaps she can join the girls' Bible circle. Its purpose is for young ladies to learn about the role of women in the Bible and to prepare them for the responsibilities of matrimony and motherhood."

"A worthy undertaking."

"Indeed, it is," the vicar replied, nodding wisely. "Too many women are embracing an ideology of selfishness and outright rebellion. A woman's only purpose is to gratify her husband and bear his children. Anything else is unforgivable egomania that should be quashed at the youngest possible age."

Daniel arranged his features into an expression of weighty deliberation, desperate to suppress the mirth that had bubbled up inside him. The thought of any woman of his acquaintance existing merely to gratify a man was absurd, since most of them, including past and future mothers-in-law, were temperamental, opinionated, and, in the case of Flora, unapologetically outspoken. The idea of Flora simpering and fussing to make him happy was as unimaginable as it was unwelcome. He didn't need a servant. He wanted a wife who would share his troubles, give him the benefit of her opinion, and help him raise Charlotte to be a woman who could be proud of herself.

What century was this relic living in? The answer was obvious. The vicar upheld sentiments many men of their generation held dear. It was Daniel who had profoundly changed, his worldview forever altered by Jason and his refusal to cleave to outmoded ideas about male and female roles. Years ago, Daniel would have been appalled by the direction of his thoughts, but he acknowledged that he could never go back to the man he had been then, nor did he want to.

Tired of the vicar's maddening discourse, Daniel interrupted. "A neighbor mentioned that St. Peter's is known for its annual fête. My wife is an accomplished archer. Do you hold a competition?"

"The fête is the highlight of the summer, Mr. Haze. We have contests, games, and refreshments. All the entries in the baking competition are served to the attendees once the judges have sampled them and made their determination. And there are many delicious entries," the vicar said with a smile that slid off his face when he recalled Daniel's inquiry. "I, myself, am vehemently opposed to instilling a sense of competition in women. It fosters pride and a desire for attention, but the bishopric sees no harm in allowing the ladies to compete once a year. And some of them are surprisingly skilled. I'm sure Mrs. Haze will fit right in."

Daniel thought that if Flora were to join in the archery competition, she would probably aim for the vicar instead of the target, and she would not miss. And given how much the man was grating on Daniel's nerves, he'd probably cheer her on and reward her with a slice of cake and a cup of tea since it would be well deserved.

"Do many ladies enter the archery competition?" Daniel asked.

"We had nine entrants last year."

"Really? Who won? I wager my wife knows the lady, if only by name."

"Our winner three years running was Cecily Carmichael," the vicar said sourly. "She tends to gloat, which is quite unseemly, but it's not for me to bring her to heel."

"My wife might be intimidated by someone who's that skilled."

"Pride is a sin, Mr. Haze," the vicar reminded Daniel with a wag of his finger. "If we only engage in activities we know we can win at, then we're giving in to vanity. And that goes double for members of the fairer sex."

"I couldn't agree more," Daniel squeezed out. He didn't think he could tolerate this pompous prig a moment longer. "Thank you, Vicar. I will be sure to convey the information to Mrs. Haze."

"The fête is held in June. And perhaps your wife should consider entering the baking competition instead. Much more becoming to a married woman."

"I will be sure to instruct her accordingly," Daniel said, and took his leave.

Talk of cakes reminded him that he was hungry. He would have liked to stop at the Three Bells, but the men from the Brentwood Constabulary frequented the pub due to its proximity to the station, and Daniel didn't want to run into anyone he knew. For one, he didn't want to explain the reason for his presence, and for another, he needed to think. He drove down the High Street until he spotted a chophouse and pulled over. The place looked respectable enough, and would no doubt offer the usual fare. Once he tied up the horse, headed inside, and found an empty table, Daniel ordered a pint of ale and a chop with crispy potatoes.

While he waited for his food, he reviewed what he had learned thus far and suddenly recalled that Flora was quite good at archery and had won several competitions before she'd relocated to London. She had been quite proud of herself and told Daniel that she kept her ribbons in pride of place, pinned to the top of the mirror of her vanity table at Ardith Hall.

Daniel hadn't considered Flora a suspect, but it would be unethical to discount her based solely on how much she meant to him. He had to treat her as he would anyone else in Birch Hill who had access to Bloody Weald. Flora owned a bow, was a skilled archer, and did not hold with people who abused others for personal gain. Tristan Carmichael appeared to be drawn to spirited women, like Moll and Cecily, who clearly wasn't as timid as Daniel had first thought. A woman like Flora would be a conquest, a prize to be won, or a potential challenge that demanded it be answered. Was it possible that Flora had had a run-in with Tristan Carmichael?

Daniel shook his head, surprising the waiter who delivered his meal and probably thought Daniel was unhappy with the appearance of the food. Daniel absentmindedly thanked the man, his mind immediately returning to his worrisome thoughts. Flora would be more than capable of hitting a target using a bow and arrow, but she wasn't the sort of woman to ambush someone in the woods and then deny all responsibility. If she had shot Tristan Carmichael, she would have marched right up to Harriet Elderman's door, asked to see him, and confessed to what she had done.

But not so long ago, Daniel would have said the same of Sarah. He had loved Sarah since she was a girl and had thought he knew her inside out. He had been confident that he could predict what she was and wasn't capable of, but Sarah had proved him tragically wrong and had all but demolished his confidence and self-esteem. She had attempted to kill a man, and had kept the truth from Daniel, a betrayal he'd never quite got over. He had just been learning to live with this new reality when Sarah had taken her own life, leaving him to wrestle with his guilt and regret until he was finally able to see that nothing he might have done would have changed the final outcome.

Flora wasn't Sarah. She was strong, capable, and above all, pragmatic, but there were moments when Daniel questioned his own cogency. He loved Flora; he knew that, and that was the only thing that explained his uncharacteristic decision to throw caution to the wind and ask Flora to marry him after knowing her only a few months. Some, like Harriet, would think that Daniel had been driven by fear of being alone and the loneliness that had become his constant companion in the years since Sarah had died, but just as Jason had known from the start that Flora was the right person for Daniel and Charlotte, Daniel understood that Flora was a rare woman and not one to be kept waiting.

His desire to be with her wasn't a result of gnawing emptiness or a need for a warm body in his bed after years of celibacy. Flora completed him in a way he found utterly astonishing and at the same time perfectly natural. In some respects, she was the female version of Jason—intelligent, compassionate, open to new ideas and ways of doing things, and at the same time completely approachable and perfectly rational.

But murder wasn't rational. It was a visceral reaction to fear, hatred, and loss of control. And Tristan Carmichael had been a man capable of inspiring all of the above even in the most sensible people because no one was immune to terror. The British judicial system was based on the principle of innocent until proven guilty, and Daniel would need to be presented with irrefutable proof of Flora's guilt to believe that she had been in any way involved, but until he was certain she was innocent, he had to keep an open mind, no matter what it cost him, and trust, if not in his own judgment, then in Flora's and Jason's.

Daniel finished his lunch, left a few coins on the table, and stepped back into the brightness of the afternoon. It was time he returned to Birch Hill.

Chapter 15

When Daniel arrived at Redmond Hall, he found Jason in the shed. Jason was in his shirtsleeves but hadn't put on an apron to protect his clothes since the body on the table was intact. The door to the shed was wide open, which allowed Jason to take advantage of the bright afternoon light that shone directly onto the table where Tristan Carmichael's body was laid out.

The corpse was now unclothed, and Daniel had to admit that Tristan had been a fine-looking man even when relieved of the trappings of wealth. His profile was worthy of a Roman bust, his limbs were long and well-toned, and his stomach was taut, the muscles clearly defined. Jason had draped a linen towel across Tristan's hips, not because he worried about the dead man's modesty but because his household was made up mostly of women and he was concerned for their sensibilities should they come striding past.

From what Daniel could see, Tristan had not suffered any other injuries except for the wound inflicted by the arrow. It was now no more than a two-inch incision that Jason had stitched after removing the arrowhead. As Jason had predicted, Tristan's feet were a mottled purple, the result of livor mortis that was also clearly evident in his hands now that they had been washed of blood. Jason pulled a sheet over the body, and the two men stepped out of the shed and into the pleasant cool of the autumn afternoon. There didn't appear to be anything more to be learned from Tristan's remains, and it was preferable to talk when not standing over a corpse.

Jason stopped walking and faced Daniel, his expression turning somber when he noticed Daniel's obvious disquiet. "What is it, Daniel? What did you discover?"

"Flora is a skilled archer," Daniel blurted out, and cursed himself for allowing his doubts to get the better of him when he had just promised himself he wouldn't jump to conclusions and would deal only with facts. But he needed to see Jason's reaction to this revelation.

"So?" Jason asked, drawing out the word as if he had expected there to be considerably more to that statement. He didn't seem particularly shocked by Daniel's revelation either, and Daniel was suddenly able to breathe a little easier.

"What if she was the one to shoot Tristan?"

"Why would Flora kill Tristan Carmichael?" Jason asked.

His tone was calm and measured, and Daniel was grateful that Jason hadn't accused him of being foolish or irrational. He was asking Daniel to explain his reasoning and would reserve judgment until he had heard all the pertinent facts.

"He might have hurt her," Daniel said, and the words lacerated his insides like broken glass. The thought of Flora feeling helpless and scared was unbearable and nearly as alarming as the knowledge that if Flora were backed into a corner, she would try to fight her way out, even if she were torn to shreds in the process. She was a lioness, his Flora, and a lioness would strike back, even if she was wounded.

Jason looked deep into Daniel's eyes and was silent for so long, Daniel thought he might be about to acknowledge the possibility, but Jason did no such thing. He stood back, folded his arms, and tilted his head to the side before asking, "Do you believe Flora capable of premeditated murder?"

"No," Daniel replied instantly, and realized that Jason had hit on the one vital fact Daniel had failed to consider.

The murder of Tristan Carmichael had been premeditated. Had it been the result of a moment of madness brought about by blinding terror, then yes, Flora could be driven to kill. She would defend herself from assault with whatever she had to hand, but what they were dealing with in this case was vastly different. The killer had either waited for Tristan Carmichael to come to the woods, which meant they had been familiar with his plans, or they had arranged to meet him and had lain in wait, knowing what they would do once Tristan appeared.

"Neither do I," Jason agreed, his calm unwavering. "I think Flora might be capable of killing someone in the heat of the moment, and in self-defense, but I can't imagine her planning an execution."

"You said many times that we're all capable of murder," Daniel reminded him.

"And we are, but our ability to go through with it depends on the circumstances. I would kill to defend my family, but I wouldn't murder anyone in cold blood, nor would I stalk them and shoot them from the cover of the trees. They would know who took their life and why."

"But a woman is more vulnerable. To face a man who'd hurt her is to take the chance that he might hurt her again. The only way a woman can shift the balance of power is by putting him at a disadvantage."

"Are you certain this crime was committed by a woman?" Jason asked, nonplussed. "I haven't come across anything that would lead me to that conclusion."

"I'm not certain, no, but these days, archery is a woman's sport, and both Flora and Cecily Carmichael won archery competitions several years in a row."

Jason sighed and nodded in understanding. "Daniel, I can certainly understand how you would be afraid to be blindsided by a woman you love and trust. Sarah's actions led you to question your judgment, and at times your very sanity, but unless you find evidence that suggests Flora and Tristan had a history we're not aware of, this is baseless speculation driven by fear, and possibly a mild case of wedding jitters," he said with a small smile. "Let's set Flora aside for the time being and focus on Cecily. I daresay she probably had a more compelling motive to want Tristan dead than your bride."

Daniel felt something unclench in his chest and sucked in a shuddering breath. He realized he had probably told Jason about Flora's skill with a bow because he needed to hear Jason say that he didn't believe Flora could have anything to do with Tristan's murder. Jason was the most intelligent, logical person Daniel knew, and if Jason saw no reason to suspect Flora, then Daniel could allow himself to move forward without worrying that once again he was being led by the nose by a woman he trusted. Perhaps this was unfair to Flora, and Daniel knew he owed her an apology, but he also admitted to himself that Jason was right, and Sarah's betrayal had led him to question not only his sanity but also his fitness as a parent. He supposed he needed to be reassured that he could trust his instincts and put his faith in another human being fully and without reservation.

"All right," Daniel said. "Let's focus on Cecily."

"We now know that Cecily Carmichael is a skilled archer. Her husband was unfaithful to her from the start and fathered at least one child that we know of with another woman," Jason said. "This gives her a valid motive for murder, especially if some other transgression had recently come to light. This gives Cecily means and motive, but I'm not so sure about opportunity."

Daniel nodded. "From what I could see, Lance Carmichael's home in Brentwood is heavily guarded, and Cecily complained about feeling caged. She might have done that to mislead me, but Brentwood is a long way from Bloody Weald, and if Tristan was murdered, say between ten and noon, Cecily would have to have set off no later than nine o'clock. She would have had to bypass the guards, avail herself of a horse from a stable that's staffed by several grooms, and bring along a bow and arrow, a sack, and enough rope to tie Tristan to the tree. She would also have needed to be certain that Tristan would be there at that precise time."

"If it was Cecily's intention to murder Tristan, then this scheme leaves too much to chance," Jason said. "I can see how she wouldn't want to ambush Tristan anywhere near Brentwood, but I find it difficult to imagine how Cecily could carry out this plan with such precision and not arouse anyone's suspicions. Were you able to identify any other suspects after calling on the Carmichaels?"

"Cecily mentioned two names. The first, Harvey Boswell, took over for Tristan here in Essex after Tristan was sent to London. Cecily thought that Boswell had much to gain by Tristan's death since he could be the one to take over the London operation. The second was Nathaniel Cavey, who Cecily claimed was a powerful rival with a devoted band of followers."

"Anything in it?"

"I spoke to Harvey Boswell, who works out of the rooms Tristan Carmichael had occupied above the Red Lantern. Boswell could have taken himself to Bloody Weald and ambushed Tristan before establishing an alibi with a local coffeehouse owner. He also has something to gain if heading up the London operation is the objective, but Boswell didn't strike me as someone who'd resort to a method that's so theatrical and uncertain. He also admitted outright that he is worried about his sister's safety and would never put Annie Boswell in harm's way. Could be an intentional misdirection, but his fondness for Annie seemed genuine."

"Could Tristan have molested Annie?" Jason asked.

"Boswell assured me that Annie and Tristan never met, which could be a lie. But if Boswell had motive to murder Tristan Carmichael, surely it would be safer and easier to dispatch him in London, where no one would suspect Boswell when Tristan turned up dead."

Jason nodded. "Might Annie have arranged to meet Tristan in the woods?"

"Again, possible, but it would have required considerable planning, especially if she didn't want her brother involved. I have it on good authority that both Boswells were in Brentwood by nine o'clock, which would mean that Tristan was murdered no later than eight."

Jason shook his head. "It's difficult to ascertain the precise time of death, particularly when the body had been left out in the open, but based on the advancement of rigor and the early stages of lividity in the extremities at the point of examination, I very much doubt Tristan was murdered that early in the day. I'd say probably closer to ten. Maybe even as late as noon."

"So, where does that leave us?" Daniel asked.

"Since we don't know where Harvey Boswell, Annie Boswell, and Cecily Carmichael were between ten and twelve o'clock on Monday, in much the same place as before," Jason replied. "Plus, we have yet to speak to Nathaniel Cavey, and we have a skilled huntsman in our midst who had cause to hate Tristan Carmichael."

"Who are you referring to?"

"Evan Jones. Squire Talbot's gamekeeper."

"Jones? What has he to do with Tristan Carmichael?" Daniel asked. This was the first time he was hearing of a connection between Tristan Carmichael and Evan Jones, who was an odd duck, according to Harriet.

"Evan Jones readily admitted that Tristan Carmichael seduced his sister and got her with child. After Jones confronted Tristan, he lost his position as gamekeeper to Lord Stanhope. According to Jones, all this happened some time ago, but that kind of resentment runs deep, especially since Brynn Jones still services Tristan Carmichael at one of their brothels," Jason said.

"Blimey, was there no end to that man's depravity?" Daniel exclaimed.

"Apparently not."

"Do you think Jones may be our man?"

Jason considered the question. "Evan Jones has a motive, happens to be proficient with a bow and arrow, and lives a stone's throw from Bloody Weald. He also has no alibi for Monday morning. Having said that, I will also say that his reaction to the news of Carmichael's death seemed genuine, and unless he wanted to be caught, he wouldn't have incriminated himself so willingly."

"Perhaps the man is a simpleton," Daniel said.

"He is rather eccentric, but I don't think he lacks intelligence. He seems fixated on his ancestral connection to the archers of Gwent, and informed me that Welsh archers were the best in the world."

"They were, actually," Daniel replied. "They were also merciless. Their antics are legendary."

"What sort of antics can an archer resort to?" Jason asked. He appeared genuinely interested in the subject matter.

"My father told me a story about something that happened after a battle. I can't recall which one it was, but that's not really important. The archers apprehended a soldier who was trying to escape, so they dragged him from his horse, made him mount the wrong way, then fired arrows into his thighs to pin him to the saddle. Then they slapped the horse on the rump, sending the unfortunate deserter back the way he had come."

"Every army punishes deserters," Jason said, a cloud passing over his face. "I've seen my share of military justice, or what passes for justice in the minds of those incapable of compassion."

"This wasn't their deserter," Daniel explained. "The archers were for hire, so there was no call to be so cruel. And given the average age of soldiers in those days, the poor sod was probably hardly more than a boy." Daniel paused, reflecting on what he had just said. "Jason, do you think it's possible that the killer was paid to murder Tristan?"

"I suppose anything is possible, but the suggestion leads me to the same question. Why would someone hire an archer to kill Tristan with a bow and arrow? I can't help but think that the method was meant to send a message, and we're missing the vital clue that would help us to decipher it."

"And who would this message be for? His father? His wife?"

"I don't know, but Tristan has a son, who might now be a target."

"Why would anyone want to murder a two-year-old boy?" Daniel asked.

"Because boys grow into men, who can bear a grudge and become bent on vengeance."

"Only if they know who's responsible," Daniel argued, then recalled once again that Lance Carmichael intended to conduct his own inquiry. If he learned who had killed his son, he would no doubt exact vengeance and teach Samuel to do the same once he came of age.

"Tristan once told me that people like him live by their own code of honor," Jason said. "They don't go after women and children, but if Lance Carmichael discovered that a rival killed his only son, he could go on a killing spree that would start a blood feud that could last for generations."

"That might explain why the killer used a bow and arrow. Lance Carmichael would expect a rival to use a pistol or a knife, weapons that are routinely used in gang warfare. A bow and arrow feels personal and, dare I say it, Biblical."

"Yes, it does," Jason agreed. "Which makes me wonder if the bow and the location were intentionally used to muddy the waters. Or perhaps the location was chosen for access. In London, Tristan was surrounded by his men. Here, he was alone. I expect he thought himself invincible."

"He's not so invincible now," Daniel said, his gaze straying to the naked man in the shed. "We're all equal in death."

"Not quite," Jason replied. "Even in death, some people are more privileged than others. Tristan's funeral will be one for the ages, and his body will be laid in the family vault, where it will be protected from grave robbers. He truly will rest in peace."

"Speaking of burials, Lance Carmichael would like to bury his son."

"I'll see the body is delivered to him," Jason said. He seemed to contemplate Tristan's remains, then said, "Daniel, it's not too late to turn the case over to the Brentwood Constabulary. Essex is Brentwood's concern, and so far, we haven't uncovered any leads that point to a London connection."

Daniel sighed heavily. "Boswell implied—no, said outright," he amended, "that DI Coleridge is on Carmichael's payroll. Can the Brentwood Constabulary be trusted to conduct an impartial investigation, or will Coleridge fit up someone for the crime and send them to the gallows to appease Lance Carmichael?"

"We don't know that what Boswell said is true, but to be frank, I wouldn't be overly surprised to discover that there was some truth to the accusation."

"You wouldn't?" Daniel balked.

"Lance Carmichael has a dozen men guarding his house, and dozens more at his beck and call. DI Coleridge can ill afford to antagonize the man."

"Are you suggesting that DI Coleridge picks his cases based on the odds?"

"Until the constabulary has enough men, and until such time as they are armed with more than wooden sticks, DI Coleridge must consider the safety of his people. Perhaps he and Lance Carmichael have an agreement."

"The police service does not make agreements with criminals," Daniel bristled.

"Misery acquaints a man with strange bedfellows," Jason replied.

"What manner of cretin said that?" Daniel demanded, outraged. "I'd like to teach him a thing or two about honor."

"Shakespeare," Jason replied with an amused grin. "And I think he's somewhat beyond your reach."

"Well, what do we do, then?"

"I think we should have a word with Nathaniel Cavey. Do you know where to find him?"

"He lives on a houseboat and docks at Foulness Island."

"If the name is anything to go by…" Jason began, then suddenly went quiet.

"What is it?" Daniel asked.

"We have something that might give us a clue to the identity of the killer," Jason said, his face brightening.

"Really? What?"

"The rope. Micah said he saw a similar knot in a picture of a boat. If Cavey lives on a houseboat, he is sure to be proficient with nautical knots. But it would help to identify the knot first. There are many different kinds."

"How many ways could there be to tie a rope?"

"You'd be amazed," Jason replied.

"So, how do we identify the knot? Birch Hill is not exactly a sailing community."

"We need to consult an expert. And we should do it before we confront Cavey."

"Do you know any sailors?" Daniel inquired.

"I do, as it happens," Jason said. "But I would have to go to London to speak to the man. And I think you should come with me."

"Do you think you will require backup?"

Jason shook his head. "I have something else in mind."

"Care to enlighten me?"

"There's one person who knew everything there was to know about Tristan's life—his butler, Simcoe. It would be remiss not to question the man in connection with his employer's murder."

Daniel nodded, annoyed that he hadn't thought of it himself. Simcoe greeted Tristan Carmichael's visitors, oversaw both incoming and outgoing correspondence, and maintained his social calendar. He knew everywhere Tristan went and whom he met with.

"Are you able to go tomorrow?" Daniel asked.

"I can get away. I will tell Dodson I'm going to visit the Royal College of Surgeons, and you should mention to Mrs. Elderman's servants that you're going to London to collect Flora's ring. No need to reveal our plans."

"Do you think mentioning it to the servants will somehow protect the integrity of our investigation?"

"Mrs. Elderman's groom drinks at the Red Stag, and Tilda has been stepping out with John Locke, who works at the livery attached to the tavern. Men tend to talk over a pint, and Davy Brody is a known associate of the Carmichaels. If Lance Carmichael hears that the investigation took us to London, he might send someone to speak to Simcoe first and either gather the information for himself or silence Simcoe before he has a chance to reveal something incriminating."

"Valid point," Daniel agreed. "And I do need to collect the ring. I was going to go on Thursday, but tomorrow should be fine."

"Excellent. Have Mrs. Elderman's groom drive you to the train station in Brentwood, and I will meet you there. We can take the ten o'clock train."

"I will be there."

"See you tomorrow, then."

Chapter 16

A fledgling sense of calm settled over Daniel as he guided the dogcart down the peaceful country lane. The sun shimmered high above the tree line in the distance, and the air was pleasantly warm. The leaves had yet to change to their autumnal colors, and the fields were golden with ripened wheat. Daniel had always loved September, when the summer seemed to linger during the day but there was a chill in the air once the sun set and darkness descended a little earlier each day. Nature seemed to hunker down with the approach of winter, while people prepared for the darkest months of the year, when they were driven inside and left to their own thoughts and the company of their loved ones.

This year, Daniel had much to look forward to. There would be cozy nights by the fire. Christmas would not be a day to be stoically borne and made artificially festive for Charlotte's sake. And the New Year would signal a new beginning rather than the continuation of the misery that had pervaded the house since Sarah had died. But before Daniel could allow himself to focus on the good things to come, he had to get through this week, which wasn't turning out as he had anticipated. Tristan Carmichael's gruesome demise reminded Daniel that ugliness always lurked just around the corner and even a beautiful, serene wood like Bloody Weald could become the scene of something dark and frightening.

Daniel allowed the tired horse to amble on at its own pace. He was in no rush to get back. He couldn't think of Harriet's house as home, not anymore. It was a place to lay his head until the wedding, and he was weary. The one thing he looked forward to at the end of this frustrating day was an hour spent with Charlotte before she went to bed. Charlotte was the only person in Harriet's household who didn't judge him or make him feel as if he were about to commit the ultimate betrayal. Daniel was ready to move on, but he couldn't do that as long as there were constant reminders of a life that retreated further into the past with every passing day.

To Daniel, Flora was the light shining through the trees, a new dawn after a period of darkness. He couldn't wait for Saturday to come and despised himself for mistrusting Flora. Because of his past, he had ample reason to be cautious, but Flora had never given him cause to doubt her. Daniel vowed then and there that he would never question Flora's motives again and would support her in every possible way. Perhaps if he had made such a vow when he'd married Sarah, things would have turned out differently and Sarah wouldn't have felt so emotionally isolated when she had needed him most. Daniel's face burned with shame when he recalled sharing his suspicions about Flora with Jason, and he wished he could take back everything he had said.

Jason was Daniel's closest friend, his only friend really, and his partner in more than a dozen investigations, but if Daniel were honest, there were times when their collaboration hadn't felt even-handed, and he had felt at a disadvantage. Daniel might not admit it to anyone else, but he couldn't lie to himself. Without Jason, he wouldn't solve half the cases that came his way or be able to claim the impressive solve rate that made him one of the most respected detectives at Scotland Yard. Jason was able to identify leads and pursue avenues of inquiry that were obvious to him but had never occurred to Daniel. As he had just done with the current case. Without Jason's foresight, the investigation would have stalled.

It had been some time since Ransome had made his pitch to Jason, but Daniel knew in his heart that if Jason showed the slightest inclination to accept Ransome's offer, Ransome would snap him up. Ransome didn't want Jason to become a police surgeon, even though Mr. Fenwick had finally retired, and the opening was yet to be permanently filled. Ransome wanted Jason on the murder squad, and he was willing to offer him the coveted title of detective inspector. It was a relatively new position, and to date, Ransome had promoted only one inspector. DI Yates strutted around the Yard like a peacock and never missed an opportunity to remind the other detectives that he was now a step above them, and they should all be impressed by his newly minted rank.

Daniel hated to admit it since it sounded prideful, but he coveted the title and wished Ransome would promote him, but Ransome held back, waiting for the right moment to tap a second man. And Daniel knew precisely who that man was. Jason's effortless ability niggled at Daniel and made him question his own worth. It wasn't Jason's fault. He was simply being himself, and Daniel could never fault him as either a colleague or a friend. The problem lay with Daniel, who felt inherently inferior. The possibility of losing Jason as a friend troubled him, but Daniel knew there would come a time when he would have to either prove himself or die trying.

Chapter 17

After he saw Daniel off, Jason re-dressed Tristan Carmichael, covered the body, and affixed the padlock after making sure the door was firmly shut. The external examination hadn't yielded any new information, so tomorrow morning, he and Joe would deliver the body to Lance Carmichael. It would be the perfect cover for traveling to Brentwood and would also prevent Carmichael's men from showing up at Redmond Hall. Once the body was safely delivered, Jason would meet Daniel at the station.

As Jason strode toward the house, his thoughts turned to Flora. He couldn't cast Flora in the role of remorseless killer, but he could hardly blame Daniel for experiencing feelings of paranoia. It would be a long while before Daniel could trust someone without second-guessing his judgment, after he had placed his trust in Sarah and been so thoroughly deceived. Perhaps facing his doubts about Flora was healthy, and either Daniel would realize he couldn't trust Flora, or he would forge ahead with a renewed sense of commitment.

Jason didn't judge Sarah's motivations for murder and had understood her desperate need for justice. It had been unbearable for her to watch the man responsible for Felix's death strut around as if nothing had happened, oblivious to the pain of the family he had destroyed and the child he had unintentionally killed. But Sarah had crossed the line between wanting to see justice done and becoming the instrument of said justice, and once she had attempted to commit murder, she had never truly been able to come back, even though she had not succeeded and someone else had got there moments before her. Sarah had evaded the hangman's noose, but she hadn't been able to escape from guilt. So she had executed herself, probably believing she had righted a wrong. But as far as Jason was concerned, Sarah had wronged Daniel and Charlotte and had left them forever damaged, even if that damage had been buried deep inside.

Did one ever completely recover from trauma? Jason didn't think so, and it galled him that modern medicine saw no good reason to delve into the workings of the mind. Some people found a way to live with their pain and buried it deep inside in order to go on, but others resorted to self-destructive behavior and thought they didn't deserve to be happy. The perfect example of this was Mary, who couldn't seem to find her place in the world and was once again talking about returning to the United States.

Micah had referred to Mary's angst as Catholic guilt, but Jason didn't think Mary's feelings had anything to do with religion. Mary had lived when her parents, her brother, Liam's father, and then her new husband and baby had died. Deep down, she didn't think she deserved to live on and couldn't make peace with everyone's passing. The two people who kept Mary tethered to this world were Liam and Micah, and if anything happened to them, Mary would surely self-destruct. Jason wished he could help Mary, but he had learned long ago that you couldn't talk people out of their feelings or try to do-good them into changing their ways. The person had to want to change and find their own reasons for living. Just as Daniel had to find his own reasons for getting married.

Jason would stand next to Daniel in church come Saturday, but if Daniel changed his mind and thought it prudent to wait, then Jason would support him in his decision, even though he couldn't think of a more perfect fit for Daniel than Flora Tarrant. Flora was intelligent, independent, and resilient—the sort of woman Daniel needed by his side. She wouldn't fall apart if things became difficult, and wouldn't allow Daniel to go to pieces if tragedy struck again. And why wouldn't it? There were no scales of justice that made certain everyone got their fair share, and no one was made to suffer more than anyone else. Some people were truly cursed, and Jason desperately hoped Daniel wasn't one of them.

Jason decided to keep his maudlin thoughts from Katherine, who had enough to worry about as her pregnancy progressed. No woman could remain serene in the face of the possible death of either herself or the child she already loved and not worry about the people she might leave behind if the worst happened. Jason would do everything in his power to ensure a smooth delivery, but sometimes life had its own plan. Every family walked through its own graveyard in their hearts, the stones etched predominantly with names of women, who died in childbirth or shortly after, and children. The Redmonds had enjoyed an idyllic summer, but winter was coming, and with it the cruel winds that had the power to chill one's soul.

Chapter 18

Wednesday, September 8

The handover of Tristan Carmichael's remains went much as expected. Lance Carmichael himself came out to inspect the body and pumped Jason's hand longer than necessary as he thanked him for looking after his boy. Jason didn't have any warm feelings toward the old scoundrel, but he could sympathize with him as a father and offered his condolences on Tristan's passing.

"You must come to the funeral," Lance said. "Tristan always spoke very highly of you."

Jason was surprised to hear that Tristan had spoken of him at all but had promised Lance he would do his best to attend. It could be helpful to see who showed up and if anyone acted twitchy in the presence of the corpse. Jason was put in mind of the ancient practice of cruentation, where an individual accused of murder was instructed to publicly touch the body of the victim. If the corpse began to bleed or if any other strange signs manifested, the accused was deemed guilty. Jason thought the probability of Tristan's killer attending the funeral was higher than average and would have liked to see Lance Carmichael demand that every mourner lay their hands on Tristan's remains. That would make for a spectacle few would soon forget, if only for the panic it was sure to cause among the attendees.

Daniel didn't seem inclined to converse on the ride to London and buried his nose in a newspaper, so Jason looked out the window, his thoughts on everything and nothing. Once they arrived, they agreed on a meeting time, then went their separate ways. Daniel was off to Upper Brook Street to speak to Tristan Carmichael's butler, and Jason headed to Bishopsgate. Captain Isaiah Needham, whom Jason had operated on shortly before removing the family to Essex, resided in a modest house just down the street from St. Botolph-without-Bishopsgate, an area of

London Jason had yet to familiarize himself with. London had so many neighborhoods, each pocket of humanity known for their characteristics and judged by their address. Jason wasn't sure what the address said about Captain Needham but knew the old sailor to be a good man and looked forward to seeing him again.

He was admitted by a servant of late middle age, who took his things and invited him to wait in the parlor. Despite the early hour, the woman looked tired and wan, and walked like someone who was in chronic pain. Her pallor spoke to a life spent mostly indoors, unlike her employer, whose skin had been tanned to leather by years spent on the captain's bridge, his face exposed to the elements.

"Would you care for some refreshment, Dr. Redmond?" the servant asked once Jason was settled before the empty hearth.

"Thank you, no," Jason said, and the woman left him on his own.

He wouldn't have said no to a cup of coffee, or even tea, but the shabbiness of the parlor was a clear indication that Captain Needham didn't have money to spare, and every little bit mattered to his survival. Yellowed antimacassars protected the tops and armrests of the chairs, and the upholstery was visibly worn. The curtains were faded, and the rug that covered only a small part of the room was threadbare. The paint was peeling in places, and there was a damp patch on the ceiling.

Jason would have expected an officer whose career in the Royal Navy had spanned decades to be more comfortable in his twilight years, but he didn't know anything about the man's personal habits. Perhaps he had spent his wages on drinking in quayside taverns or had gambled it away. Or maybe he had never expected to find himself living ashore for any length of time and had never bothered to make a home. It was only recently that Captain Needham had been forced to retire, after a cut on his calf had turned gangrenous and Jason had removed the leg from the knee down to save the man's life.

Captain Needham smiled in greeting when he entered the parlor. His crutch tapped on the wooden floorboards as he made his way across the room and settled in a chair across from Jason. He was in his early fifties, a tall, lean man with an angular face and thinning dark hair that was more liberally streaked with silver than when Jason had last seen him. The captain's most striking feature was his bright blue eyes that shone with good humor even when he wasn't in the best of spirits. He had been clean-shaven when Jason had first met him, but now he wore a short beard, possibly because he had difficulty balancing himself while shaving and didn't care to shave sitting down.

"Dr. Redmond, what a pleasure it is to see you," Captain Needham said once he was comfortably seated, and his crutch was positioned against his chair and within easy reach. "Have you come to check on me? I didn't think you made house calls."

"It's good to see you too, Captain. How are you feeling?"

"The leg is healing nicely, but sometimes in the night I feel the most awful pain in my calf. I wake, and it takes me a moment to remember that my calf is no longer there."

Captain Needham's expression was one of deep sadness as his hand went to his knee, and he caressed the stump as if he could feel the pain in his absent calf at that very moment, the limb as real to him as if it were still there.

"The phenomenon is known as phantom pain," Jason explained. "It's all in the mind, but I know it feels real and very painful."

"It does," Captain Needham agreed. "Will it go away in time?"

"The episodes will become less frequent, but the time frame varies from person to person."

Captain Needham nodded. "I miss my ship, Dr. Redmond."

"I thought you might. Will you go to sea once you're fully recovered?"

The captain shook his head. "The Royal Navy doesn't believe I'm fit to captain a ship. I've been decommissioned, like some old, leaky tub of a boat. I don't know what to do with myself to fill the days."

"I'm sorry to hear that," Jason said.

He felt awful for the man. Captain Needham wasn't married and didn't have children. His crew had been his family. Jason supposed he must have had friends, but people tended to drift apart once a common interest had been removed and one person was no longer fully mobile.

Captain Needham smiled ruefully. "But it's not all doom and gloom. I was told there are plans to open a Royal Naval College in Greenwich and I will be able to apply for a teaching post. So you see, I can still be useful."

"I'm happy to hear it."

"An old sea dog like me needs to be on the water, but if I can no longer go to sea, I can offer my knowledge and experience to a new generation of officers."

"Will you relocate to Greenwich?" Jason asked.

"There's nothing to keep me here, and I'm told there will be staff accommodation. I would like to live among sailors. It's the only life I know."

"Then I hope it all goes to plan," Jason said.

"Me too, Doctor. Me too."

"Captain, I was hoping I might consult you on something I've come across."

"Of course. Happy to help," Captain Needham exclaimed. "Is it to do with sailing?"

"It might."

Jason pulled out the sketch he'd made of the knot used to bind Tristan Carmichael to the tree and passed it across. Captain Needham studied it for a moment, then handed the sketch back to Jason.

"Is this a nautical knot?" Jason asked.

The captain shook his head. "I've never seen a knot like this. Where did you come across it?"

"It was used to secure a dead man to a tree."

"Where?"

"In Essex. Near Brentwood."

"So not a sailing community, then."

"No, but my ward thought he had seen a similar knot in a drawing of a medieval ship."

"It is possible that this sort of knot was used in centuries past. Or in other parts of the world. I really can't say for certain. I only know the type of knots that were used during my time in the Navy and on British ships." Captain Needham tilted his head to the side, his expression one of patent curiosity. "Would identifying the knot help you to track down the killer?"

"I hoped it might narrow the field of suspects."

"Are there that many?"

"This man had a habit of making enemies," Jason explained.

Captain Needham nodded. "I've known a few of those in my day. Some men just rub others the wrong way."

Tristan Carmichael had actually been quite charming and could play the gentleman when it suited his purposes, but any man in a position of power who held sway over the lives of others had his share of enemies, and Tristan had been no different. He'd held the power of life and death in his hands when it came not only to his own men, but also to those who dared to cross him or challenge his authority.

"How did the victim die?" Captain Needham inquired. Jason thought the captain hoped to prolong the conversation, since Jason was most likely the only visitor he'd had in a long while.

"He was shot with an arrow."

Captain Needham's eyebrows rose in astonishment. "With an arrow? Not a commonly used weapon these days."

"No, but there are those who still use it when hunting, and it's something of a sport."

"It takes great skill to shoot an arrow," Captain Needham said. "Focus, strength, and excellent aim."

"I expect the killer had honed all three. We didn't find any other arrows in the vicinity, so the first arrow probably found its mark."

"Unless your man cleaned up after himself," Captain Needham pointed out.

"I don't think an individual who's not confident in their ability to hit the target would opt for that particular method."

"You're right there. Plenty of ways to kill a man, especially when near a tree."

"You mean hanging?"

"Well, if one means to murder someone and has rope…" He made a gesture meant to invite Jason to draw his own conclusions.

"To hang a man, one has to get close enough to get the noose around his neck. An arrow can be shot from afar."

"But the killer did get close, didn't he? He tied the victim to a tree."

"I think perhaps the victim was propped up against the tree after death."

"To what end?"

"Perhaps the killer wanted to make sure the body was discovered. They covered the head with a sack."

"Interesting," Captain Needham said, his gaze pensive.

"Interesting how?"

"It shows a degree of regard, wouldn't you say?" Captain Needham asked. "I've seen men flogged and hanged, but the same men who had administered the punishment were sometimes the first ones to look after the wounds they had inflicted or prepare the body for burial at sea. They wrapped the deceased as if they were swaddling a baby, with love and tenderness."

"Why do you think that was?" Jason asked.

"They did what had to be done because they had no choice in the matter. They were following orders. But they had a choice about how they treated the victim afterwards. Something to chew on, at any rate," Captain Needham said. "Your man might have had his own reasons for propping the body up or for pulling a sack over the head. Perhaps he wanted to hide the man's identity, if only temporarily, or maybe he couldn't bear to look upon the victim's face a moment longer."

Captain Needham sighed with what was obviously a painful memory, his face creasing with what could be regret. Perhaps he had been the one to perform the gruesome task when he was a lowly sailor and had watched his friends die and get tossed overboard, their bodies consigned to the deep.

"Was the victim someone close to you?" the captain asked at last.

"Not close, no, but we did have history."

"Then I wish you the best of luck, Dr. Redmond. I know you're a practiced hand at unraveling tricky cases."

"Thank you, Captain," Jason said.

He was about to stand when the captain said, "Would you care to join me for luncheon? Esther promised me cold beef and salad. I know that probably doesn't sound too appealing to a man of your stature, but it's good enough for me, especially when I'm homebound and can't move around as I used to. I prefer to eat light these days."

"I thank you for your kind offer, Captain, and I would love to join you, but I have arranged to meet a colleague and cannot be late."

"Of course. I understand," Captain Needham said. "Another time, then."

"I'll look forward to it," Jason replied.

He shook the captain's hand and walked toward the door. He could almost taste the man's loneliness and his grief at losing the life he'd loved, and hoped Captain Needham would find new purpose at the future Naval Academy.

Chapter 19

Daniel knocked on the door of Tristan Carmichael's Upper Brook Street residence several times before Simcoe finally answered. He looked bleary-eyed, and the smell of strong spirits emanated from his pores. Not so upstanding when the master wasn't around, then, Daniel thought, then wondered if Simcoe had been informed of Tristan's death and had given in to his sorrow.

"What do you want?" Simcoe asked. He'd recognized Daniel and was understandably wary to find a policeman at the door.

"I need a word."

"Mr. Carmichael is not at home."

"I know."

"And how do you know that?"

"Because his body was delivered to his father's house early this morning."

Simcoe stared at Daniel, dumbfounded. "What are you saying, man?"

"Tristan Carmichael was murdered, Mr. Simcoe, and I'm investigating the case. Look, do we have to do this on the doorstep?" Daniel asked irritably.

"No, of course not. Come inside."

Simcoe stepped aside to let Daniel in, then shut the door behind him and gestured toward the drawing room. Normally, a butler would receive a visitor in the butler's pantry, but Simcoe had evidently realized that he wouldn't remain in this house much longer, and unless he was reassigned, his employment with the Carmichaels was probably at an end.

Since Simcoe hadn't bothered to take his things, Daniel took off his hat and unbuttoned his coat before settling on the settee. The room was lovely, the furnishings exquisite, and still new. Daniel would have expected Tristan Carmichael to flaunt his wealth, but the décor was tasteful and understated, the room comfortable without appearing overstuffed. Daniel wondered what it would be like to be able to afford such luxury and not have to worry about money. Tristan Carmichael wouldn't be worrying about anything anymore, but he had enjoyed his life while he was able and had taken what he'd wanted, whether it was goods or women. And despite his failings, he had been loved and would be missed.

"How did Mr. Carmichael die?" Simcoe asked. Daniel explained, and the butler stared at him, his mouth falling open with shock. "Is that really true?"

"Would I make it up?" Daniel asked.

"Probably not. You're not known for your sense of humor."

"Is that so?"

Daniel wasn't sure why he found that insulting. He didn't think of himself as someone who was witty and amusing, but he still resented being told he was dry as toast.

"So, why are you here, Inspector? Surely you didn't come all that way just to tell me in person."

"No. I have some questions to put to you."

"Go on, then, but first, let's drink to Mr. Carmichael's memory," Simcoe said as he strode toward the drinks cabinet.

"A bit early for me."

"Come, Inspector. Join me," Simcoe said in a tone that bordered on pleading.

"All right," Daniel reluctantly agreed.

He had to admit that he felt sorry for the man. This morning, he had been safe in the knowledge that his position was assured, probably for the rest of his days. Now, nothing was certain, and he was understandably upset and unbalanced by the news. Daniel also thought that Simcoe had cared deeply for his employer. Tristan was an easy man to like as long as one didn't cross him, and he had probably been good to Simcoe, who had been as devoted to Tristan Carmichael as a faithful dog.

The butler handed Daniel a tumbler of brandy and raised his glass in a silent toast. Daniel didn't want to drink to Tristan Carmichael, but it seemed churlish not to acknowledge a man's death, so he raised his own glass and tossed back the contents. It was good brandy, very smooth, and probably very French. It slid down Daniel's throat like the smoothest silk, warming his insides and calming him, although that was probably just the side effect of drinking so early in the day. Normally, Daniel put off the pleasure until after dinner, when he allowed himself a well-deserved tot of brandy.

"Another?" Simcoe asked eagerly.

"No, thank you. And I think you've had enough. You reek, man."

Simcoe defiantly poured himself another drink and tossed it back, then took a seat. His shoulders were slumped, and his eyes became so moist, he had to look away.

"What will you do?" Daniel asked once Simcoe seemed more composed.

"I will write to Mr. Carmichael and ask for instructions. I expect he'll want to sell the house, or lease it. The poor man must be crushed. Tristan was everything to him."

"He has other children."

"Girls," Simcoe said dismissively. "Hardly the same as a son."

"There's a grandson." Two, though Lance might not know about Tristan's illegitimate child.

"Samuel is still a baby, but I expect Mr. Carmichael will keep a close eye on him. If Tristan's widow wishes to remarry, she'll probably have to relinquish all rights to the boy," Simcoe said.

"What about the other boy?" Daniel asked.

Simcoe didn't insult Daniel's intelligence by denying knowledge of another child. "The child's mother got married and left London."

"Where is she? Do you know her name?"

Simcoe nodded. "Felicity Sweetman. Dixon before she married. She now lives in Philadelphia, and before you ask, Mr. Carmichael and Felicity had a cordial relationship. Felicity was his mistress for at least a year, and although Mr. Carmichael stopped visiting her once she got with child, he saw to her upkeep and provided for the boy."

"Did he see his son?"

"He did. Mr. Carmichael loved the boy, but he didn't begrudge Felicity a chance at happiness. They parted on amicable terms, and Mr. Carmichael even settled a sum on Philip. Something for his future, he said."

"So, you don't think Felicity Sweetman might have held a grudge?"

Maybe moving to Philadelphia was just a story Tristan's former mistress had told him to get him out of her life.

"Nah," Simcoe said.

"Do you have an address for her?" Daniel asked.

"I can show you one of her letters."

"I would appreciate that."

Simcoe shook his head in disgust. "You're grasping at straws, Inspector."

"That's the nature of policing. Ask question after question until you get an answer that makes sense." Daniel wasn't sure why he was explaining himself. He didn't need a reason to ask about Tristan's love life. "Was there a current mistress?"

"Not that I'm aware of. Mr. Carmichael spent most of the summer in Essex. I expect Mrs. Carmichael kept him busy in that regard."

A pretty young maidservant peeked into the drawing room. "Do you require anything, Mr. Simcoe?"

"No, we're all right," Simcoe answered gruffly. "I'll come find you later."

The maidservant seemed surprised but didn't question the man and beat a hasty retreat, presumably to the kitchen.

"Are there any other servants in the house?"

Daniel seemed to recall that Tristan Carmichael had a manservant named Freddy but wasn't sure if he still employed the man.

"No, it's just me and Lizzie."

"What about Freddy?"

"Freddy moved on. He wanted to remain in Essex."

"Does he still work for the Carmichaels?"

"I don't know. He might."

"Is there no groom or coachman?" Daniel asked.

Daniel had expected Tristan Carmichael to maintain a bigger staff, but if he wished to protect his privacy, it was best to keep domestic retainers to a minimum since servants, even the most devoted ones, tended to talk. Daniel would have a word with Lizzie as well, but for now all his attention was on Simcoe. He had thought Simcoe was older, but now that he wasn't putting on airs, Daniel realized that they were probably of an age. Simcoe had neatly trimmed light brown hair and eyes that fell somewhere between brown and gray. Like mud. He had good bone structure, though, and was in enviable physical shape, which made Daniel wonder if Simcoe had been more than just a butler. A bodyguard of sorts? It was possible.

"The coachman went to Brentwood with Mr. Carmichael," Simcoe said.

"Did Mr. Carmichael have any enemies?"

"Everyone has enemies."

"Not everyone."

"You think there isn't anyone who'd like to shoot you through the heart and tie you to a tree?" Simcoe retorted.

"I'm sure there are a number of people who'd like to hear of my passing, but I'm not sure many of them would risk their lives to kill me themselves."

"Well, this bloke didn't risk his life, did he? You have no idea who did it."

"Not yet, but I will. And Lord Redmond is assisting in the investigation."

"Good. Mr. Carmichael would have liked that. He trusted the man. Lord only knows why," Simcoe grumbled.

"Perhaps because Lord Redmond has a sense of honor." *Unlike some* seemed to hang in the air between them.

"Mr. Carmichael had a sense of honor, Inspector. You might not think so, but he looked after those he cared about."

"That's really not the same thing."

"It is to some. To know that someone will take care of you when you are in need means a lot to most people."

"Did Mr. Carmichael look after you?"

Simcoe nodded. "He did. He sent my boy to a good school and made sure my Will had everything he needed, so he'd fit in with the other boys."

"I didn't realize you had a son."

"Why would you?"

"Only child?"

"I had a daughter, but she died in infancy."

"I'm sorry. And your wife?"

"Died five years ago, when Will was seven."

Simcoe didn't say what his wife had died of, and Daniel didn't ask. It wasn't pertinent to the investigation, and Daniel saw no reason to pry into the man's personal grief.

"What will happen to your boy now that Mr. Carmichael is gone?" Daniel asked.

"I don't know. I hope Mr. Lance Carmichael will look after him, but I was more Mr. Tristan's man."

"So tell me, who do you think would have reason to want Tristan Carmichael dead?"

"I really don't know. There were rivals, sure, but I don't think they'd murder him in the woods."

"Why not?"

"That's not how these things are done," Simcoe said.

"How are they done?"

The man shook his head at Daniel's naivete. "If someone's going to top a rival, Inspector, they'll do it in such a way that everyone knows it was them. It's a show of strength, a challenge. They're not going to shoot him with an arrow and leave him tied to a tree. That would be pointless."

"So you think this was personal rather than professional?"

"Don't you?"

"Maybe," Daniel conceded. Simcoe made a good point that Daniel couldn't easily dismiss. "Was there anyone Mr. Carmichael had wronged? A husband? A woman? An underling?"

"Mr. Carmichael wasn't much interested in married women, so I doubt a jealous husband's your man. And he dealt fairly with his underlings, at least as far as I'm aware. Unless they crossed him, of course—then he was vicious."

"Had anyone crossed him of late?"

"He didn't see eye to eye with Harvey Boswell."

"Why was that?"

"I don't know, but he did say the man was a wily devil. I expect their paths crossed while Mr. Carmichael was in Brentwood." It was obvious from Simcoe's expression that he felt slighted and would have liked to join Tristan in the country.

"Why didn't Mr. Carmichael take you along?" Daniel asked.

"Because Mr. Carmichael's father has his own people, and someone had to stay behind and look to his post and various other interests."

"I see. Can you think of anyone else Mr. Carmichael didn't get on with?"

That was a euphemism if Daniel had ever heard one, but he wasn't sure how to ask what he wanted to know without causing Simcoe to clam up and ask him to leave. He needn't have worried. Simcoe seemed eager to talk.

He nodded, his heavy-lidded gaze growing even more somber. "Clarence Tipton."

"And who's he?"

"Tipton was a warehouse manager. He left the side door of the warehouse unlocked when he went home one night. An entire shipment of opium that had just arrived from China, thousands of pounds' worth, was stolen by members of a rival gang. And several other items were taken."

"What sort of items?"

Simcoe looked uncomfortable, as if anything Tristan Carmichael had kept in his warehouse could be worse than opium. "There was a crate of pistols from America," Simcoe admitted.

"So, Tristan Carmichael thought Mr. Tipton had left the door unlocked on purpose?"

"Tipson said he received a note that his wife was unwell and forgot to lock the door in his hurry to get home, but Mr. Carmichael thought he was on the take."

"Whoever stole the opium and the guns could have just as easily broken in. Why bribe the manager?"

"To make a point, and force Mr. Carmichael to question the loyalty of his men."

"And who runs this rival gang?"

"I don't know. Mr. Carmichael never said."

"Have you ever heard of Nathaniel Cavey?" Daniel asked.

133

Simcoe nodded. "He's one to watch out for, but I don't know if he was involved."

"So, what happened to Mr. Tipton?"

"Don't ask." Simcoe grimaced as if in pain.

"I'm asking."

"Mr. Carmichael disemboweled him. That was the punishment for traitors in the old days."

"Yes. Drawing and quartering."

"Well, he didn't go that far, but he assembled his men in the empty warehouse, had Tipton suspended from the rafters, then slit his belly open. Everyone had to stand and watch Tipton's guts slither out onto the floor and the man writhe in agony until he died."

"Were you there?"

Simcoe nodded. "Mr. Carmichael asked me to come along."

"Did he think you needed to learn a lesson?"

"I was loyal through and through, Inspector. I wasn't worried."

"You said Mr. Tipton had a wife?"

"Yes. The Tiptons were married less than a year."

"Do you know his wife's name?" Daniel asked.

"Naomi. Comely little thing. I met her once."

"And would you say Naomi was capable of avenging her husband's death?" Daniel inquired, thinking that shooting Tristan with an arrow and tying him to a tree would be a fitting punishment for what he'd done to her husband.

"I honestly don't know. As I said, I only met her once. She seemed feisty enough, but that doesn't mean she's capable of murder."

"Where do I find Mrs. Tipton?"

"The Tiptons lived in Royal Mint Street. I don't know if she's still there."

"How long ago was she widowed?"

"In June, just before Mr. Tristan went to Essex."

If Tipton had died in June, his widow could be long gone, especially if word got out of how her husband had met his end. Naomi Tipton would be persona non grata among people who valued loyalty and relied on each other for support. She could have gone back to her parents or moved in with a sibling. She would be in mourning, but if her husband hadn't left anything of value behind, she would have needed to find a way to support herself, so perhaps she'd had to get a job. The neighbors might know.

"Was there anyone else you can think of who might have had a grudge against Tristan Carmichael?"

"I'm sure there were people who felt slighted and who wouldn't have minded seeing Mr. Carmichael fall, but I can't think of anyone who'd take it upon themselves to murder him."

"Who will take his place here in London?"

"I couldn't tell you. Mr. Carmichael doesn't share his plans with me."

"Who was Tristan Carmichael's second?" Daniel pressed.

"Michael O'Keefe. Mr. Carmichael trusted him implicitly."

"How far would O'Keefe go to move up the ranks?"

Simcoe shook his head. "Not that far. Lance Carmichael would not allow him to live another day if he thought O'Keefe killed his son."

"But if the murder was dressed up as a personal vendetta, Lance Carmichael would never know, would he?"

"He'd know. The men would know. These things have a way of getting out."

"So, you think O'Keefe couldn't possibly have had anything to do with his boss's death?"

"I don't, but I'm just the butler, Inspector Haze."

"*Were* you just a butler?"

Simcoe shrugged. "I was also Mr. Carmichael's bodyguard, but he didn't ask me to come to Essex. He said there were plenty of men there already and I should enjoy the time off."

"And did you?" Daniel asked.

"Didn't know what to do with myself, if I'm honest, and couldn't wait for him to get back, but he won't be coming home now," Simcoe said miserably.

"I'm sure Lance Carmichael will take care of you," Daniel said a tad derisively, but Simcoe didn't seem to pick up on his tone.

"I'm getting old, Inspector. Mr. Carmicheal wants strong, young men, but if he ever needs a butler…"

Daniel pushed to his feet. "Show me that letter from Mrs. Sweetman, and let me know if you hear anything else."

"Even if I do, I can't be seen to be working with the police," Simcoe said, and stood as well.

"So send an anonymous note to Scotland Yard. It'll find its way to me."

"All right," Simcoe said, but Daniel knew he wouldn't.

He waited until the butler returned with the envelope. Daniel checked the address and made certain the missive inside really was from Felicity Sweetman, then read the letter and handed it back before heading to the basement kitchen to have a word with Lizzie.

The maid gave in to hysterics when she heard that her employer was dead and swore blind she didn't know anything about his personal dealings. She was just the servant, and now she would be unemployed and left without a character unless Mr. Simcoe was willing to help.

Daniel wished her luck finding a new job and took his leave.

Chapter 20

It was still early in the day when Jason and Daniel met at a chophouse in Fenchurch Street. They had planned it that way in case they intended to pursue another London lead. The idea was to have a meal, compare notes, and set off from the train station, which was a central location and the best place to find a hansom during the busiest time of the day. And they could return to Essex if there was no good reason to remain in London.

Once they had ordered roast duck with a cherry glaze, scalloped potatoes, and pints of ale, they exchanged news, which did little to help the investigation when it was Jason's turn. He was glad to have seen Captain Needham and was assured of the captain's continued recovery, but Jason's hunch about the knot had proved a disappointment, and he was glad to hear that Daniel had fared better with Simcoe.

"What are your thoughts on Naomi Tipton?" Daniel asked after the waiter had brought their drinks and disappeared into the kitchen.

"Naomi Tipton certainly has a motive. Her husband was publicly disemboweled," Jason said grimly. He'd thought he had understood what Tristan Carmichael was capable of, but to hear that he had tortured a man to death still came as a shock. "But even if Mrs. Tipton is skilled with a bow and arrow, I find it hard to imagine that she traveled to Birch Hill with a bow, a quiver of arrows, and a length of rope, contacted Tristan Carmichael, lured him to Bloody Weald, which is nowhere near the Carmichael home in Brentwood, then shot him through the heart and tied him to a tree once he was dead."

"That does sound a bit far-fetched," Daniel agreed. "But we can't discount her out of hand. If anyone would want to murder Tristan Carmichael, it would be her. Were you able to get a lead on the knot?"

"The knot is a dead end," Jason said with a shake of his head. "Captain Needham wasn't able to identify it, but he did say it could be known to foreign sailors."

"I can't think of anyone in Birch Hill who is or was a sailor. And we don't have any suspects who are foreign."

"O'Keefe is an Irish name, is it not?" Jason asked.

"Yes. What of it?"

"Might Irish sailors have used knots different to those of Englishmen?"

"I suppose that's a possibility," Daniel agreed. "But we don't know anything about his background."

"No, we don't," Jason agreed, "but as Tristan Carmichael's second, O'Keefe has much to gain from his boss's death, but only if Lance Carmichael allows him to remain in charge. Carmichael could just as easily bring in his own man."

"Harvey Boswell might be a candidate," Daniel mused. "Simcoe did say that he and Tristan Carmichael didn't see eye to eye, but that doesn't mean Lance doesn't trust the man." Daniel looked thoughtful. "Boswell made it sound as if moving up the ranks was the furthest thing from his mind, but he could have been playing a part."

Jason nodded. "You don't get far in a criminal organization without showing some initiative. I'd like to speak to Boswell and O'Keefe and get a measure of the two men," he said just as the waiter reappeared with two steaming plates and headed toward their table. The duck looked very appetizing and smelled divine.

"We know where to find Harvey Boswell, but O'Keefe is not likely to agree to a meeting, especially if he realizes he's a suspect," Daniel pointed out as soon as the waiter was out of earshot.

"Both men are sure to attend the funeral. If either of them doesn't, that will not only be a grave insult to Lance Carmichael but an indication that they're afraid."

"Do you know when the funeral is to be?"

"Friday at St. Peter's Church in Brentwood. Lance Carmichael informed me when Joe and I delivered the body."

"Do you think he expects you to attend?" Daniel asked.

"Perhaps. Lance Carmichael quizzed me about the injury and asked who I thought would be capable of committing such a crime against his family."

"He trusts your judgment, and your presence at the funeral would be an acknowledgment of his authority," Daniel said.

"I have no intention of paying homage to either Carmichael, but I do think I should attend," Jason replied. "If the killer comes from the ranks of the Carmichael organization, he's sure to be present."

Daniel pushed his spectacles up his nose as he studied Jason across the table. "And you think that you would be able to spot the culprit just by looking at them?"

"No, but the funeral will present me with an opportunity to size up Boswell and O'Keefe, and anyone else who might now be in the running for the much-coveted promotion. The higher these men are in the pecking order, the closer they will sit to the front. And, of course, there's Cecily Carmichael. She certainly had a motive, and it is possible that like her husband, she was carrying on with someone else."

"Do you think she would conduct an affair under her father-in-law's nose?" Daniel asked, clearly unable to believe that Cecily would have the audacity to even try.

"She would if the person had valid reason to spend time with her."

"And what reason would that be?"

"I think it's safe to assume that Lance Carmichael has guards on the property at all times. I saw at least four guards on the grounds, and I expect there were more men inside the house. If Cecily began a relationship with someone who was always there, Lance Carmichael would not notice if they were discreet."

"Lance Camichael is many things, but oblivious is not one of them," Daniel replied.

"No, but we have to assume that Tristan's wife and son are protected round the clock, and Lance is not a man who likes to leave the running of his enterprise to others. I'm sure he is frequently away from the house, which would allow Cecily to spend time with her lover."

"If she has one," Daniel reminded him.

"If she has one," Jason agreed. "But we can't discount the possibility, not when Cecily had good reason to resent the man she had probably married in good faith."

"Good faith and Tristan Carmichael don't quite go in the same sentence, do they? What a nest of vipers that family is," Daniel said with disgust.

"Which brings me to my next point," Jason continued. "Lance Carmichael has two daughters, does he not?"

"Yes."

"What is the role of their husbands within the Carmichael organization? Might either of them aspire to a position of leadership?"

"That is a very good question. I'm embarrassed to admit that I never considered Tristan's brothers-in-law. How do we find out where they stand?" Daniel asked. He had finished his meal and had laid his cutlery atop his plate.

"All the players will be in the same place for the duration of the funeral. And I think it's highly likely that the killer will be present."

"You can hardly question the suspects at the funeral," Daniel pointed out.

"No, but I can observe. And I can approach them after the service. The English are ridiculously impressed with rank. Even if they don't wish to speak to me, they will not have the cheek to walk away. I'm their *better,* after all. Even Lance Carmichael was deferential," Jason said mockingly.

The very idea that someone was a better man simply by virtue of their birth was still foreign to him, but the idea was so deeply ingrained in the minds of the people he met that at times, Jason was astounded by how much he could get away with if he so wished just because his grandfather had been a viscount, and the title had been passed down to Jason when Giles Redmond had died shortly after the premature death of his only son, Jason's father.

"Why are you so sure that the killer will attend the funeral?" Daniel asked.

"I can't help but think that Tristan trusted whoever killed him. Why else would he agree to meet them in the woods?"

"Because he didn't want to be seen talking to them," Daniel replied.

"Or maybe the killer was the one who didn't wish to be seen talking to Tristan Carmichael. It was an added layer of protection since they knew damn well what they were going to do. The difference between freedom and capture is one witness." Jason sighed as he folded his napkin. "Thank God Micah and Tom didn't come that way earlier or they could have witnessed the murder. That would make them a liability."

"I hadn't even thought of that," Daniel said. "But are we certain they are safe? What if the killer was still in the vicinity when the boys came upon Tristan's body?"

Jason considered the question. "I think the killer would have acted by now if he or she believed that the boys had seen something."

"Should we involve Ransome, do you think?" Daniel asked. "Tristan Carmichael might not have been murdered in London, but he was London-based."

"Let's hold off," Jason said as he took out his wallet and took out enough money to pay for them both. "We can always ask for reinforcements if more men are needed."

"All right," Daniel agreed. "So, what do we do now?"

"Let's have a word with Naomi Tipton," Jason said, and pushed away from the table. "She might know more than Simcoe gives her credit for."

Chapter 21

Royal Mint Street, which Daniel still remembered as Rosemary Lane from when he was a boy, had been renamed in 1850 to reflect its proximity to the Royal Mint. Despite the grandiose name, the street was flanked by shabby buildings and home to Rag Fair, an open-air market that sold secondhand goods. The street was lined with rickety tables piled high with gowns, coats, trousers, and previously owned undergarments. Several vendors sold shoes, and there were some who dealt exclusively in bedlinens and towels. Many sellers, most of whom were women, operated without a license, but the police turned a blind eye since any form of intervention was useless. They would chase away one seller only to find three more in their place the following week. And the original seller would eventually return and set up in a different spot, optimistic that the bobby who ordered her to leave wouldn't be able to recall her face.

Daniel found it surprising that Clarence Tipton, who must have earned a fair wage as a warehouse manager, would have chosen to live in this chaotic, disorderly place, but perhaps he'd thought it best to hide in plain sight if he was dealing in stolen goods and sought to make connections with people who could make the merchandise disappear without a trace. The opium might have been stolen by a rival gang, but Tipton could have been the one to take the pistols. Their street value would be in the hundreds of pounds, and if each pistol went to a different owner, their whereabouts would be impossible to trace.

It didn't take Jason and Daniel long to locate the correct address. Everyone seemed to know Naomi Tipton, and the vendors they asked were only too happy to direct two well-dressed gentlemen who didn't appear to be bailiffs to her door. They probably thought Naomi was about to come into an inheritance or benefit from a visit from pious do-gooders. When Naomi opened the door, it became instantly obvious that she couldn't have murdered Tristan Carmichael. She was so heavy with child, she had to lean back in order to not tip forward. Her black skirts created a flowing tent around her legs and distended belly, and made her narrow shoulders and modest breasts seem even more dainty in comparison. Naomi was a lovely young woman, but she looked tired and worn, and her soulful eyes were like dark pools of sadness.

"Mrs. Tipton, I'm Inspector Haze of Scotland Yard, and this is my associate, Dr. Redmond. Can we have a word?"

"What do you want with me, Inspector?" Naomi asked.

She hunched her shoulders and pulled in her neck in obvious fear, and Daniel felt a wave of pity for her, despite her husband's affiliation with the Carmichaels.

"Tristan Carmichael—I believe you're familiar with the name?—was murdered, his body discovered in the woods," Daniel began.

Naomi stared at him, seemingly uncomprehending, but Daniel could see she was pleased. He couldn't say he blamed her. Naomi's shoulders relaxed, and she let out a slow breath. Then the realization must have dawned that a policeman had come to her door, and she stared up at him, tensing like a frightened cat once more, her gaze sliding to Jason as she tried to figure out what exactly was happening.

"Why have you come here?" Naomi asked, her voice barely audible.

Daniel had to raise his own voice to be heard over the din of the market. "We thought you might have some insight into who might want him dead. Would it be possible to speak inside?"

Naomi moved away from the door, and the two men stepped inside. The house was small, the two rooms at the front in near-darkness since the light was obscured by the stalls set up directly in front of the house. There didn't appear to be anyone else in the house, so either they were out, or Naomi Tipton had lived alone since the death of her husband. Jason hoped she had someone to turn to in her time of need, since she would be needing help sooner rather than later.

They could still hear the back and forth between vendors and customers as brisk trade took place in the street, but it was cooler and quieter in the parlor. Even though the furniture and curtains looked well used, there was a colorful carpet covering the faded boards of the wood floor, and a cheerful painting hung above the mantel. This was a comfortable home, or had been while the man of the house had been alive. The mirror was covered with black crape, and a photograph frame lay face down on the mantel.

Lowering herself into a chair, Naomi Tipton motioned for the men to sit down. Jason took the other chair while Daniel settled on the settee.

"So, what is it that you think I know, Inspector?" Naomi asked bitterly. "And why did you bring a doctor along? Did you think I would succumb to the vapors?"

"Tristan Carmichael murdered your husband," Daniel said. "I thought you might want justice."

"Justice? For whom? Tristan Carmichael? I hope he rots in hell."

"Fair enough," Daniel replied. As far as Naomi Tipton was concerned justice had already been served. "But we still need to find out who killed Tristan Carmichael, in case the killing was the first move in a bid to overthrow the Carmichaels and gain control of their territory. You might think that has nothing to do with you, but as someone whose husband was part of the Carmichael organization, you might still be in danger because of what you know."

That was overstating it a bit, since Naomi Tipton and her child were hardly a threat to a new crime family, but Daniel's explanation seemed to have the desired effect, and Naomi Tipton sat up straighter, her attention eagerly fixed on the two men.

"Can you think of anyone who'd want to murder him?" Jason asked.

Naomi hadn't asked how exactly Tristan had died or where he had been found. She didn't seem to care, but the light of vengeance burned in her eyes.

"Tristan Carmichael murdered my husband on the word of someone who held a grudge. Clarence never put a foot wrong, but Carmichael's mind was made up as soon as he heard the accusation. He didn't believe Clarence when he swore that he had locked the door before leaving. Carmichael tortured him," Naomi exclaimed, her agitation painful to watch. "And now his child will never know its father, and I will never again see his beloved face."

"Who was it that betrayed your husband to Carmichael?" Jason asked gently.

"Michael O'Keefe."

"Why would Michael O'Keefe want your husband dead?" Daniel asked.

"Because he is a Fenian," Naomi cried.

"What's that got to do with it?"

"My Clarence was in the army, Inspector. He was stationed in Ireland and participated in putting down a Fenian uprising in 1866. O'Keefe held a grudge on account of losing both a brother and a cousin," Naomi said. "Once Clarence was dead, he convinced Carmichael to install one of his relations as the new warehouse manager. He means to take over the whole enterprise, and I wouldn't be surprised if he was the one to unlock the door and have his men move out the merchandise."

"Would he murder Tristan Carmichael to clear the way?" Jason asked.

"I don't know," Naomi said, resting a pale hand on her belly. "I can't speak to what he would or wouldn't do. I only know the man has his own agenda."

"Which is?" Daniel inquired.

"To bring in his own," Naomi said, giving Daniel a look that clearly meant to imply that he wasn't the sharpest knife in the box. "London is heaving with Irish immigrants. If they take control of East London, that will give them a firm foothold. And if O'Keefe was behind the robbery, he now has opium and guns."

Naomi was most likely repeating her husband's words, but the information was still useful, and could potentially endanger Naomi if she shared these views with individuals who reported to O'Keefe. And if that was what Clarence Tipton had believed, then it was clear why Michael O'Keefe had taken issue with him and wanted him out. Perhaps he hadn't thought Tipton would be tortured to death, or perhaps he hadn't cared, especially if he'd held Tipton responsible for the deaths of his brother and cousin.

Jason had known plenty of men during the American Civil War who had enjoyed the carnage and taken great pleasure in torturing captured enemy soldiers and the womenfolk left behind at the Southern plantations. Some men had been court-martialed for their involvement, but many had got away with their crimes, claiming they had been following orders issued by their commanding officers and didn't have any say in the matter.

It was difficult to say if someone who worked for the Carmichaels had a conscience, but there were as many personal circumstances as there were men. Michael O'Keefe might have his eye on Tristan Carmichael's turf, but others might only want to make a living and support their families in a city where they were despised because they were Irish. It seemed the Carmichaels did not discriminate, which was an unexpected point in their favor but perhaps also a fatal flaw in their plan.

"Did your husband ever mention Nathaniel Cavey?" Daniel asked.

Naomi looked thoughtful. "Yes, he did. He said something about Cavey coming to London to recruit."

"Was Cavey in direct competition with the Carmichaels?"

Naomi shrugged. "I'm afraid I know nothing about the man."

"Is there anyone else you can think of who might have meant Tristan Carmichael harm? Any women?" Jason asked.

"Women?" Naomi asked, clearly taken aback by the question.

"He was shot with an arrow," Jason replied. "So it could have been a woman. Someone he'd scorned, perhaps."

Naomi laughed and clapped her hands in delight. "That's perfect. Shot by Cupid's arrow."

Her mirth died away as quickly as it had come, and her expression grew somber. "Tristan Carmichael was a despicable man, but I don't think he was the sort to force himself on unwilling women. Clarence said he liked to be admired and basked in the admiration of beautiful women. It is possible that he had wronged one of them, but my money would be on his long-suffering wife. If anyone had a reason, it would be her. There's only so much humiliation a woman can be expected to bear."

"Did you ever meet Mrs. Carmichael?" Jason asked.

"No."

"So, what makes you think Cecily Carmichael was even aware of her husband's infidelity?"

Naomi scoffed. "A woman always knows the truth in her heart, Dr. Redmond. And it hurts like the devil to admit you don't matter to the one person who should cherish you most." Tears glittered in her dark eyes as she smiled wistfully and caressed her swollen belly. "At least I know I was loved," she said quietly.

"Do you have any family, Mrs. Tipton?" Jason asked as he glanced toward the empty corridor.

"Just my mother. She's out there." Naomi jutted her chin toward the market beyond the window. "Selling second-hand linens. Without Clarence, we had to find a way to survive."

"Any male relations to look after you?" Jason asked solicitously.

Naomi shook her head. "My father died when I was a child, and I don't have any brothers or uncles."

Her reply seemed truthful and served to confirm what Jason had already suspected. Naomi Tipton might be glad Tristan Carmichael was dead, but she didn't have anything to do with his murder.

"Thank you, Mrs. Tipton," Jason said, and stood. Daniel followed suit. There was nothing more they could learn from Naomi Tipton, and it was time they were on their way.

Chapter 22

"Unless Naomi Tipton lied about her connections, I think we can safely cross her off the list," Daniel said morosely once they boarded the Brentwood-bound train and found an unoccupied compartment where they could speak privately. "Even if she's a skilled archer, she could hardly hunt down Tristan Carmichael in Essex in her condition." Daniel seemed perplexed as he fixed Jason with a quizzical stare. "Nathaniel Cavey appears to be well known among the Carmichaels' associates, but I'm unclear as to his affiliation since we have yet to hear of a powerful gang run by someone other than the Carmichaels."

"It's quite possible that Cavey and O'Keefe are working together to weaken the Carmichael organization from within."

"Yes, I suppose it is. And I hope we get some answers when we go out to Foulness Island. Shall we go tomorrow? And perhaps I should go to the funeral on Friday," Daniel mused.

Jason stared at Daniel in surprise. "You're getting married on Saturday. Surely there are things you must attend to."

"There isn't much for me to do," Daniel replied sulkily. "Other than hide from my mother-in-law's reproachful glare."

Jason shook his head in disbelief. He could, of course, understand Harriet Elderman's feelings. She had lost her only daughter and probably blamed Daniel for everything that had gone wrong in Sarah's life since her marriage, but Daniel was not at fault. He had done nothing but support Sarah and try to help her in any way he could. To begrudge him personal happiness after years of emotional torment was not only uncalled for but downright cruel. But like most people who saw only their own pain, Harriet feared the future and probably thought she would lose the granddaughter she loved and find herself alone in her twilight years.

Jason could sympathize with her plight, but his loyalty was to Daniel, and Daniel deserved to have love in his life. It wasn't only the women who knew when they were loved. Jason knew without a shadow of a doubt that Katherine adored him with all her heart, and he was certain that Flora loved Daniel in the same way. Their courtship had been quick, but when the heart knew, it knew, and even though Daniel still questioned his judgment, Jason thought that what he really couldn't come to terms with was the idea that someone could love him so fearlessly.

Daniel didn't believe he was worthy of such devotion and was bracing his heart for bitter disappointment. Perhaps that was the reason he had chosen to involve himself in the investigation. The case occupied his mind in the days leading up to his marriage and kept him from giving in to the fear that Flora would change her mind and leave him broken. And if he could convince himself that Flora was somehow involved, it would make it easier to justify her betrayal. It was utter nonsense as far as Jason was concerned, but in Daniel and Flora's relationship, Daniel was the one with prewedding jitters, and as the best man, Jason was ready to do his job.

"Daniel, you cannot allow anyone to mar your happiness," he said with all the conviction he could muster. "Death is part of life, and those left behind must move on if they hope to keep on living. Charlotte deserves a mother who loves her, not a string of nannies who will never provide the security she needs, and you deserve a loving wife. And Flora will be a loving wife, even if you think she's capable of murder," Jason added, a smile tugging at his mouth.

"I don't really think that, and I'm thoroughly ashamed for allowing my fears to get the better of me," Daniel said softly. "I suppose after what happened with Sarah and then after Rebecca was murdered, I can't help but always brace for the worst possible outcome."

"Neither death was your fault," Jason said.

"Maybe not, but the two women I loved died on my watch. My mother always used to say that death comes in threes."

"Three what? Wives? Lovers? People you happen to know? Beloved pets?"

"I don't know," Daniel admitted with a rueful grin. "I just keep thinking that come Saturday, something will go terribly wrong."

"We will deal with whatever happens," Jason promised as the train pulled into the station and they gathered their things.

Jason registered two things as soon as he and Daniel exited the station. The first was that Inspector Pullman was standing next to his brougham, his gaze scanning the arriving passengers, and the second was the headline of the *Brentwood Informer*, a small local newspaper that was published daily and sold for a penny, probably with a view to increasing circulation. The newspaper was a cross between a reputable chronicle and a broadsheet, whose sole intention was to frighten and shock passersby into purchasing a copy. Jason never bought the *Informer*, but today was going to be the exception.

Local Businessman Brutally Murdered

Jason would have ignored the headline if not for the lurid drawing beneath that depicted a man seated behind a desk, a knife sticking out of his chest and a bag over his head. The story did not appear to be about Tristan Carmichael, which could mean only one thing. A similar murder had taken place in the past twenty-four hours.

Daniel stared at the newspaper in shock, his mouth opening slightly as his gaze slid toward Inspector Pullman. Jason handed the newsboy a penny and scanned the story for a name.

"Who was it?" Daniel exclaimed as he tried to read the article over Jason's shoulder. "Who was murdered?"

"Harvey Boswell. His body was discovered this morning. According to the article, there were no witnesses, and the police have no leads."

"Who discovered the body?" Daniel asked just as Inspector Pullman grew tired of waiting and approached them.

"Gentlemen," Pullman said.

"Inspector," Jason replied. "Were you waiting for us?"

"Indeed, I was." Inspector Pullman had the decency to look shamefaced. "DI Peterson has asked me to pass on a message."

"Oh?" Daniel asked, his eyes narrowing and his jaw tensing as he studied his one-time protégé. It seemed change was afoot at the Brentwood Constabulary.

"He requests that you kindly terminate your inquiries forthwith. You have no authority in Essex, Inspector Haze."

"And what are DI Coleridge's thoughts on this matter?" Daniel asked.

Inspector Pullman's face fell. "DI Coleridge is no longer with us."

"Has he finally taken retirement?" Daniel asked. "Or was he pushed out?"

Pullman shook his head. "DI Coleridge passed away yesterday."

"Was it a suspicious death?" Jason asked. He was watching Inspector Pullman intently and appeared to be asking if DI Coleridge had been murdered.

"Not at all," Inspector Pullman replied. "His heart gave out while he was dining with his wife and daughter. His physician had warned him that he needed to step aside and engage in more peaceful pursuits if he hoped to stabilize his blood pressure."

"I'm sorry to hear it," Jason said.

"Thank you, sir," Pullman replied.

"Please pass my condolences to DI Coleridge's family," Daniel said once he'd finally recovered from the shock. "And Peterson? How did his promotion come about?"

"As the highest-ranking officer after DI Coleridge, it was only right that Inspector Peterson should assume charge of the station."

Daniel opened his mouth to inquire about the investigation, but Jason stuffed the folded newspaper beneath his arm and tipped his hat to Inspector Pullman. "Please convey my regards to DI Peterson, Inspector. I wish him the best of luck in his new post. And do let me know when the funeral for DI Coleridge is to be held."

"Erm, yes, sir," Inspector Pullman said, his surprise evident. He had clearly expected to encounter opposition to his request. "But Mrs. Coleridge did say she would prefer a private affair."

"Of course. Now, if you will excuse us…" Jason strode toward the brougham, greeted Joe, and climbed inside the carriage.

Daniel followed suit. "Why did you agree to stop investigating?" he hissed as soon as the door closed behind him.

"I didn't agree to anything. I simply wished DI Peterson luck with his investigation."

"But he expects us to drop the inquiry," Daniel pointed out.

"DI Peterson has no authority where we are concerned, and has no inkling what we have planned. By the time he realizes we're still investigating, the case will either be solved to our satisfaction, or we will be ready to turn it over to the Brentwood Constabulary."

Daniel sighed and chuckled. "You really are wily."

"I simply choose to pick my battles."

Daniel was silent for a few moments, then said, "I was shocked to hear about DI Coleridge. His wife and daughter must be devastated."

"I'm sure they are, and my heart goes out to them, but I can't say I'm overly surprised," Jason admitted.

"What do you mean?"

"The last time I saw DI Coleridge he really didn't look well. His face was red and puffy, he was morbidly overweight, and seemed to be chronically short of breath. He was under a great deal of pressure, and he clearly overindulged in both food and drink without the benefit of taking regular exercise."

"Are you saying his death was inevitable?"

"Not inevitable, but not completely unexpected."

Daniel sighed heavily and looked out the window at the passing countryside. The death of someone one knew and liked was always shocking and was sure to make one reflect on one's own mortality. "Do you think DI Peterson is taking over the investigation at the behest of Lance Carmichael?" he asked once the silence had gone on for too long.

"I think it's likely. If Carmichael had Boswell murdered because he believes he was responsible, then the case will remain unsolved until Boswell's death is all but forgotten."

"Which means that as far as Lance Carmichael is concerned, his son's death has been avenged and there's no case left to investigate."

"I'm not convinced Harvey Boswell was responsible," Jason replied. "Are you?"

"I am not, but maybe Lance Carmichael knows something we don't."

"Perhaps. I would still like to speak to Nathaniel Cavey and see how he fits into this puzzle."

"And if he's working with O'Keefe."

"Nathaniel Cavey might be armed," Jason said. "And I doubt he will welcome us onto his boat."

"Are you suggesting we arm ourselves?"

"You should not come armed, but I will bring my Colt."

"Why not me?"

"Because you are an inspector with the police, and to come armed would be seen as an act of aggression. I'm a civilian, and an American. You Brits think all Americans are savage outlaws, so I don't think Mr. Cavey will be too shocked if he discovers I'm armed."

"I would prefer that he didn't discover it," Daniel said.

"I don't plan to go in brandishing a weapon," Jason replied. "I will wear a discreet holster. Unless Cavey's men pat me down, they will never know it's there."

"All right," Daniel agreed. "I will stop by the Stag and ask Davy Brody how to find Cavey. I have a feeling he might know precisely where his boat is docked."

"You think Davy Brody is working both sides?"

"With Davy, anything is possible," Daniel said. "Some people never learn."

"No, they do not," Jason said. This seemed an opportune moment to mention what he'd been thinking since they'd left the station. "Daniel, if we are no further in our inquiries by Friday afternoon, I mean to step away from the investigation."

"Yes, I think that would be wise," Daniel agreed.

They had never walked away from an investigation, and Jason wouldn't propose they quit if he cared about the victim and their family, but this time, he not only found it difficult to engage with the victim's plight, he also worried that in their quest for the truth, they were kicking a hornet's nest that was best left undisturbed. Perhaps justice had already been served, brutal as it might seem, and it was time to let the Carmichaels move on under new leadership. Jason had meant what he'd said. It was important to pick one's battles, and even DI Coleridge, whose judgment Jason trusted and respected, had chosen to turn a blind eye to gang warfare. His already thinly stretched resources had been better allocated elsewhere, and if Jason were honest, so were his and Daniel's.

"Shall I ask Joe to drop you at the Stag?" he asked.

"Please," Daniel said.

"I will collect you tomorrow morning at nine."

Daniel nodded. "I will be ready and waiting."

Chapter 23

"It's too dangerous, sir," Joe Marin said when Jason alighted from the brougham at Redmond Hall and informed Joe that he and Daniel intended to go to Foulness Island the following morning.

"What makes you say that?" Jason asked.

"I may have been born and raised in Birch Hill, but my mother's father was from Rochford. He was a fisherman and a smuggler in his day. I spent several summers with my grandparents when I was a lad. My grandsire, he told the best stories," Joe reminisced.

"Have you ever been to Foulness Island?"

Joe nodded. "I have at that. It's cut off from the mainland by deep creeks, and the only way to reach it is by either the Broomway or a boat."

"What's a broomway?" Jason asked.

Jason suddenly pictured several cloaked figures, their pointy hats silhouettes against the faint glow of a full moon, bent low over their brooms as they raced over the marshlands. He knew it was ridiculous. Tales of witchcraft had become part of American folklore thanks to the stories brought over by European immigrants and the now-famous Salem witch trials. The image of the witch had become synonymous with Halloween, the drawings and costumes as common as jack-o'-lanterns and tales of the headless horseman. Jason deplored superstition and baseless fear, but the stories had appealed to his imagination when he was a child, and he had looked forward to the Halloween party their neighbors in Washington Square had thrown every year. It was a long time ago now, those childhood Halloweens, and he knew better, but the images were so deeply embedded in his mind, they sprang forth unbidden.

"The Broomway is a walkway that runs for about six miles along the outer edge of the island and can only be accessed at low tide," Joe said.

"Why is it called the Broomway? And come to that, why is the island called Foulness?"

Jason was fascinated by English names. Monikers that sounded odd to his American ears always had a long history and a perfectly logical explanation, just like Bloody Weald, which brought to mind a terrifying landscape but was actually named after harmless, colorful flowers.

Joe chuckled, his dark eyes creasing with amusement. "It's really not what you think, your lordship. Foulness is for the birds—the fowl that nested on the island. And the Broomway is named after the posts. In the old days, the head points—that's where you could turn inland—were marked by posts that looked like twig brooms. Hence, the Broomway."

"What happens if the tide starts to come in?"

Joe gave Jason a look that spoke volumes and reminded him that as someone who hadn't grown up in accordance with the dictates of nature, he had no business setting foot on a tidal path, since he wasn't likely to return.

"Do you even know where this fella is docked, sir?" Joe asked.

"I admit, I don't."

"I reckon the only reason anyone would tie up at Foulness Island is because that's where they grew up and know the terrain."

"Not because it's difficult to reach?"

"That too," Joe said with a nod. "If you ask me, this cove doesn't care to be found."

"So how do we find Nathaniel Cavey?" Jason asked.

"My suggestion would be to travel overland to Burham-on-Crouch and see if you can find a local who'll take you out in his boat. If anyone is willing, that is."

"Do you think they would refuse?"

"That largely depends on what they have to lose."

That didn't sound encouraging at all but made Jason want to speak to Nathaniel Cavey all the more. If he had grown up in a place that to Jason sounded like the wilderness, he would be comfortable with homemade weapons, and he'd be at home on both land and sea. A man who lived on a boat would know all about knots and would be difficult to locate if he decided to lie low for a while. He also wouldn't have any problem reaching Brentwood if he had access to a horse. Jason had no proof that Cavey was responsible for Boswell's death, but if he had killed Tristan Carmichael, there would be a case to be made for the second murder as well since the method was quite similar. It would be difficult to shoot an arrow indoors, but a blade to the heart wasn't so very different, and the sack over the head was identical.

"If I may, sir," Joe said, interrupting Jason's thoughts. Jason nodded. "I've heard of the Carmichaels and the Plimptons, and of most other families that have had the run of Essex since their smuggling days, but I've never heard of the Caveys. If this cove is gunning for the Carmichaels, he can't have come from around here."

"Or he's going by a different name," Jason said.

Of course, Cavey could have come from anywhere, and might rely on a local to navigate the marsh.

"Thank you, Joe," Jason said, and went inside. He'd clean and load the Colt after dinner. He had no intention of going into the wilderness unarmed.

Chapter 24

Daniel didn't think he'd learn anything from Davy Brody, who clammed up as soon as Daniel brought up the Carmichaels. Davy seemed scared, and probably had good reason to be, since he'd just heard about Harvey Boswell's murder and the Stag had been buzzing with speculation about Tristan all week.

"Lance Camichael releases his hounds first and asks questions later," Davy said, lowering his voice so that his regulars, who appeared to be glued to their stools, wouldn't hear what was said.

"You don't think Harvey Boswell murdered Tristan Carmichael?" Daniel asked.

Davy shot Daniel a derisive look. "Why would he?"

"Someone obviously thought there was a reason."

"Ye drip poison into someone's ear long enough, and they'll believe anything ye tell them."

"And who's dripping this poison?" Daniel asked.

Davy shook his head. "I ain't naming names. Ye can figure it out for yerself. Or better yet, get yerself married and go back to London. Take it from me, Haze. This won't end well for ye if ye keep poking about. And ye should tell Lord Redmond as much. Some things are best left alone. He should think about the safety of his womenfolk, and so should ye."

"Are you saying our families might be in danger?"

"The easiest way to bring a man to his knees is by threatening what he loves best."

"Understood," Daniel said, and left the tavern.

He hadn't bothered to ask Davy about Nathaniel Cavey. Given what the barkeep had said, it was best not to show his hand.

Someone could be listening, or watching. Daniel's spine tingled with apprehension as he walked down the lane, the darkening sky casting the path in deep shadow. The Carmichaels had woven a web of violence and deceit, and anyone who got caught in their clutches was either absorbed into their network or killed.

Daniel couldn't help but wonder if DI Peterson would stand his ground or kowtow to Lance Carmichael. Peterson was considerably younger than DI Coleridge and typically more mulish and direct in his approach, but he had a young family whose welfare could be used as leverage if it came to it. Even Peterson wasn't stubborn enough to risk the lives of his wife and children in order to bring Lance Carmichael and his disciples to heel.

Jason was right. Perhaps it was time they walked away from this case and focused on the people who depended on them. Having made his decision, Daniel immediately felt lighter and less apprehensive about the next day. He would send Harriet's groom with a note first thing in the morning and tell Jason that he had changed his mind about going out to Foulness Island. Instead, he would spend the day with Charlotte. They could go for a drive in the country, or maybe Charlotte would prefer to visit with Lily and Liam, and they'd spend time with the Redmonds. He wouldn't mind a peaceful day himself. It had been so long since he'd had nothing to do but walk, read, and reflect. And perhaps he would visit Felix's and Sarah's graves. He thought he should tell them himself that he was to be married, and that Charlotte would soon have a new mother.

A few months ago, he would have thought the idea ludicrous, but Daniel had come to accept that perhaps there were things beyond his understanding. A line from *Hamlet* sprang to mind.

> *There are more things in heaven and earth, Horatio, than are dreamt of in your philosophy.*

Daniel smiled to himself. Perhaps it was the height of hubris to compare himself to Hamlet, but the notion that human beings had contemplated similar ideas for centuries brought him comfort and helped him to feel less alone. He stopped walking and gazed at the rising moon. It was hardly more than a crescent, and the pale glow did little to light his way, but the celestial light was a symbol of hope and continuity and would see him home tonight.

He had barely taken two steps when a dark shadow floated into his path. The breath caught in Daniel's throat as he came to an abrupt stop, his heart hammering with fear as his mind registered the shock. With the moon behind the figure, all Daniel could see was a female silhouette surrounded by a shimmering halo of weak moonlight. He couldn't make out any identifying features, but the woman's hair looked wild against the backdrop of the night, and when she raised a hand and held it out to Daniel, the limb fluttered like a frantic moth that had flown too close to a flame.

"Please, help me," a thin, croaky voice called.

For one mad moment, Daniel thought he had come face to face with a restless spirit, but then common sense prevailed. This was no ghost, this was a frightened girl who needed his help. Daniel stepped forward just as the girl turned her face an inch toward the light. He saw huge, terrified eyes, pale cheeks smudged with dirt, and a chin that wobbled as she fought to hold back tears. The girl wore no coat and shivered violently as a cold wind swept the exposed path and whipped her hair about her head. Daniel shrugged off his coat and wrapped it around her, then held her close as she threw herself at him and buried her face in his chest, her thin body quaking with desolation.

"It will be all right. I'll look after you," he said quietly, even though there was no one to hear them. "I'll see you safe."

"I saw my brother die. Harvey was murdered before my eyes," Annie Boswell sobbed into Daniel's shoulder.

Daniel waited until Annie finally calmed down, then wrapped his arm around her as he guided her down the lane. "Tell me what happened," he said softly.

He didn't think it was a coincidence that Annie had found him. She had been waiting for him, and by the looks of her, she'd been there a while and had been hiding in the woods.

"He didn't do it," Annie cried, her desperation painful to behold. "Harvey didn't kill Tristan Carmichael. He didn't have it in him to hurt anyone."

"Do you know who did?"

Annie shook her head.

"So why did Harvey have to die? Did you see who killed him?"

Annie began to cry again. "Harvey told me to hide when he heard footsteps on the stairs. He knew something was wrong."

"Where did you hide?"

"There's a window seat in the office. It opens and locks from the inside, and there's a peephole. I was in there, when…" Annie's voice trailed off, and she gulped miserably.

Daniel waited. He needed to know what Annie had seen and why she was so certain Harvey had not murdered Tristan Carmichael, but he couldn't rush her. She was as fragile as a snowflake on a warm fingertip, likely to melt into nothingness if pressed too hard. At long last, Annie was able to speak.

"I was two when my parents died. I went to bed having a family and woke up to three dead bodies. My mother and baby sister died during childbirth. My father walked into his study, locked the door, and shot himself in the head. He couldn't bear the loss of my mother," Annie explained. "He loved her that much."

Or he loved you that little, Daniel thought, but didn't comment aloud.

"Harvey was fourteen. He couldn't find a job that would allow him to care for me, and he wouldn't take me to an orphanage. He said he would always take care of me, and he has."

"By working for the Carmichaels."

"Yes. Harvey was good with numbers, so Lance Carmichael hired him to work in one of his betting shops. Harvey left me in the back while he worked and brought me food and books to look at." Annie glanced at Daniel, her eyes shining in the moonlight. "He never hurt anyone. I swear it, Inspector Haze."

"So, why would someone want to hurt him?" Daniel asked.

"Victor Roy had his eye on the Red Lantern ever since Mr. Carmichael made Harvey manager. Roy wanted to move up the ranks, to have more control. He said as much to Harvey and tried to frighten him off, but Harvey wouldn't leave. He thought Mr. Carmichael would protect him, but it seems he couldn't even protect his own son," Annie said quietly. "And now that Harvey is dead, Lance Carmichael will give Roy the Red Lantern as a reward for avenging Tristan."

"Was there anyone else there that night, Annie?"

"No. Roy wouldn't want any witnesses. He searched for me after he murdered Harvey. He turned the flat over, and then he probably went to our house. He knows I'm the only one who can convince Mr. Carmichael that Harvey had nothing to do with Tristan's death. Roy is not going to stop looking for me as long as he believes I'm a threat to him."

"How did you come to be in Birch Hill?"

"I stayed hidden for hours, until I thought it was finally safe to come out, and then I ran. I knew you lived in Birch Hill. Harvey told me. And I asked a farmer's wife where to find you. She gave me some milk and bread."

"Which farm was it?" Daniel asked, worried that Annie would be betrayed if someone came looking for her.

"It was the one with the apple orchard."

The Caulfields, then. They were good people and kept themselves to themselves. Mrs. Caulfield would never betray a frightened young girl.

"You are the only one who can help me, Inspector Haze," Annie said, her voice pleading. "I have nowhere else to go."

"Don't worry. Tonight, you will stay with me."

"And then?" Annie whimpered.

"And then we'll figure something out. I will not turn you over to Victor Roy, Annie, so you needn't worry."

"You promise?" Annie asked, her expression so trusting, it choked Daniel up.

"I promise."

"Harvey said you were a good man, someone I could trust."

"I'm sorry for what happened, Annie."

Tears slid down Annie's filthy cheeks. "Harvey was the only family I had. How will I manage on my own?"

"I will help."

"Do you have a wife?" Annie asked as they approached the house. The windows glowed welcomingly and cast a pool of light onto the drive. "Will she be cross with you for bringing me into your home?"

"I'm getting married on Saturday."

Annie's mouth formed an O of surprise. "This Saturday?"

"Yes."

"And then you will go off on a wedding trip?"

"I'm afraid so."

"What will happen to me?" Annie cried.

"I will leave you in safe hands."

Daniel handed Annie his handkerchief, and she dabbed at her streaming eyes, rubbed at her cheeks, and blew her nose. She stuffed the handkerchief into the pocket of Daniel's coat and took a steadying breath as Daniel knocked on the door.

Chapter 25

Once Daniel briefly explained the situation, he braced himself for Harriet's anger, but Harriet took one look at Annie's tear-stained face and sprang into action.

"Come, my dear," she said, and drew Annie into the parlor. "Tilda, tea, and add a generous dollop of brandy. Also sandwiches," she called out. "My dear child, you must have had quite an ordeal. Don't you worry. You are safe here with us."

Harriet appeared more animated than she had in years, and her gaze was filled with purpose. She watched Annie sip her tea, then placed two ham sandwiches on a plate and handed it to her. "You must eat."

"Thank you, Mrs. Elderman," Annie whispered. "You are so kind."

"I'm nothing of the sort. I had a daughter once, and I would like to think that someone would have helped her if she were in trouble."

Annie nodded and bit into the sandwich. It was obvious she hadn't eaten anything since the bread and milk Mrs. Caulfield had given her, and that was likely that morning. Her hands were trembling, and her eyelids drooped with fatigue.

"Tilda, prepare the spare room, and make sure there's an extra blanket. It promises to be cold tonight. And lay out one of Sarah's old flannel nightdresses for Annie. There are several gowns in Sarah's old trunk." Harriet caught sight of Annie's mournful face and instantly amended her instructions. "The black satin, the one Sarah wore after her father died. That will do nicely since Miss Annie is in mourning."

"Of course, Mrs. Elderman," Tilda replied, and hurried from the room.

"Thank you," Annie said, her eyes brimming again.

"No need to thank me, my girl. Mourning must be observed." She cast Daniel a sharp look, then turned away. "Inspector Haze will see your brother receives a proper burial."

"A word," Daniel hissed, and strode from the room.

"What is it, Daniel?" Harriet demanded once she had followed him out into the corridor.

"Annie's brother worked for Tristan Carmichael and was murdered before her eyes. Funeral arrangements are not at the top of my list, and I don't think we should tell anyone Annie is here. Her very presence can put us in danger."

Harriet clearly hadn't considered the consequences of hiding Annie. All she had seen was a helpless young girl who had nowhere to go. She paled, her eyes widening as she no doubt thought of Charlotte, who was sleeping upstairs.

"What do we do?" Harriet asked.

"We look after Annie tonight, and tomorrow I will consult with Jason and see what he thinks."

"Good. That's good," Harriet said, nodding to herself. "Lord Redmond will know what to do. He's such a clever man. I trust his judgment implicitly."

Which was another way of saying she didn't trust Daniel's, but he didn't mind. In this instance, Daniel was more than happy to defer to Jason's judgment since Annie could bring untold trouble on all of their heads. Victor Roy might have taken advantage of an opportunity, or he might have created one. If he had murdered Tristan Carmichael and killed Harvey Boswell to cover his tracks, then made certain to benefit from both deaths, he was far smarter than Daniel had first given him credit for. And if there was only one person who could ensure his downfall, Roy wouldn't stop until he found Annie.

Daniel didn't think Victor Roy would ever think to look for Annie Boswell at the former home of a police inspector, but Daniel had no way of knowing who'd seen Annie as she made her way to Birch Hill.

"We must impress on Tilda that she's to tell no one Annie is here," Daniel said. "Especially not her beau. One careless word at the Stag, and Annie is as good as dead."

"I completely understand. I'll speak to her straight away."

Tilda was a good woman, but she had a propensity to gossip and would likely spill the beans regardless.

"Tell her if Roy comes looking for Annie, she will be next, since she now knows the truth."

Harriet nodded and hurried upstairs.

Daniel returned to the parlor. Annie was huddled in her chair, fast asleep, the empty plate still in her hands. Daniel took the plate from her and set it down, then carefully lifted Annie into his arms. Her head rested on his shoulder, and she pressed herself closer to him, as if she instinctively knew that he represented safety. Daniel felt something stir in his soul, but now wasn't the time to give in to sentiment. He carried Annie up the stairs and settled her on the bed. Harriet clucked in disapproval when the dried mud from the hem of Annie's gown soiled the clean sheets, but Annie looked so exhausted, Harriet decided not to disturb her. She unlaced Annie's boots and pulled them off very gently, then folded the counterpane over her and added the blanket Tilda had brought. Harriet brushed a lock of hair out of Annie's face, then bent down and kissed her on the forehead.

"She's not Sarah," Daniel said softly once Harriet had shut the door behind them.

"I know that. Goodnight, Daniel."

Harriet didn't return downstairs but walked into her own bedroom and shut the door firmly behind her. Left to his own devices, Daniel decided he could use an early night himself. He locked up, asked Tilda for supper on a tray, then checked on

Charlotte and headed to his own room, his decision to abandon the investigation quite forgotten.

Chapter 26

Thursday, September 9

Annie looked considerably better when she came downstairs in the morning. She had washed and arranged her hair in a neat bun. The gown Tilda had laid out for her didn't quite fit but would do until the bodice could be taken in and the skirts hemmed. Annie smiled at Daniel gratefully when she found him in the morning room, a cup of tea halfway to his lips.

"Were you able to sleep?" Daniel asked.

"Yes, thank you. I was so tired, I don't even remember going up to bed."

"I'm glad you're feeling better," Daniel said, and realized how foolish that sounded. Food and rest weren't all this sad girl needed. "I would like you to meet Lord Redmond," he said when he saw Jason's brougham through the window. "He's the nicest man I know," he hurried to add when he saw the fear in Annie's eyes.

"All right," she muttered.

Daniel stepped outside and filled Jason in on what had been happening. When the two men came inside, Jason took off his hat and bowed to Annie, as if he were the commoner and Annie a noblewoman. Annie became flustered and looked to Daniel for guidance. He nodded encouragingly.

"Miss Boswell, it's so good to meet you," Jason said. "And I'm so very sorry for your loss."

"Erm, thank you," Annie replied. "My lord."

"Please, Dr. Redmond will do just fine. How are you feeling?" he asked as he took a seat next to her. Jason reached for

Annie's hand, his fingers resting lightly on her wrist as he took her pulse.

"I am… I am…" Tears shimmered in Annie's eyes, and she looked away, as though embarrassed by her grief.

Jason withdrew his hand and poured Annie a cup of tea. He added two lumps of sugar and a splash of milk and set the cup before her. The simple, domestic gesture seemed to soothe Annie, and she gave him a watery smile before taking a sip.

"Annie, my home is on the other side of the village. You will be safe there until Inspector Haze and I return."

Annie had just opened her mouth to reply when Harriet swept into the room. "Annie will be perfectly safe right here."

Daniel was shocked to see Thomas, an old-fashioned rifle slung over his shoulder, his gaze fixed on Annie, standing behind Harriet.

"Thomas is an excellent shot and will look after us should we have any unwelcome visitors."

"Mrs. Elderman," Jason began, but Harriet held up her hand.

"We have no reason to suspect anyone knows Annie is here. She will remain in the house, with me. We have much to do, don't we, Annie? I hope you're a deft hand with a needle."

Annie stared at Harriet, clearly mystified.

"We have several gowns to alter. And I think Sarah's kid slippers should fit. You'll need something to wear while Thomas cleans your boots. Can't have you tracking mud all over the carpets, can we?"

"No," Annie muttered, and turned to Daniel again.

Daniel would have liked to take Annie to Redmond Hall, if only to get her as far away from Charlotte as possible. He thought

Annie and Harriet could take care of themselves, but he worried about leaving Charlotte unprotected and around a man who was clutching a rifle.

"Why don't we drop Charlotte at Redmond Hall," Jason suggested, as if reading Daniel's mind. "I'm sure she would enjoy spending the day with Lily and Liam, and you can collect her once we return."

Relief surged through Daniel. "Yes, I think that's an excellent idea," he said. "I'll just tell Tilda to get her ready."

Jason turned to Annie once more. "You are not alone, Miss Boswell. We will see you safe and appropriately housed."

"Housed where?" Annie whispered.

It was clear she thought Jason might be referring to a workhouse, since she had never been employed and had no skills or character references that would help her to secure her first position.

"You leave that to me and Inspector Haze. In the meantime, I think Mrs. Elderman could do with your help."

Jason stood, bowed to Annie, and left the room. Daniel followed.

A few minutes later he heard Charlotte's gleeful chattering as Tilda laced her shoes, then helped her with her coat and the ribbons of her bonnet. Charlotte shot a curious glance at Annie, whom she could see through the parlor door, but then she shrugged and grinned happily at Daniel, clearly thrilled to be going to Redmond Hall.

Well, at least someone is happy this morning, Daniel thought morosely as he took her by the hand and led her toward Jason's waiting brougham.

Chapter 27

Once Charlotte had been delivered to Redmond Hall and had been reunited with her friends, the two men finally got on their way.

"There are several possibilities I can think of," Jason said as the carriage bumped along a rutted track. "One: Victor Roy murdered Tristan, then blamed Harvey Boswell, and killed him to facilitate his rise and possible incursion into London. Two: Victor Roy is working with Cecily Carmichael. Perhaps they are romantically involved and hatched a plan to rid themselves of individuals who stood in the way of their goals. Three: Tristan's death presented Roy with an unprecedented opportunity, and he decided to make it work to his advantage by framing Harvey Boswell for the murder and clearing the way for himself. Which would mean that Tristan was murdered by someone we have yet to identify."

Daniel nodded. "I agree. And there's another possibility as well. Victor Roy might be working for someone else, someone like Nathaniel Cavey." Daniel sighed. "Last night, I was ready to abandon the case, happy to let these thugs duke it out among themselves, but when I saw Annie…"

"I see no reason for Annie to lie to us about the identity of her brother's killer. So as long as Victor Roy is at liberty, Annie is in danger."

"How do we keep her safe without endangering our own families?" Daniel asked.

"We solve the case, tie all the loose threads together, then make sure all the players are safely behind bars and awaiting trial."

"But in order to do that, we need the cooperation of the Brentwood Constabulary," Daniel pointed out.

"And we will have it," Jason replied. "DI Peterson will have no choice but to arrest the culprit if presented with irrefutable evidence of a crime. If he doesn't, then we'll take it to Ransome, and he will involve the home secretary. The killings might have taken place in Essex, but the Carmichaels are steadily expanding their operations in London, which should give the home secretary a kick in the pants."

Daniel couldn't help but chuckle at Jason's choice of phrase. He would think that the rise of organized crime would give any high-ranking public servant a kick in the posterior, but it was becoming increasingly clear that everyone either had their price or could be intimidated into turning a blind eye.

"This needn't affect your plans."

"I'm starting to doubt the honeymoon will even happen," Daniel replied dourly.

"Are you having second thoughts about the marriage?" Jason asked. "Surely you don't still think Flora is involved."

"No. That was a moment of madness, but I am worried about leaving. Perhaps it would be wise to postpone the wedding. I'm sure Flora will understand."

"Will she?"

Jason's expression was very clear on what he understood—that Daniel would be digging his own grave with both hands.

"You're right," Daniel said. "I refuse to allow the Carmichaels and their dirty dealings to ruin a happy occasion. There are too few joyful moments to take for granted. But I do have reservations, Jason," he admitted. "In some ways, it was my work that destroyed my life with Sarah. I don't want the same to happen with Flora. She understands and supports my commitment to the police service, but she might feel differently if the situation were to change."

"You mean if she gets with child?"

Daniel nodded. "A policeman who's sent men and women to the gallows is never safe, is he? There are always those who crave what they perceive as justice and will not rest until they see it done."

"What would you do if you were to leave the service?" Jason asked.

"My future father-in-law offered me a job. He's in need of an accounting clerk. It would be steady work, decent pay, and fixed hours."

"Oh? When was this?"

"A few weeks ago. I refused then and there, but perhaps I was too hasty."

"I'm sure the offer still stands."

"The very thought of spending my days staring at columns of numbers makes me feel ill, but when I think of Charlotte and Flora and their well-being, I am forced to admit that perhaps I'm being selfish, and I need to man up and face my responsibilities."

"You must consider every aspect of Mr. Tarrant's proposal," Jason said. "There might be room for advancement."

"There's room for advancement at Scotland Yard as well, but a promotion is not guaranteed, not when Ransome has his eye on you."

"I made it clear to him that I am not interested in becoming a detective inspector," Jason replied.

"Things change, Jason. Feelings change."

"Prospects change as well," Jason replied. "Mr. Tarrant has no one to leave the company to once he's gone. You could have much to gain by accepting his offer."

Daniel nodded. "I know. And Flora would like me to join her father in the business, but she won't press me. She understands what it is to feel trapped."

"So does Katherine," Jason said. "But she is not happy with my involvement either. I can see it in her eyes and in the set of her mouth when I tell her about some of our more dangerous cases. And with another child on the way…"

"You could always open that private practice you spoke of."

"I could, but my work at the hospital is enough for now. I always wanted to become a doctor and help those in need, but I find that investigating crimes offers something I never imagined I'd need."

"What's that?"

"An intellectual challenge. Surgery is physically taxing and emotionally demanding, but it no longer offers the same intellectual stimulation it once did, not unless I move away from treating patients and focus on groundbreaking procedures."

"What sort of procedures?" Daniel asked, giving Jason a worried side glance.

"Open heart surgery, for one."

"But that's never been done."

"It has been attempted, many times, but with little success. The patients always die, either during surgery or after."

"Would you be willing to take such a risk, knowing the odds?" Daniel asked.

Jason shook his head. "I've seen so much death, Daniel. I don't think I can experiment on living patients and tell myself it's for the greater good, even though successful surgeries will save lives in the future."

"So we're both right back where we started," Daniel said glumly. "Perhaps this is our vocation."

"Yes, I suppose it is," Jason agreed. "But there are turning points in life. The last one led me here, and the decision to come to England truly transformed my life. Perhaps it's time to consider another change."

"Perhaps," Daniel said thoughtfully, and they both fell silent.

Chapter 28

The ride to Burnham-on-Crouch took a long while but was relatively smooth most of the way, since Joe kept to the road the coaches used to reach the previously out-of-the-way town. When they arrived, Jason and Daniel eagerly got out of the carriage, ready to stretch their legs and get their bearings. Burnham was a picturesque waterfront town surrounded by a defense wall. Stone steps led down to the quay, where a number of vessels were moored in the harbor and several boats sailed on the River Crouch. The air smelled of the river, and gulls wheeled overhead, diving into the water when they spotted a fish.

The men who milled on the quay instantly spotted the newcomers and watched their progress, some warily and others with bland curiosity. There were also two scruffy boys, but they paid Jason no mind, their attention on a large gull that was holding a squirming mouse in its beak. Jason descended the steps and approached a man who smiled in welcome, unlike the one next to him, who was scowling, his eyes shadowed by the brim of his flat cap.

"Good afternoon," Jason said. He didn't need to consult his watch to know it was noon, since the sun was riding high in the sky and the chilly morning had turned into a mild afternoon.

"Good afternoon, sir," the man said. He was around forty and was dressed in a well-worn black coat and trousers, tweed waistcoat, and woolen cap. A pipe dangled from the side of his mouth, the scent of tobacco pleasantly sweet. "How can I help?"

"Is this your boat?" Jason asked, pointing to the rowboat the man was standing next to.

"Yes. I just brought in the morning catch," the man said.

"May I know your name?"

"Marty Lambe, sir. And this is my brother, Malcolm."

The scowling man nodded in greeting, but his expression of belligerence remained firmly in place.

"I would like to visit Foulness Island," Jason announced.

"Foulness Island?" Malcolm Lambe echoed. "Why'd ye want to go there?"

"I hear it's lovely this time of year and there are all sorts of birds." Jason thought he heard Daniel chuckle behind him and continued. "Would you be able to take us, Mr. Lambe? I'm happy to pay whatever amount you think is appropriate."

The other men glared at Marty Lambe with ill-disguised jealousy, probably thinking that they should have smiled like loons at the eccentric American who was willing to throw good money around to look at birds he could see on the mainland. Marty looked tired and would have no doubt rather adjourned to the pub, but the promise of easy money was enough to sway him, as it would most of these men.

"Well, it's rather a long way and hard going, sir," Lambe said, doing his best to justify whatever amount he was about to name.

"You would know best, Mr. Lambe," Jason said. "Is the Broomway walkable just now? Such whimsy," Jason added, attempting to look delighted. "I'm so very curious to see it."

"The Broomway will emerge in about an hour, once the tide goes out," Lambe said.

"Are ye visiting from America?" one of the boys asked. "Ye talk funny." The boy's blue eyes sparkled with curiosity, and he smiled widely, revealing two missing milk teeth.

Lambe jabbed the boy in the ribs and hissed to him to shut it, but Jason smiled, eager to show that he wasn't offended in the least.

"Please don't chastise the child," he said. "It's a perfectly reasonable question. And I suppose my speech would sound funny to you." He smiled at the boy. "I live in London these days, but my accent always gives me away."

"It sure does," the boy said with a chuckle. "I never met an American afore."

"How much, Mr. Lambe, or should I ask someone else?"

The rest of the men watched them intently, their initial hostility replaced by looks of hunger. If Lambe wasn't going to name a price soon, one of them would be sure to preempt him and try to steal the rich American away from him.

"One pound," Lambe announced. He had the look of a man who thought he was asking for an enormous sum and was wondering if he had overstepped.

Jason nodded happily. "Done."

"Are you ready to leave now, or were you going to have luncheon first? There's a fine pub just there." Lambe pointed toward a building that was just visible through a gap in the houses that fronted the shore, his expression hopeful. He was probably hungry and needed to fortify himself before rowing for what could be hours.

"If we could leave in an hour, that would be most convenient," Jason replied. "Shall we meet back here?"

"If you wouldn't mind leaving a small deposit, sir," Lambe said, probably realizing that Jason could change his mind, and he would miss out.

"Of course. Will six shillings do?"

"Yes, sir. And your name?"

"Redmond. And this is my associate, Mr. Haze."

"Pleasure to meet you both," Marty said, and touched the visor of his cap.

Jason, Daniel, and Joe made their way to the tavern, which was half full, the patrons clearly locals. The owner suggested they try the oyster stew and assured them that the oysters had been brought in just that morning and were plump and fresh. Jason didn't think it wise to consume a heavy meal before getting on a boat, but they were all hungry and weren't sure when they would return to shore. Joe took a table in the corner and ordered the same. He'd have to find a way to pass the time until they came back, and Jason had asked him to see if he could discover anything about Nathaniel Cavey without appearing too obviously interested.

Marty Lambe did not follow them to the tavern. He probably lived in town and had gone home to get something to eat and rest a while before setting off again. Malcolm Lambe was at the bar, enjoying a pint with his friends and casting frequent looks in Jason and Daniel's direction, as if to make sure they were still there and not trying to sneak out the back door and find a cheaper fare. Jason thought any of Marty Lambe's friends would be happy to undercut his price, but Jason wasn't there to bargain or cause a rift between life-long mates. He wanted to get on their way and hopefully come back before the sun began to set. He was worried about Annie and hoped Victor Roy wouldn't think to look for her in Birch Hill. It was far enough from Brentwood to not immediately spring to mind, and few people would assume that Annie was hiding out at the home of a Scotland Yard detective, but Birch Hill was Carmichael territory, and if someone had spotted Annie, they just might turn her over to Roy if he came looking.

Jason and Daniel arrived at the quay at the appointed time. Lambe smiled happily as Jason and Daniel stepped into the boat and took their seats. Daniel sat in the prow, while Jason took the seat across from Lambe, who reached for the oars as soon as they were ready to go.

"Sit back and enjoy the ride, gents. It should take us about an hour to get out to Foulness Island, and we should get back no later than four o'clock, as long as the weather holds."

"Is a storm expected?" Daniel asked worriedly.

"Nah, you're all right, Mr. Haze," Lambe replied. "I don't foresee any trouble."

Chapter 29

Marty Lambe rowed steadily for about half an hour, until they were well away from the town and nearing what he said was Foulness Point. From what Jason could see, Foulness Island was nothing but marsh and farmland, no manmade structures visible from the water. Lambe said there were farms further inland and a public house at Courtsend. The tavern had served the locals for generations and was probably the only meeting place on the island besides the church.

Having lived in a bustling city all his life, Jason couldn't imagine growing up in a community of a few dozen. It had to be socially limiting and emotionally stifling, but he supposed there were those who might think that living in a city the size of London or New York was unhealthy and overwhelming. The multitudes offered little to any one individual, who was surrounded by their chosen few and followed an established routine of home and work. Still, Jason preferred the options a big city had to offer and looked forward to returning to London. Life in the country held no appeal, especially when one discovered the danger that lurked beneath the unspoiled idyll.

"I do hope this is what you were expecting, Mr. Redmond," Marty Lambe said as they rounded Foulness Point. Several birds had just erupted from the marshland, their pale wings beating frantically as they cleared the tall grass and rose into the cloudless sky.

"Charming views," Jason replied, but his attention was fixed on Daniel, who sat very still, gripping the sides of the boat and gazing longingly in the direction of the town.

It was plain to see he didn't enjoy being out on the water in this small craft, with nothing but the desolate island and the North Sea before them. Lambe suddenly stopped rowing and turned sideways so that he could face both Jason and Daniel.

"So, why did ye really want to come here?" he asked. "And don't tell me it was for the charming views and the pretty birds. I know who ye are. I read the papers, and it wasn't so long ago that ye dug up human remains on the estate of the Earl of Ongar."

Daniel looked startled, his face instantly taking on a defiant expression, but Jason decided that honesty was the best policy since Marty Lambe already knew he was being deceived and probably thought it his duty to protect his close community.

"We're looking for Nathaniel Cavey," Jason said. "We were told he ties up his boat at Foulness Island."

"And who told ye that, I'd like to know," Lambe said.

"It doesn't matter who told us," Daniel said angrily. "Are you going to take us or not?"

"What do ye want with Nathaniel?"

"Know him, do you?" Daniel demanded.

"I do, as it happens, and I wouldn't want to bring the enemy to his door."

"We're not the enemy, Mr. Lambe," Jason said. "But we do need to speak to him."

"What about?" Lambe demanded. "And ye'd better start talking, or we'll sit here all day." The threat was addressed to Daniel, either because Marty Lambe respected Jason's noble station or because he thought it was the policeman who was the real threat.

"Tristan Carmichael was murdered several days ago," Jason said. "Shot with an arrow in Bloody Weald and left for the animals to feast on. Cavey's name came up in the course of our investigation."

Marty Lambe shook his head and scoffed. "You think Nathaniel would shoot Carmichael with an arrow? Talk about barking up a wrong tree, if you'll pardon my saying so, your lordship," Lambe said sarcastically.

"We only want to speak to him."

"Ye're not going to find him here," Lambe said.

"And where would we find him?" Jason asked.

Daniel remained silent, since Jason had the situation in hand.

Lambe made a show of thinking, then gripped the oars once more and began to turn the boat around.

"We're not going to pay if you don't take us to the island," Daniel snapped.

"I am taking ye, Inspector. Nathaniel ties up on the other side of Courtsend, on the River Roach. Ye clearly don't know anything about sailing if ye think he'd tie up near the Broomway."

"So, why are you taking us to him if you don't trust us?" Daniel demanded.

"Because once ye speak to Nathaniel, ye'll see how wrong ye are to suspect him."

"How long have you known Nathaniel Cavey?" Jason asked, hoping to learn as much as he could by engaging Lambe in conversation.

"Since I were a boy. His father was a great one for learning and brought Nathaniel to school in Burnham most days. He always knew Nathaniel wasn't one for farming."

"Does his family still work the farm?" Daniel asked.

"Nathaniel's brothers inherited the farm when their father passed."

Marty Lambe rowed around the way they'd come, then turned into the mouth of another river, presumably the River Roach. Once they'd traveled a short distance, Jason spotted a canal boat tied to a short dock. The long, narrow boat was painted brown and red and sat low in the water, its shape reminiscent of a fat slug. He couldn't begin to imagine how something so unwieldy could be propelled or steered, but as Marty Lambe had pointed out, Jason was no sailor. He'd gone sailing in Newport, Rhode Island, during his university days, but the boats they'd taken out in Narragansett Bay had been sleek and elegant, and not meant for long-term habitation.

Pulling up to the canal boat, Lambe called out, "Ho, boat!"

Nothing happened, so he called again. After a while, a short, stocky man appeared through a narrow door and came up on deck. He was dressed much like Lambe and couldn't be mistaken for anything but a working man. A younger man appeared at the back of the boat. He was tall and wiry, and his cap was pulled down low, but Jason could still see the dark eyes that moved from Jason to Daniel and back again. He seemed set to charge them should the situation call for it, and Jason thought he'd spotted a pistol tucked into the front of the young man's waistband.

"Visitors for ye, Nat," Lambe called out.

Nathaniel Cavey scowled at him. It was evident he wasn't pleased but didn't care to berate Lambe in front of strangers.

"How can I help you, gentlemen?" Cavey asked instead. He did not invite them to come aboard and continued to glare at Lambe in a way that suggested they would be having some very heated words in the near future.

"I think ye'll want to hear this," Lambe said. "I wouldn't have brought them otherwise. That there is Lord Redmond and Inspector Haze."

Cavey's eyes widened in surprise. "Are you really?" he asked as he stepped onto the dock where Jason and Daniel had just disembarked and peered at Jason in the way of a man who usually wore spectacles but didn't have them on hand.

"Jason Redmond," Jason said, and held out his hand.

Cavey looked baffled but took the proffered hand and gave it a firm shake. Daniel made no move to come forward.

"Nathaniel Cavey. That there is Hank." He didn't explain who Hank was, but he was clearly someone to watch out for.

"Pleased to meet you, Mr. Cavey. We won't take much of your time."

There was something about Cavey that inspired trust, but Jason couldn't say precisely what that was. He'd met plenty of men he'd thought honorable but had quickly realized that his trust had been misplaced. He wasn't about to underestimate a man whose name had been mentioned in connection with a murder, but he was willing to keep an open mind. The fact that Marty Lambe thought they should speak to Cavey piqued his interest.

Nathaniel Cavey seemed momentarily conflicted, then said, "Come aboard, gentlemen. The kettle's just boiled." He shot Lambe a look that clearly said, *Not you, mate.*

Jason and Daniel stepped aboard, passed through a low doorway at the front of the boat, and found themselves inside a cabin. The space wasn't large and smelled strongly of damp wood and creosote, but it looked fairly comfortable. There was a small stove, a table and two chairs, and a neatly made cot. There was also a shelf stacked with several books and an open pantry stocked with provisions.

"Tea?" Cavey asked once Jason and Daniel were seated at the table.

"No, thank you," Jason said.

"Please," Daniel replied. "Milk and sugar, if you have it."

Cavey poured two mugs of tea, added a bit of milk from a pewter jug and two lumps of sugar he'd taken from a narrow canister, then brought the mugs to the table. He pulled a stool from beneath the table and set it some distance away from Jason and Daniel.

"So, what's this about, then?" he asked after he had taken a sip of tea.

"Mr. Cavey, Tristan Carmichael was murdered on Monday. He was shot with an arrow and tied to a tree, his body left in Bloody Weald."

Cavey looked sincerely shocked. "Was he now? Who'd do a thing like that?"

"That's what we're trying to find out. Your name came up."

"In what context?" Cavey asked.

"We were told you and Tristan Carmichael were rivals."

Nathaniel Cavey laughed at that, the sound rich and vibrant. "Rivals? Is that what we were?"

"If not rivals, what were you, exactly?" Daniel asked.

"We weren't anything, Inspector, but I often mentioned the Carmichaels in the meetings."

"What meetings would those be?"

"The meetings I organize for working men."

"And how do the Carmichaels fit into your agenda? Do you recruit for them?" Jason asked.

"I do not," Nathaniel Cavey said, and it was clear he found the question offensive. "The Carmichaels, and other organizations like theirs, have no trouble finding willing men. Do you know why?" Cavey didn't wait for an answer. "Because they take care of their own. They offer a fair wage and whatever support the men need in order to secure their loyalty. If a man or his wife and children get ill, the Carmichaels will send a doctor. If a man gets hurt on the job, they will continue to pay his wages until he's well again. And if a man is killed as a result of his involvement, they will support his family."

"You make them sound like living saints," Daniel scoffed.

"They're not saints, Inspector Haze. They're men who understand that if they want loyalty, they need to treat those who work for them like human beings. I don't hold with their activities, but I respect their employment model, and I think companies across England should offer the same benefits to their workers."

"You're a bloody socialist," Daniel exclaimed.

"And what's wrong with socialism? What will happen to your family if you're killed in the line of duty, Inspector? Do you have inherited wealth for them to rely on? Will your wife and children be able to survive without you, or will your woman have to marry the first man that comes along in order to keep out of the workhouse?"

Jason could see the questions had hit home, since, like any thinking man, Daniel had considered what would happen if he were to die suddenly. Once he and Flora were married, Flora would get legal custody of Charlotte, and the Tarrants would look after their daughter, but if not for the Tarrants' wealth, Daniel's family would be left in dire straits, like so many other families who'd lost their breadwinner.

"Does your employer pay your expenses," Cavey went on, "or do you dip into your wages to pay your way? And will your employer continue to pay you if you become ill and can't work?"

"We're not talking about me," Daniel replied gruffly.

"But we are. You are a working man, although you're probably better off than most men I meet with. Factory workers, ship builders, navvies, miners, and anyone else who does an honest day's work is expected to work ten to twelve hours a day. They earn barely enough to live on, and get no benefits from their employers. If they get hurt or fall ill, their families don't eat, and sometimes, even lose the roof over their heads. So if the rich were asked to be held accountable for the lives that depend on them, would that be so wrong?"

"So you're a modern-day Robin Hood. He was skilled with a bow and arrow, if I recall correctly," Daniel said acidly.

"I'm no Robin Hood, Inspector, nor do I shoot people full of arrows. I'm just someone who advocates for better conditions for people who keep this country running."

"Advocates?" Daniel echoed. "You mean you're urging workers to unionize."

"I am. Are you going to arrest me?" Cavey seemed more amused than worried.

"As long as you're not in the act of causing civil unrest, I have no cause to arrest you, but I do think you should mind yourself. The powers-that-be will not stand for unions," Daniel replied.

"Not yet, but times are changing, Inspector. Times are changing."

"Mr. Cavey, where were you Monday morning?" Jason asked.

"I was in London. I arrived on Sunday evening and returned to Essex yesterday."

"Can anyone vouch for your whereabouts?" Daniel asked.

"Only the two hundred men or so who attended the meetings I had organized in the East End. I spoke at the Swan, the Ivy, and the Sailor's Knot. You can check with the publicans. They will confirm I was there."

"Presumably you held these gatherings in the evenings," Daniel mused. "You could have sailed to Essex, murdered Tristan Carmichael, and returned to London in time for your meeting."

Cavey chuckled. "The pubs in the East End open as early as seven o'clock in the morning, and I was there to speak to the pre-shift drinkers, Inspector. I was there in the afternoons, and I was there in the evenings. I was seen by dozens of men in each location. And I assure you, I had no motive to murder Tristan Carmichael. Whoever told you I did was sending you on a wild goose chase, and it doesn't get wilder than this." Cavey made an expansive gesture intended to encompass the isolated location.

"Where are you off to next?" Jason asked.

"Birmingham."

"How do you power and navigate this boat? Surely you don't rely on the currents," Jason said, looking around. "And how would you get to Birmingham from here?"

Cavey chuckled. "These narrowboats used to be pulled by horses or donkeys, who walked along the canals. I expect some still are. But I had this boat outfitted with a steam engine some years back. It's not fast, but it gets me where I need to go. And to answer your question, my lord, I can reach the Midlands by way of the canal system. There's one that runs from London directly to Birmingham. It will take me a few days, but I'll get a warm welcome once I arrive. Full of working men is Birmingham. Working men who are tired and fed up and ready to hear what I have to tell them."

Daniel looked at Jason to see if he had any more questions, but Jason was more than ready to leave.

"Thank you for your time, Mr. Cavey," he said, and stood. "Best of luck with your endeavors."

"Although I doubt your wishes for my success are sincere, I thank you, nonetheless, my lord," Cavey said.

"You're quite mistaken," Jason replied. "I wholeheartedly agree with what you're proposing and think that not only the working man but also the employers would benefit. Loyalty goes a long way, and it's a two-way street."

"Indeed, it is, my lord, but I doubt your brethren would agree with you. Perhaps as an American, you are able to see the situation from a different perspective, but the English have an inherent fear of democracy. We've seen what happened to the French."

"As you said, Mr. Cavey, times are changing," Jason replied.

"Not quickly enough for my liking."

"Nor mine," Jason said. "Good day to you."

Jason lowered his head as he passed beneath the lintel, relieved to be out in the fresh, marshy air. He hated closed spaces and found that he couldn't breathe normally until he was outside. He and Daniel disembarked, then walked the short distance to where Marty Lambe was waiting for them, his dark eyes watching them intently, as if he could reconstruct the conversation that had taken place inside the boat.

"Got what ye came for?" he asked as he waited for them to take their seats.

"Not really, but it was illuminating," Daniel said sulkily.

"He's quite charismatic, isn't he?" Jason asked once Marty Lambe had rowed them out into the river.

"He always was, even as a boy. Nat has some big ideas," Lambe said, his admiration obvious.

"Ideas that will get him killed," Daniel muttered under his breath.

"We're all going to die, Inspector," Lambe said. "Better to die doing something worthwhile, wouldn't ye say?"

Daniel did not reply.

Chapter 30

"Another wasted journey," Daniel grumbled once they were back in the brougham. It was nearly four o'clock, and they had learned nothing that would bring them closer to solving the case.

"Not necessarily," Jason said.

"Did we not hear the same thing?" Daniel asked.

"We did, but from where I'm standing, a clear suspect is beginning to emerge."

Daniel gaped at Jason, utterly baffled by that unexpected statement. "Care to enlighten me?" He felt foolish in the extreme for having to ask for an explanation.

"Who pointed you in the direction of Nathaniel Cavey?"

"Cecily Carmichael."

"And who first mentioned Harvey Boswell?"

"Cecily Carmichael."

"And who won the archery competition three years running?"

"Cecily Carmichael."

"Perhaps she mentioned Boswell to Victor Roy as well."

Daniel sighed with frustration. "But how does Cecily Carmichael benefit from her husband's death?"

"As Nathaniel Cavey helpfully pointed out, going out to Foulness Island was meant to send us on a wild goose chase. And telling you that Harvey Boswell was intent on moving up the ranks provided an explanation for his subsequent murder."

"And?" Daniel asked, feeling the idiot.

"And there are two people who stand to benefit from both murders. Cecily Carmichael is now free of a husband who didn't want her and left her to molder under the watchful eye of her father-in-law, and Victor Roy can now get out from under Lance Carmichael's thumb and take over the Red Lantern. Perhaps the two are in cahoots, or maybe they had conspired to do one another a favor."

"Except that Cecily will lose her son if she tries to leave, and Victor Roy was seen by Annie," Daniel replied.

"Perhaps Cecily is willing to relinquish the rights to Samuel in exchange for freedom, and Victor Roy knows that Annie will resurface sooner or later. All he has to do is bide his time."

"Victor Roy is also in charge of guarding Cecily, so if she slipped out and shot her husband, he would cover for her," Daniel supplied.

"Precisely. And Cecily might have been the one to suggest getting rid of Boswell so that Roy could take his place."

"How could she be sure Lance Carmichael would appoint Victor Roy the new manager of the Red Lantern?" Daniel asked.

"She might have suggested that as well and told Lance that Roy's talents were wasted on patrolling the grounds."

Daniel nodded. Jason's theory incorporated all the main points and provided the suspects with feasible motives. "Neither Cecily Carmichael nor Victor Roy has ties to London, which means they would need to be arrested by Essex police," he pointed out.

"What we have right now is speculation," Jason said. "We need to present DI Peterson with irrefutable evidence."

"And if he passes the information to Lance Carmichael, neither Cecily nor Victor will ever see the inside of a courtroom," Daniel said. "Lance Carmichael will mete out his own justice."

"I don't care about Victor Roy, but I won't send a young mother to her death unless I'm absolutely certain she shot that arrow," Jason replied.

"So how do we find the evidence we need?"

"I will start by attending the funeral tomorrow," Jason said. "Presumably both Cecily and Victor will be in attendance, as well as Michael O'Keefe."

Daniel nodded. "I will collect Charlotte, take her back to Mrs. Elderman's, and make sure Annie is all right. Then I will call at Ardith Hall."

"I thought you weren't going to see Flora until the wedding."

"I wasn't, but I feel as if a part of me is missing when I can't speak to her."

Jason smiled. "I feel the same way when I'm away from Katie."

"I never thought I'd say this again, but I found someone who completes me," Daniel said, and a silly grin spread across his face.

"I'm happy for you, Daniel, and I will be happier still if we can wrap up this case before your wedding."

"Which leaves us one day."

"Then let's put it to good use."

Daniel would have liked to put forth a brilliant suggestion but had no idea what to say. Jason was going to the funeral, where he might be in the presence of Tristan Carmichael's killer, but short of keeping Annie safe, Daniel didn't know how to proceed. Jason seemed to sense his conundrum and came to the rescue.

"I doubt Lance Carmichael will leave the house and the child unprotected during the funeral. Samuel's nanny is sure to remain behind, and there will be men to guard the property. Perhaps you can find out more about Cecily and Victor Roy's whereabouts at the time of the murder and the extent of their personal relationship. If we can prove they were working together, we will have enough to present our findings to DI Peterson, or a magistrate, if Peterson is unwilling to make an arrest."

"Okay," Daniel said. Using the American term made him feel sophisticated and modern.

"Okay, then." Jason grinned at his friend. "We have a plan."

Chapter 31

Daniel felt the usual twinge of apprehension as the dogcart rolled through the wrought-iron gates of Ardith Hall and made its way down the drive that bisected the manicured lawns. Ardith Hall had belonged to the Ardith family for centuries and, in its heyday, had been the seat of influence and great wealth. The last scion of the Ardith family had sold up and followed his mistress to the south of France. An odd choice for a member of the nobility, but some men were either foolish in the extreme or brave enough to break with tradition and grab whatever happiness they still could in their twilight years.

Daniel could understand the logic that had driven John Tarrant to buy the hall. His future father-in-law had planned to elevate the family's position and acquire a country seat in which generations of Tarrants could raise their families in a style no Tarrant had hitherto enjoyed, but after their only son Hector had died, John Tarrant had lost interest in the estate and spent most of his time in London, where his business interests lay.

Flora had made it clear to her parents that she would not be moving her new family into the hall, and Daniel was immensely grateful not to have to begin his marriage with a disagreement. He had no intentions of living with his in-laws, and in a place he had been glad to escape. As Daniel maneuvered the cart down the circular drive and pulled up before the massive doors, he hoped Flora's parents would not keep him from seeing his bride. It was unorthodox to call on Flora before the wedding, but given that they had shared a house for several months, albeit platonically, before becoming engaged and were a family in all but name, Daniel didn't think a brief conversation would doom their marriage to failure.

The Tarrants' new butler, Wiggins, greeted Daniel politely but permitted himself a brief look of astonishment before instructing a maidservant to take Daniel's things. Wiggins led him to the drawing room and invited him to wait while he informed Flora Daniel wished to see her. No doubt Flora would be surprised as well, but that couldn't be helped.

Daniel settled into one of the damask wingchairs and wished Wiggins would have offered him a drink. He was tired and cold, and if he were honest, more than a little resentful. This was supposed to be his time, but the past kept intruding on the present and constantly reminding him that everything was connected and there was no escaping one's doubts and fears. Daniel had always thought life was linear, but every time he moved forward, he found himself looping back to a place where he was kept hostage by memories, guilt, and people who would prefer to keep him where he was.

Daniel didn't suppose anyone could outrun the past. All they could do was try to build a future worth fighting for and hope that tragedy didn't derail them again just when their life was finally on track. He knew it was morbid to think of tragedy on the eve of a happy occasion, but perhaps that was the best time to acknowledge one's worries. Happiness made a person vulnerable and reminded them that they now had something precious to lose. And Daniel didn't think he could bear any more loss.

He turned toward the door, eager to see Flora's beloved face, only to find John Tarrant striding into the room.

"Daniel, to what do we owe the pleasure?" Tarrant asked once he had settled stiffly in the chair opposite. "I thought we had agreed that we wouldn't be seeing you until the wedding."

Noting the tense line of John Tarrant's shoulders and the grim set of his jaw, Daniel suddenly realized that his future father-in-law was bracing for bad news. Did he imagine Daniel was there to call off the wedding? The Tarrants had given up all hope of Flora marrying one of her father's aging business associates or the eligible but not very desirable men that Mrs. Tarrant had put in Flora's way in the hope that she would make a respectable marriage before she got too old to attract a husband.

Had Daniel and Flora found their way to each other sooner, Mr. Tarrant would most likely have refused Daniel's proposal, but at this point, to marry a penniless policeman was better than to remain a spinster. No one cared what Flora wanted or had asked what would make her happy. Unlike her brother, who had been the child of his parents' dreams, Flora was an embarrassment, a daughter who refused to conform and do what she was told. Daniel could sense John Tarrant's fear that Flora would remain unwed despite the sizable sum he had settled on her in the hope of attracting a suitor. And now Daniel was there, a day before the wedding, and probably looking rather grim, but not for the reasons John Tarrant imagined.

"I'm sorry to have disturbed you, Mr. Tarrant, but might I have a moment with Flora?"

"Look, Haze, if you've changed your mind at this late stage…" Mr. Tarrant began, his already mottled skin turning a darker shade of red. "That would be bad form. Bad form, indeed. If it's a matter of money…" John Tarrant's voice trailed off, and Daniel had the sick feeling that Tarrant was about to whip out his checkbook and offer him a bribe.

"It's not a matter of money, and I'm not here to break the engagement. I love Flora, and I would marry her if she didn't have a penny to her name," Daniel exclaimed.

John Tarrant looked dubious, his gaze sweeping over the grand drawing room and the paintings that adorned the walls. They alone would probably pay Daniel's rent in St. John's Wood for a decade or more if sold, but Daniel wasn't interested in John Tarrant's wealth. He had never given Flora's inheritance a thought, at least not in the way her father imagined. Daniel wanted no part of Ardith Hall. The gloomy wood-paneled rooms with their coffered ceilings made him feel like he was inside a coffin, and the silent corridors echoed with loneliness and the bitter tang of the Tarrants' disappointments.

"I need to consult Flora regarding an unrelated matter," Daniel said, and hoped John Tarrant wasn't going to demand to know the nature of said matter and feel he had the right to decide if it was important enough to bring to Flora. Daniel's hope was in vain.

"What could possibly be so urgent?" Tarrant asked irritably.

"It's to do with a case I'm investigating."

"And you thought this would be a good time to discuss something so sordid with my daughter?" John Tarrant shook his head, as if marveling at Daniel's shocking lack of sense. "I really think this isn't the time or the place to confer on police matters." He pushed to his feet but remembered his manners and gave Daniel a tight smile. "I will be sure to tell Flora you called. Good night, Mr. Haze. Wiggins will see you out."

Daniel did his best to keep his tone mild and his expression bland, but he was angry and frustrated, and felt as if a roadblock had been erected in his path. Why shouldn't he speak to Flora? They were both adults and perfectly capable of deciding what was and wasn't worth talking about. And given that they were about to marry, why was John Tarrant so determined to maintain control over his daughter? Flora should be able to decide for herself. If she didn't wish to see Daniel before the wedding, he would respect her decision and leave, but what right did her father have to show Daniel the door?

"I'm certain Flora won't mind," Daniel replied, and remained seated.

John Tarrant's brows rose in amazement, and he seemed unsure what to do. Daniel mused that the man should be used to opposition, given Flora's propensity for argument, but didn't think he should engage in a battle of wills with his future father-in-law. If Tarrant held his ground, Daniel would be forced to leave.

"Flora won't mind what?" Flora asked as she swept into the room. She smiled at Daniel after shooting her father a narrow-eyed look. He glared back in obvious disapproval.

"I wanted a quick word," Daniel said, smiling back at her. "I didn't think you'd mind."

"Father, would you give us a moment?" Flora said.

"I can't very well leave you unchaperoned," John Tarrant protested. He sat back down and crossed his legs.

Flora planted her hands on her hips, and an angry flush bloomed in her cheeks. "You can't leave us unchaperoned?" she repeated slowly. "Father, you do realize that I live in Inspector Haze's home and am about to become his wife." Flora turned to Daniel. "I trust you're not here to jilt me?"

"I'm not," Daniel assured her.

"Then I think it's perfectly safe to leave us alone, unless you realized you can't wait another minute and mean to ravish me on the carpet," Flora said, turning to Daniel. She smiled in a way that made him think she might not object if he were.

"Flora, stop torturing your father and sit down," Daniel said. He was barely able to keep a straight face at the sight of John Tarrant's apoplectic expression and almost felt sorry for the man.

A few years ago, he would have thought Flora's behavior outrageous and would have labeled her common and unladylike, but now he found her enchanting and wished he could pull her into his arms and kiss her in a way he had been dreaming of since she'd first walked into his life. *Not long now*, he reminded himself as John Tarrant finally capitulated and heaved himself out of the chair. He made a point of checking the time, then turned to Daniel.

"I will have the groom bring your cart around in ten minutes."

"Thank you. That's very thoughtful," Daniel replied only a tad sarcastically.

"Not at all. Goodnight to you."

John Tarrant walked out of the room without a backward glance but left the door wide open, in case Daniel and Flora should throw caution to the wind and, as Daniel's mother used to euphemistically say, put the cart before the horse.

"Oh, Daniel, I'm so glad to see you," Flora gushed as she sank into the chair her father had just vacated. "My parents are driving me to insanity. I cannot wait to leave this house for good."

"Mrs. Elderman is not making things easy for me either," Daniel confessed.

"And why would she, the poor dear? She has legitimate concerns. Did you tell her we would never think of keeping Charlotte from her?"

"Of course."

"Still, it's not easy to be old and alone, is it?"

"No, I don't suppose it is, but living to old age is a privilege so many are not granted," Daniel said, and instantly regretted his words. Flora would think he was referring to Sarah and Felix.

"No, they are not," Flora agreed with a sigh. "I do wish Hector was still with us. I miss him terribly, and I know he would be so happy for me."

Daniel had wondered what Hector had been like and if they would have got on had Hector lived. If he had been anything like Flora, perhaps he would have been a friend and an ally in this new family.

"The dead are always with us, aren't they?" Daniel mused.

Flora nodded. "But I'm sure you didn't come here to talk about death."

"I did, actually." Daniel smiled apologetically. "Did you hear what happened to Tristan Carmichael?"

"No. Do tell."

Daniel filled her in on everything that had happened thus far but intentionally left out the part about suspecting her. Even Flora wasn't that understanding.

"Would it make me an awful person if I were to admit that I'm not sorry that reprobate is dead?" Flora asked.

"No, it wouldn't, and I feel much the same. Everyone deserves fair treatment before the law, but Tristan Carmichael forfeited his right to justice. I can't begin to imagine how many families have suffered because of the Carmichaels."

"Perhaps losing his son will take the wind out of Lance Carmichael's sails."

"Lance Carmichael still has a lot of good years left in him, so he will simply groom his grandson to take over when the time comes. I believe he began to involve Tristan by the time he was ten."

Flora sighed heavily. "How cruel people are to their children."

"I don't suppose he saw it as cruelty. Tristan lived in a fine house in a prestigious part of town and passed himself off as a gentleman. And if Lance Carmichael bribed or intimidated enough politicians, Tristan would have probably been ennobled," Daniel said with disgust.

"Lance Carmichael could have purchased him rank, if he were so minded. If he acquired land that was tied to a title, he could have made a claim on the title."

"Really? Is that possible?"

Flora nodded. "My father attempted to do just that when he bought Ardith Hall. He wanted the title for Hector, but since the Duke of Ardith was alive and could still sire an heir, the request was denied. Little good a title would do my father now, with only a daughter left," Flora said bitterly. "I'm the last Tarrant, and only until Saturday at that."

"Will your parents remain in this house?"

"Most likely, although my mother would like to return to London. She's lonely here."

"So why stay?"

"Because Father will never agree to sell. He will see it as an admission of defeat."

"An admission before whom?"

"His business associates and the friends he has made since moving from London. He plans to host a fox hunt next month. He's quite taken with the pursuits of the country squire."

"Good thing we'll be back in London, then," Daniel said. He couldn't think of anything he wanted to do less than hunt some terrified creature.

Thinking of frightened creatures put him in mind of Annie Boswell. He would like to see her settled before he and Flora left on their honeymoon. "We have to find a safe place for Annie," he said.

"My father's Aunt Eleanor is in need of a companion. She's a kind soul and would welcome Annie into her home."

"Where does she live?"

"In Basildon. She has a great big house and a lovely garden that she looks after herself. She's a great one for gardening. Annie would be well looked after."

"I'm not sure how safe Annie would be in Basildon. It's too close to Brentwood. Perhaps we need to find her something further afield, deep in the country. And speaking of country living, whom did you compete against in the archery competition at last year's fête?"

If Flora was surprised by the question, she didn't show it. "There weren't that many contestants. It was me, Arabella Chadwick, Belinda Cressy, and Lauren John."

"And were the rest of them any good?"

"Belinda and Lauren didn't even graze their targets, but Arabella Chadwick proved quite a surprise, a dark horse you might say. With her sister not there to overshadow her, she finally got her chance to shine. She almost won, actually. The judges had to measure the arrow's proximity to the center to determine whose was closer. I was quite vexed, I don't mind telling you," Flora said with a smile. "Imagine, that little mouse almost getting the better of me." She chuckled. "Really, I think it did Arabella a world of good. She looked proud for about five minutes, until her mama stole her thunder."

"Caroline Chadwick is good at that. It should be a sport," Daniel replied.

"Then my mother would pose quite a threat to her talents." Flora reached out and laid a hand over Daniel's. "I hope you don't think I shot Tristan Carmichael."

"The thought did cross my mind. I'm so sorry, Flora," Daniel said, and hoped she would be able to forgive him for his inexcusable disloyalty. "My mind went to a very dark place, and I imagined he'd hurt you."

"So, what made you change your mind? Or do you still think I killed him? Is that why you came here, to feel me out?"

"I realized you would never do anything sneaky. If you were to murder someone, you'd do it face to face, and then you would own up to it."

"You're right there," Flora said. "But let's hope it never comes to that."

"Can you forgive me?" Daniel pleaded.

Flora smiled indulgently, then leaned closer to Daniel and took his face between her hands, looking deep into his eyes. "You have every reason to doubt me after what happened with Sarah, and if you were a lesser man, you would have denied suspecting me. But you told me the truth, and that's what matters. Let there be no secrets between us, ever."

"I'm okay with that," Daniel said, and smiled.

"I'm okay with that too, although I'm still not exactly sure what that means."

"Neither am I, but it seems to cover a wide range of conditions." Daniel's vision blurred as tears pricked the backs of his eyes. "I love you so much, Flora. I would happily murder Tristan Carmichael myself if he ever hurt you."

"Good thing he never noticed me, then," Flora said. "And I love you as well. Suspicious mind and all," she added.

Daniel took Flora's hands away from his face and kissed each one in turn. They weren't the soft hands of a lady but hands that knew what it was to work and to care for oneself and others. "I will see you on Saturday."

Flora smiled. "I'll be the one walking down the aisle."

"And I'll be the one waiting at the altar."

"I can't wait."

"Neither can I," Daniel said. He glanced at the clock on the mantel, then stood with great reluctance. "I better go before your father has me thrown out."

"He wouldn't dare," Flora said with a smirk. "He's too desperate for you to take me off his hands."

"Which I will happily do."

Flora walked Daniel to the door, and he hurried down the steps toward the waiting cart. *One day more*, he thought giddily as he climbed onto the bench and reached for the reins. *Only one day more*.

Chapter 32

After Daniel and Charlotte left, Jason spent an hour with Lily, who told him all about the game she had played with Charlotte and Liam, and about the fairy cakes Mrs. Dodson had sent up with their afternoon milk. He then joined Katherine in the drawing room for a pre-dinner drink. Katherine had a small sherry, and Jason poured himself a large whisky. Even though the drawing room was pleasantly toasty, he couldn't seem to warm up after the time spent on the open water.

"It doesn't sound like Cavey was involved in Tristan Carmichael's murder," Katherine said after Jason had told her about the visit to Foulness Island. "But he does have some interesting ideas."

"He does, but I very much doubt any employer would be willing to implement them unless the workers were to go on a prolonged strike."

"That can be quite risky for the workers," Katherine said.

Jason nodded. "They will lose their jobs if the employers decide to replace them with new hires."

Katherine sighed heavily. "Why is it that men never listen to reason?"

"Because they are vain and greedy, and too shortsighted to see the benefits even the most minor changes can bring about in the long term."

Smiling sweetly, Katherine said, "I can think of a few others who won't listen to reason."

Jason chuckled. "Might you be referring to me and Daniel?"

"Jason, Daniel is getting married on Saturday. Surely he deserves a bit of inner peace as he sets out on this new chapter in his life." When Jason didn't immediately reply, Katherine continued. "My dear, I know it's important to you to know justice was done, even when the victim was someone as reprehensible as Tristan Carmichael, but perhaps it's time to turn the case over to the Brentwood Constabulary."

Jason reached out and took her hand. "You're absolutely right, Katie. In the coming days, we need to focus on Daniel and Flora."

"And Charlotte," Katherine reminded him. "I'm sure she will feel a bit forlorn once they leave on their wedding trip. Charlotte adores Flora, but this will be a big change for her, and she will have to learn to share Daniel with his wife and possibly a new sibling."

"Do you think we should invite Charlotte to stay with us while Daniel and Flora are away?" Jason asked.

Katherine shook her head. "I expect this will be the last time Mrs. Elderman will have uninterrupted time with Charlotte. We shouldn't infringe on that."

"No," Jason agreed.

Katherine tilted her head to the side and smiled innocently, but Jason could read the question in her eyes and knew he had to give her an answer. He couldn't help but smile back. When Katie did that, she reminded him of his mother, who had been able to bend his father to her will with a sweet smile and a few carefully chosen words.

"I will call on Daniel tomorrow morning and inform him of my decision to close the case. He will not continue to investigate without me," Jason said confidently.

"No, he won't. Daniel follows your lead and worries about disappointing you."

"Daniel is his own man, Katie."

Katherine smiled at him as if he were a naïve child. "When I was a girl, my mother told me that in every relationship, someone has the upper hand. At times, they don't even know it, but there's a delicate balance that must be maintained because a sudden shift can cause a surprisingly deep fracture."

Jason squeezed her fingers. "We know who has the upper hand in this relationship, and I wouldn't have it any other way."

Katherine gently pulled her hand away and stood, her hands going to her lower back and offering Jason a glimpse of her expanding belly as she leaned back, stretching her spine. "It's time to change for dinner. And I want to give Lily a kiss before she goes to sleep."

"I will be up in a moment," Jason said. "I'll just finish my drink."

Katherine nodded. "Mrs. Dodson made beef Wellington. I'm rather looking forward to it. I've been unusually hungry these past few days."

"A robust appetite is a sign of a healthy pregnancy," Jason said.

"Mary says it means I'm carrying a boy. I wasn't very hungry with Lily, so perhaps there's something to it."

Jason was about to say that every pregnancy was different and there really was no way to foretell the sex of the child but quickly realized he shouldn't be too quick to crush his wife's hopes. What was the harm in believing in portents? Once the child was born, Katherine would cherish it whether it was a boy or a girl, as would Jason. He would be just as happy with another daughter, but it would be nice to have a son.

"I'm sure Mary is right," Jason said, and watched Katherine's eyes crease at the corners as she grinned.

"Thank you for humoring me. I know you think it's absolute tosh."

"Ancient wisdom is not to be discounted, especially when it applies to beef Wellington. Maybe we should rename it beef Washington in this house," Jason quipped.

"Silly Yank," Katherine said affectionately, and left the room.

Chapter 33

Jason finished the whisky and resisted the urge to top up his drink. He looked forward to dinner, but the whisky and the warm fire had relaxed him, and he had enjoyed the few minutes of quiet solitude after spending the day around other people. Despite what he'd told Katherine, Jason wasn't mentally prepared to close the case, but he would keep his promise and call on Daniel tomorrow. If Daniel needed them to step away from the case in order to focus on his personal life, then Jason was happy to oblige. Katie was right. Justice mattered to Jason, more than he cared to admit, but there were degrees of justice, and Tristan Carmichael didn't deserve it as much as the individuals he'd harmed.

Did Harvey Boswell?

Boswell had worked for the Carmichaels for years and had spent the final year of his life peddling opium to people who were unable to resist their craving for the pipe. Was Boswell guilty, or did the blame lie with the people who found their way to the Red Lantern and spent their hard-earned money to purchase a few hours of oblivion? Jason supposed the blame went both ways, but from what Annie had told Daniel, her brother had gone to work for the Carmichaels in order to care for her and had never personally engaged in acts of violence. That hardly made him a saint, but it seemed he'd had some redeeming qualities and had cared for his sister. Without Harvey, Annie would most likely founder and wind up dead or in a workhouse unless she found respectable employment.

But who would hire her? Employers demanded impeccable references and hands-on experience, and Annie had neither. Perhaps, if she was interested, Jason could help her secure a place at the nursing school at St. Thomas's, but not every woman was cut out for nursing, and Annie was too young to be faced with the responsibility of caring for the sick and dying. Perhaps Mrs. Dodson could be prevailed upon to train her as a scullery maid since Kitty was long overdue for a promotion and hoped to take over for Mrs. Dodson once she was ready to retire. Jason supposed there was no sense making plans until he consulted Annie on her wishes for the future. And perhaps Daniel would have a suggestion.

His mind returning to the conversation with Katherine, Jason had to admit that her summation of his relationship with Daniel had surprised him, but he supposed he'd always known that their partnership wasn't truly even. Katherine's mother had been right—in every relationship, someone held more sway, and although Jason had never set out to gain the upper hand in his friendship with Daniel, he supposed this was the way their personalities aligned, and they were both fine with that. At least for now. But as with every relationship, change was unavoidable.

Jason had lost his best friend, Mark, when Jason had joined the Union Army and Mark had opted to stay behind to continue his education. By the end of the Civil War, Jason had been half dead of starvation in a Confederate Prison camp in Georgia, and Mark had been happily married to Jason's fiancée in New York. Jason had resented Mark bitterly until he'd found out that Mark and his baby son had died of cholera not long after Jason had arrived in England. But such was the nature of life. Fortune didn't always favor the brave or the clever. Sometimes, lives were lost on a roll of the dice.

Had Cecily Carmichael been the one to roll the dice on her husband's fate? Jason considered the theory as he stared into the leaping flames in the grate. Cecily and Victor Roy were the most likely suspects, but Jason still wasn't convinced. Just because a supposition fit the facts didn't necessarily mean it was true. And would Cecily truly benefit from Tristan's death? She would if she was romantically involved with Roy and thought she would get out from under her father-in-law's thumb once Victor rose to power. Still, the logistics didn't quite fit.

It would have been easy enough for Victor Roy to murder Harvey Boswell. The Red Lantern wasn't very far from the Carmichael mansion, and no one would have thought to ask too many questions if Roy went out for an hour. Taking control of the Red Lantern could be the first step in his bid for control and would put him in line to become Lance's second. With Roy stepping up in Essex and Michael O'Keefe taking over in London, Lance Carmichael was sure to lose ground and possibly even go the way of his son. But Jason still had questions about Tristan's death.

In order to shoot Tristan in Bloody Weald, Cecily would have had to arrange a meeting with him for Monday morning. And why would Tristan agree if he could just as easily see her at home in Brentwood? Had Tristan thought he was meeting someone else, a lover or a business associate? It seemed a strange place to meet, since it was so out of the way, but perhaps Tristan had hoped to conduct his affair entirely unobserved, whether it was a romantic assignation, or a meeting intended to hatch a plan or come up with a means to neutralize a threat.

Cecily would have needed to get away unobserved, not an easy thing to do in a house guarded around the clock, and bring a bow and a quiver of arrows. Then she would have had to wait for Tristan to arrive, execute her plan, and get back to Brentwood before anyone realized she was gone. There were too many variables, and even if Cecily had had help in the form of Victor Roy, Lance Carmichael was sure to have got wind of her absence.

No, there was something else at play here, Jason decided as the clock chimed the half hour, and he hauled himself to his feet, ready to go up and change for dinner. He and Daniel just weren't seeing it and weren't likely to solve the mystery now. It was too late. Tristan Carmichael would be buried tomorrow, Daniel would be married on Saturday, and next week Jason and his family would return to London. Whoever had killed Tristan Carmichael would be in the clear, their mission complete or only just beginning. There was little point in going to the funeral, so Jason would go see Daniel first thing in the morning.

He had just reached the stairs when Micah and Tom stepped out of the library. Micah had to change for dinner, and Tom would be on his way home. Tom had a standing invitation to dine with the Redmonds, but he preferred to join Micah for tea, which was a less formal affair and didn't require a change of clothes or intimate knowledge of cutlery. Tom looked incredibly pleased, which usually meant he'd beat Micah at chess, probably more than once, and planned to do it again tomorrow.

"Did you two have a good day?" Jason asked.

"Yes, sir," Tom said.

"The Romani are back in Bloody Mead," Micah announced. "We went by their camp. They have such beautiful ponies."

"How long have they been there?" Jason asked. He hadn't realized the Romani came in the autumn as well since they normally camped in Bloody Mead in late spring.

"They were there Sunday morning," Tom said. "I saw their caravans through the trees when we passed the mead on our way to church. They always appear as if by magic." Tom was clearly in awe of the travelers' ability to arrive unnoticed and set up camp in a matter of minutes.

Jason didn't suppose it was too difficult, given that the Romani simply circled their colorful vardos around the clearing and congregated at the center. The older women cooked over open fires, the younger ones looked after children who were too small to mind themselves, and the men saw to the animals and firewood. Jason thought he might stop by and say hello before heading to Mrs. Elderman's house. The Romani didn't welcome *gorjas*, which was what they called outsiders, in their camp, but Jason was well known to the travelers since he'd cared for them after their camp had been raided by angry locals who hadn't wanted the Romani near Birch Hill. The animals had been slaughtered, and several vardos had been set on fire. Although most of the caravans had been saved from destruction, the inhabitants had suffered burns and dangerous levels of smoke inhalation.

"Why did you go to the camp?" Jason asked when the boys exchanged conspiratorial looks.

"No reason," Micah replied, but Jason didn't buy his nonchalant demeanor for a second.

"Did you have your palms read, or did you want to look at the pretty girls?" he teased.

"Both," Tom replied, his tanned cheeks turning deep crimson. "Zemphyra is always up for a bit of *dukkerin*, but for us, she does it for free."

"Does she, now? And what did she see in your future?"

Tom kept quiet, but Micah said proudly, "She said I would become a respected doctor and marry the woman of my dreams."

"That sounds like a very desirable future to me," Jason replied.

Micah's brow creased with consternation. "The thing is, she said I've already met my bride, but I don't know any girls."

"Perhaps the sister of one of your school friends?" Jason suggested.

Micah instantly brightened. "That must be it. Several boys have younger sisters, but some of them are hardly more than babies."

"Babies grow up," Jason said. "But you have years yet until you have to worry about looking for brides."

"I don't ever want to get married," Tom said.

"Really? Why not?" Micah asked.

"I don't know too many married people who are happy. Uncle Joe has the right idea. It's best to remain on one's own."

"It must get lonely," Micah replied.

A sly look passed over Tom's face. "Uncle Joe always finds willing company when he wants it."

Jason decided not to ask who Joe was keeping company with. Two members of Jason's staff were already courting, and even though he was happy for Fanny and Henley, it made things a little awkward since Henley had yet to propose, and Dodson, who was Henley's uncle by marriage, was seething with disapproval and putting pressure on the couple to make things official.

"Well, I'll be off home now," Tom said. "Goodnight, your lordship."

"Goodnight, Tom," Jason said.

"Beef Wellington," Micah said happily as he and Jason walked up the stairs together.

"So I hear. What did Zemphyra tell Tom?"

Micah snorted with laughter. "She told him he was going to marry Aggy Locke and have six daughters. You should have your palm read, Captain. You might learn something."

"I don't care to know the future, Micah."

"Why not?"

Because it's rarely as bright as we hope, Jason thought, but didn't say so to Micah.

"I prefer to be surprised," he said instead, and they walked the rest of the way in silence.

Chapter 34

Friday, September 10

Gauzy tendrils of fog swirled past the windows as Jason and Katherine sat down to breakfast. Katherine looked well rested, her hair loosely tied with a blue ribbon and her pregnancy on display in a flowing morning gown.

"Oh, I do hope the weather will be fine tomorrow," she said as she peered out the window. "The girls are so looking forward to the wedding."

Flora had asked Charlotte and Lily to be flower girls, and the children were bursting with excitement at the prospect of attending their first wedding. They would walk down the aisle before Mary, who was Flora's only bridesmaid. Liam, who hadn't been given a role and was a bit grumpy about being left out, would sit with Jason and Katherine.

"Even if the weather will be gloomy, it will still be a sunny occasion," Jason reassured Katherine.

"Seems like it was just our wedding day," she said dreamily.

"So much has happened since, and will happen still," Jason said, and smiled at his pregnant wife.

"Shh. Let's not speak of it," Katherine said.

Jason couldn't blame her for not wanting to tempt fate. So much could go wrong. So much did for so many people.

"I'm glad you're not going to Tristan Carmichael's funeral. It would be like entering a den of thieves," Katherine said grimly. "I wager come tomorrow, it will be business as usual for the

Carmichaels. Will these people never stop indulging man's every vice?"

"Not as long as the money keeps flowing," Jason said. "And it will. Everything in life is supply and demand, and there's constant demand."

"Is there really?" Katherine exclaimed, dismayed.

"I'm afraid so, darling. Men are not known for governing their desires."

"I worry about what sort of world we will leave for our children." Katherine's hand went to her belly, as if she could protect the child within from the sins of the world.

"Every generation worries about that, but the world is still spinning," Jason said.

He drank the remainder of his coffee and pushed to his feet. "I'm sorry, but I must leave you. I must catch Daniel before he leaves for Brentwood."

Jason kissed Katherine and stepped into the foyer, where Dodson waited with his coat, hat, and a covered basket, his face as impassive as ever. Dodson's sense of self-importance seemed to reflect his surroundings, and returning to Redmond Hall brought out the haughty, self-aggrandizing retainer Jason had first met upon arriving in England. Perhaps it was the imposing hall, or maybe old age was creeping in, and Dodson was becoming even more rigid than usual. Jason reflected that in some people, rigor set in well before physical passing, but the process seemed to affect their minds, slowly eradicating mental flexibility and good humor. The knowledge that Jason was going to visit the Romani camp seemed to set Dodson's teeth on edge, but Jason didn't much care. He didn't hold with prejudice.

Jason hadn't asked Joe to bring the carriage around; it was too unwieldy to navigate the narrow woodland lanes. He could either ride or walk. Since there were few well-trodden paths between Redmond Hall and Bloody Mead, he thought it would be safer to walk, as some branches hung so low, they could cause serious damage if one was on horseback and didn't duck fast enough. Heading into the nearly impenetrable fog, he worried he might become disoriented in the woods but hoped the sounds of the camp and the smoke from the cooking fires would lead him to the Romani campground.

The forest that was so lovely on a clear day seemed sinister and unnaturally quiet. The animals were hidden in their burrows, and the birds were ominously silent. Without the sun to guide him, Jason could only hope he was walking in the right direction, but just as he thought he might be hopelessly lost, a shimmering orb glowed eerily through the fog, and within a few minutes, the mist began to clear. The forest came to life, and the air seemed lighter and more fragrant as Jason drew it into his lungs. He smelled the camp before he saw it. Someone was frying sausages, and the appetizing scent wafted on the gentle breeze and guided Jason toward the clearing.

When he saw the meadow through the trees, Jason was instantly reminded of the first time he'd visited the Romani camp. It had been in utter disarray, the travelers milling about in confusion between the charred vardos. Their faces had been covered in soot, and their hair and clothes had reeked of smoke. Today, the camp looked vastly different. The colorful vardos looked cheerful and well maintained. Small children were chasing each other around the clearing as an excited dog followed closely on their bare heels. Several women called to their neighbors in Romani, their postures relaxed as they carried on a conversation while cooking. Meat and eggs sizzled in the pans, and there was a small stack of flatbreads on a wooden sideboard.

The women tensed momentarily when they spotted Jason coming out of the woods, then recognition dawned and they smiled in welcome, calling out, "*Kushti divvus.*"

Jason knew it to be a greeting and called back, "Good morning."

As he approached the women, Jason noticed that the cooking pans were half-empty, the food not nearly enough to feed the entire camp. Perhaps some of the travelers had already eaten or would have something later. It was early autumn, a time of abundance before the lean months of winter. Jason thought he'd call on Bogdan Lee, the Romani elder, but then decided that the person he really wanted to see was Zemphyra. And maybe her cousin, Luca, if he had time.

Zemphyra was one of the most beautiful women Jason had ever seen and in some ways reminded him of Alicia Lysander. The two women were as different as night and day, in their demeanor if not in coloring, but there was an otherworldliness to them both that reminded anyone who came to know them that they were able to see things the average person couldn't.

From time to time, Jason still wondered if Alicia had been able to foresee her own death and had put his card in her reticule on the night she was attacked because she'd hoped he'd be able to save her, but now he'd never know. And if he were honest, he wasn't sure he really wanted to. He'd meant what he'd said to Micah. He had no wish to know what the future held, and if his death was imminent, he'd rather enjoy the time left to him and be taken unawares rather than worry about his impending demise. His family would be well provided for, and that was all he really cared about.

Jason picked Zemphyra out right away. She sat on the steps of her vardo, her black curly hair cascading down her back and contrasting with the reds, greens, and yellows of her clothing. Gold hoops swayed in her ears, and although he couldn't hear the jangle of her many bracelets, Jason could see them slide up and down her wrist as she moved her arm. Zemphyra held a small child, and her bodice was pulled down on one side, exposing a full breast. The child nursed contentedly, while a handsome man who was brushing down a dappled mare nearby watched mother and child, a warmth in his eyes that told Jason everything he needed to know. Zemphyra was happy and loved, and the Romani had moved on, both literally and figuratively, from the traumatic events following the murder of Imogen Chadwick.

Jason was glad he'd brought a gift. The basket Mrs. Dodson had packed didn't contain enough food to go around, but it was an offering of goodwill and would go a long way toward ensuring cooperation. A few more people called out a greeting, and Jason stopped to speak to them and ask after their families. By the time he reached Zemphyra, she had finished nursing her child and had buttoned her dress. Jason couldn't tell if the child was a girl or a boy since it wore a loose smock and had short dark curls, but he thought it absolutely charming. Zemphyra smiled and beckoned him over.

"Your baby is beautiful," Jason said.

"He is, isn't he?" Zemphyra agreed. "Looks just like his father." She glanced toward the man with the horse, who was now studying Jason, his dark eyes narrowing with suspicion. Zemphyra called something out to him, then turned back to Jason, who set the basket next to her on the step. She smiled in thanks. "You always know the right thing to say and do, my lord."

"I really don't," Jason said, "but I know what I like, and I think others are not so different."

"You must like cheese," Zemphyra said when she peered beneath the linen towel Mrs. Dodson had used to cover the food. "And honey."

"Guilty as charged," Jason said with a chuckle. "I also like bread."

Zemphyra laughed, a rich, melodious sound Jason remembered so well.

"How's Luca?"

"He's well. He has a daughter now, and another baby on the way."

"I'm glad to hear it. I'd like to say hello."

"Luca's not in camp just now," Zemphyra said, and Jason sensed an instant change in her demeanor. A wariness that was miniscule but definitely there.

"Where is he?"

"Getting supplies," Zemphyra said rather tersely.

Jason noticed an older woman watching Zemphyra and recognized her as Bogdan's wife, Luca's mother. He raised a hand, but Mrs. Lee did not return his greeting.

"A man was murdered in Bloody Weald on Monday. Did you hear about that?" Jason asked Zemphyra.

She inclined her head. "I also heard that he got what was coming to him."

"I don't think anyone deserves to be murdered. Do you?" Jason asked.

"Aren't people murdered when they're executed? Or does it not count when it's by the order of the court?"

"It counts, and I don't necessarily agree with it."

"You are in the minority. There are those who'd like to see all of us Romani strung up. They think we're thieves and murderers," Zemphyra said bitterly.

Jason didn't try to talk Zemphyra out of her viewpoint and attempt to convince her that not everyone was ruled by prejudice. It would be condescending and disrespectful of her feelings. "Your people have survived for centuries and will continue to thrive," he said instead. "You are clever and resilient."

Zemphyra nodded, and Jason knew he'd said the right thing.

"Tom Marin said you arrived on Sunday. Did you happen to see anyone in the woods on Monday morning?"

"Yes. I saw a man."

"Might he have been Tristan Carmichael?"

Zemphyra shrugged. "It was difficult to tell."

"Why?"

"The man wore a black cloak and a tall hat. Could have been anyone, but he put me in mind of that clergyman from St. Catherine's—your father-in-law," Zemphyra added.

"You think you saw Reverend Talbot in the woods on Monday?"

Zemphyra shrugged again. "Could have been him. I don't know."

"Did anyone else see him?"

"I don't think so. I was in the woods alone, gathering kindling."

"Did this person have anything on him?"

"Such as?"

"A weapon."

"Who knows what he had beneath that cloak. Why are you so interested in Tristan Carmichael's murder?"

"Because if there's a killer on the loose, others might be in danger."

"Pfft," Zemphyra said. "If Tristan Carmichael was murdered, then I'm sure whoever did it had good reason to want him dead. Why would they want to harm anyone else?"

Jason could see he wasn't going to get anything more from Zemphyra. She was probably afraid she'd be expected to testify should the killer go to trial. Jason couldn't say he blamed her. The accused's counsel would tear her apart if she took the stand.

"I'll leave you in peace, then," Jason said.

"I'm sorry," Zemphyra replied. "I know you mean well, but I can't get involved."

"I understand. Thank you for telling me about the man."

Zemphyra acknowledged his thanks with a small nod. "We'll be here for a fortnight. Come back anytime. It's always a pleasure to see you."

"We're returning to London next week," Jason said.

"Shame," Zemphyra said, but Jason could see that her mind had already drifted away from him and returned to the dark-eyed man, who was striding toward them, a scowl on his face. Jason had clearly overstayed his welcome.

He nodded to the man politely and walked away. There was nothing more to be learned at the Romani camp, and he had no proof that the man Zemphyra had seen had been in any way involved in Tristan's death. Jason oriented himself and turned in the direction of Mrs. Elderman's home in the opposite direction.

On his way out, he passed a vardo he hadn't seen before. It was painted bright blue and red, and the windows and roof were marigold yellow. A young woman, no older than seventeen, sat on the steps, her hands moving quickly as she wove a basket. She looked up and peered at Jason, then went back to her work. As he passed the back of the neighboring caravan, this one green and purple, Jason noticed a crate strapped to the back, probably an additional storage space for items that could be left out in the open. His gaze went to the knots that held the crate in place. They were just like the knot on the rope that had bound Tristan Carmichael to the tree. In itself, it meant nothing. Jason was sure people the world over made similar knots. But then he saw Luca Lee striding out of the forest. Several rabbits hung from his belt, their ears brushing the tops of his boots. Luca stopped walking, his eyes widening in fear and surprise.

Luca's unexpected reaction to Jason's presence explained Zemphyra's prickliness and her refusal to tell him where Luca had gone. The Romani did not grow their own food or own many domestic animals. To constantly move camp with cows and goats and pigs in tow was too cumbersome. Instead, they bred horses, told fortunes, and sold trinkets and charms to impressionable women and girls. And they poached. Bloody Mead was adjacent to the Talbot estate, and the rabbits Luca was carrying belonged to the squire. But the Romani needed to eat and clearly didn't have sufficient stores to get them through the coming days.

Jason made a point of looking away from Luca's kill to let the young man know he wasn't going to tell the squire about the rabbits. It wasn't as if Squire Talbot had need of the food. His family and staff had plenty, whereas these people were probably always hungry. Luca skirted the meadow and approached his mother, handing her the brace of rabbits. She glanced at Jason, then immediately stepped inside her vardo and shut the door.

As Luca turned away, Jason spotted a bow and a quiver of arrows worn in a sling on his back. Luca didn't own a gun and had no time to set traps. He went into the forest and hunted with a weapon that was easy to make, never ran out of ammunition, and made no sound as it pierced the air and found its mark. And the fletching on Luca's arrows looked similar to the fletching on the arrow that had killed Tristan Carmichael, at least from a distance.

Zemphyra walked toward Jason, her face tense, her baby held tightly against her body. The Romani put on a show of friendliness toward him, but he was still an outsider, someone who could do them irreparable harm.

"I won't tell anyone," Jason said as soon as she approached.

"See that you don't. No one should own the woods or the streams. People need to eat."

"You can always hunt and fish on my land. I will not report you."

"Thank you. You're a kind man, Lord Redmond. Kinder than most."

Jason wasn't doing it to be kind. He didn't feel a sense of ownership. He hadn't been reared on the land, with his grandfather there every step of the way to nurture and inflate Jason's sense of entitlement. As far as he was concerned, it was public land, and anyone who was hungry was welcome to its resources.

Jason wished Zemphyra well and turned back, surprising both her and Luca. Jason crossed Bloody Mead and strode into the woods, setting off on the path to Redmond Hall. He needed to speak to Daniel but couldn't afford to spare the time. There was someone else he needed to speak to first. He thought he now knew who had killed Tristan

Carmichael, and he could guess why, but it was nothing more than a theory if he had no proof.

Chapter 35

Daniel gazed at himself in the shaving mirror. The man who looked back was serious, his dark gaze intense, his face half-hidden and aged by the beard he'd worn for years. Three horizontal lines had appeared on his forehead seemingly overnight, and there were several silver strands at his temples. What on earth did Flora see in him? She was so lovely and vibrant, and he was a few years from being called an old man. Did Flora find him desirable? He wasn't sure he was ready to hear the answer.

Suddenly desperate to look younger and—dare he even think it—more handsome, Daniel lathered his face and lifted the razor, positioning it just below his sideburn. His hand jerked when a piercing scream shattered the silence.

Setting down the razor, Daniel lurched toward the window. He thought the scream had come from outside, but he couldn't see anything amiss. The front yard was empty, the gates were firmly shut, and the lane beyond stretched into the distance with nary a person or conveyance in sight. As Daniel hurriedly wiped the soap from his face, he wondered if he had imagined the whole thing, but then he heard it again. This time, the cry was muffled and accompanied by bumping and dragging. Daniel yanked open the door and pounded up the stairs to the nursery.

"Charlotte," he cried. "Charlotte, are you all right?"

Charlotte was still in bed, her face framed by the frilly nightcap and the high collar of her nightdress. She clutched her doll to her chest, her knuckles white with tension.

"Papa, what's happening?" she cried. "I heard a scream."

"I don't know, but you must stay here no matter what you hear," Daniel said. "I'll be back in a few minutes."

Charlotte nodded mutely, then dove under the covers and pulled the counterpane over her head. She was still at the age when she thought that if she couldn't see someone, they couldn't see her either. Daniel hoped they wouldn't have to test this theory, at least not today. He shut the door behind him, locked it, and slid the key into his pocket, just in case.

The landing had an arched window that offered a view of the garden. It wasn't as well maintained as it had been in Sarah's day, but the rosebushes she had planted were still in bloom, the colors bright and cheerful against the green grass. The paths were a bit overgrown, and the bench where Sarah used to sit on fine days was nearly hidden from view by tall grass. The garden backed onto the forest, and a wooden fence with a gate marked the boundary between the property and the outskirts of Squire Talbot's estate.

For a second Daniel thought the garden was empty, but then he spotted movement near the back door and watched, frozen with horror, as Victor Roy dragged a struggling Annie down the path toward the gate. Roy had one hand over Annie's mouth and the other around her waist. Annie was no match for Roy, but she put up more of a fight than Daniel would have expected of such a slight girl. Her hair had come loose, and the hem of her gown was dusty. The heels of Annie's boots had carved a dual track in the garden path as she fought to slow Roy's progress.

Annie elbowed Roy in the ribs and must have hit him hard enough to cause him pain because he grimaced and hissed something in her ear. He loosened his grip on Annie's waist and shoved his hand between her legs, his fingers pushing through the fabric of her gown. Annie went limp, her eyes shimmering with tears as she tried to squirm away from the probing digits. Roy was letting her know precisely what would happen if she continued to resist, so she had a choice to make. Go quietly into the woods or fight until someone heard her and came to the rescue. Once Roy got Annie into the woods, he would either take her away or kill her there and then.

Daniel raced down the steps until he reached the ground floor, then sprinted down the corridor toward the back door and erupted into the garden, startling both Annie and Roy. Roy's left arm tightened around Annie, and his right hand reached inside his coat, emerging with an unsheathed blade. Daniel froze, his heart in his mouth, when Roy pressed the blade to Annie's pale neck, angling it beneath her chin. The tendons in Annie's neck tensed, and she swallowed hard as she tried to control her terror. Her gaze was fixed on Daniel, silently pleading for help.

Just then, it didn't matter how Roy had found out where Annie had been hiding or how he'd managed to get into the house unobserved. The only thing that mattered was getting Annie away from him before he hurt her. And he would hurt her. Daniel could see it in his eyes. Roy wasn't leaving until he got what he'd come for, and if he had to improvise, he would do so without hesitation.

"Turn around and go back inside, Inspector, and we'll say no more about it," Roy called out.

He clearly wasn't worried about what Daniel might see or do because as far as he was concerned, Daniel was harmless. He had no official jurisdiction in Essex, so Roy would never see the inside of a cell or face the hangman unless Daniel could provide DI Peterson with incontrovertible evidence. Annie, on the other hand, could rat Roy out to Lance Carmichael, and if Lance thought Roy had murdered not only Harvey Boswell but also Tristan, Roy wouldn't live to see another sunrise.

"This is not your fight," Roy said when Daniel failed to comply.

"I think it is," Daniel replied.

He didn't have to look up to sense that Charlotte was watching from the nursery window, probably terrified out of her wits. Daniel briefly wondered where Harriet and Tilda might be but prayed they'd remain inside. It would be helpful if Thomas made an appearance, but he was probably in the kitchen, enjoying his breakfast. That left Daniel and Roy, with Annie between them. And Roy had all the power. Even if Daniel had been armed, there was little he could do. Any attempt to get to Roy would result in Annie's death. All Daniel had at his disposal were words, and they had never seemed more useless than they did at this pivotal moment. What could he say? Roy felt cornered, and a cornered man would always try to fight his way out and take down anyone who stood in his way. And Daniel wasn't much of an obstacle.

"Why did you kill Tristan Carmichael?" Daniel called out.

The question seemed to take Roy by surprise, and for a brief second Daniel saw genuine confusion in the man's eyes. Then his mouth twisted into an ugly grin. "I didn't kill him. I'm not that stupid, but I'll gladly thank the man who put him down. Makes my life that much easier."

"Easier how?" Daniel asked.

Roy sniggered. "Lance Carmichael is an old man. If something were to happen to him, there's be an opening, wouldn't there?"

"That you would try to fill."

"Clever you," Roy taunted.

"Annie is no threat to you," Daniel said.

"Oh, but she is. And now so are you, Inspector."

"Then let her go and face me man to man."

Roy laughed. "You really are a pompous fool, aren't you, Haze? I wager you always dreamed of being a hero, but you're nothing more than a rich man's flunkey. It's Lord Redmond who always gets the credit and gets his name in the papers. And there's poor Inspector Haze, hovering in the background."

"I'm not interested in being a hero," Daniel replied.

"Right. Tell that to your daughter. Is that her I see up there? Sweet kid. How old is she? About three?"

Panic raced up Daniel's spine as Roy's words found their mark. Roy knew about Charlotte, which meant Charlotte would never be safe.

As if reading his mind, Roy said, "If you've no objections, Inspector, Annie and I will be on our way."

"And if I do?" Daniel snapped.

"Then I will come for you when you least expect it. It will give me great pleasure to know you're always peering over your shoulder, thinking, *Is today the day I'm going to die?*"

"You don't scare me," Daniel shot back, but he was lying. He was scared. Not for himself but for Charlotte and Flora. And, of course, Annie.

"Then maybe I'll take your kid instead," Roy replied, that twisted grin splitting his face again. "She's a bit young, but in a few years, she'll be ready to service the gentlemen at my brothel. Annie here will show her the ropes. I could auction off her maidenhead," Roy mused. "Won't that be fun? There are those who will pay handsomely for a child. Tristan Carmichael could tell you just how much, if he was still with us."

Daniel's blood roared in his ears, and his stomach clenched with rage as he balled his hands into fists. His every thought and need evaporated, leaving behind nothing but a single-minded determination to keep Annie and Charlotte safe. It didn't matter if Daniel died defending them. He had to rid the world of this vile parasite who preyed on young girls and clearly meant to expand his influence now that Tristan Carmichael was gone.

Daniel lunged forward just as Victor Roy pushed the blade deeper into Annie's neck. She screamed in terror, frantically repeating, "Please, please, no…"

Blood welled on Annie's skin as the blade bit into her throat, a thin trickle sliding down her neck. Annie was panting now, her eyes rolling in her head like those of a terrified horse. Victor Roy was no longer grinning. He looked feral, his teeth bared as he pulled Annie tighter to him, gripping the handle of the blade with deadly intent.

"One more step and she dies. One more word and she dies. You call out and she dies," Roy ground out.

He released the pressure on Annie's throat and began to drag her backward toward the garden gate. Daniel's heart pounded, his breath coming in short gasps. He had no idea what to do. Another few minutes and Annie would be lost to him forever, and now he knew what Roy had in store for her. Annie was choking on her tears, her chest heaving with terror, but as long as Annie was still alive, there was hope. If Roy killed her, there'd be nothing Daniel could do for her. He would go for reinforcements as soon as Roy left. He'd get Annie back. Daniel tried to convey that to Annie with his gaze, but she was in a blind panic, her fingers digging into Victor Roy's forearms as he pulled her along like a sack of turnips. He was nearly at the gate when Daniel heard a strange sound, and then Roy's grip on Annie slackened.

Sensing her chance, Annie threw herself sideways, falling onto the ground in a heap of skirts. She righted herself and tried to scoot away on her backside, her gaze fixed on Victor Roy should he come after her. But Roy wasn't looking at Annie. His gaze was filled with horror, and the knife slipped from his hand, falling onto the path. Daniel seized his moment and ran toward Annie, pulling her to her feet and pushing her behind him as Roy turned his gaze on him.

Daniel had no idea what had happened, but Roy seemed paralyzed, his legs buckling as he fell to his knees, his arms coming around his sides to feel his back. It was only then that Daniel saw the arrow. The arrowhead had penetrated Roy's lower back, most likely finding a target in his kidney. There was another whoosh, and a second arrow pierced the air and buried itself in Roy's neck. Blood spurted from the wound, and Roy's eyes rolled in shock as blood trickled from his mouth and onto the collar of his shirt. He tried to say something, but his mouth was filled with blood, his teeth stained bright red. His skin turned gray, and he lifted his gaze to the sky, looking up at the sun as if seeing it for the first time. Daniel saw the exact moment the light went out of

Roy's eyes, and he fell sideways, the two arrows protruding from his body like porcupine quills.

Annie was still panting, her arms wrapped around Daniel's middle as she pressed her cheek to his back. She was trembling hard, and Daniel covered her hands with his in an effort to soothe her. He raised his eyes, grateful to note that Charlotte was no longer in the window. Daniel hoped she hadn't watched Victor Roy die, but if she had, there was nothing he could do about it just then. Instead, his gaze slid to the arrows. The fletching was white, like the feathers of a barn owl.

Daniel peered into the woods. A man stood unmoving next to an ancient tree, his buckskin shirt and leggings and dark green hood blending with the hues of the woodland. His bow was lowered, his still-full quiver slung over his shoulder. He looked like some medieval huntsman, or Robin Hood. The man nodded to Daniel, then turned and disappeared into the forest. Evan Jones, the archer of Gwent.

Daniel barely noticed when Harriet and Tilda came running from the house, Thomas bringing up the rear. Harriet wrapped Annie in a fierce hug and held her while she cried, while Tilda bent over the dead man. Daniel thought he saw her take his pocket watch and slip it into the pocket of her apron but didn't much care. Someone may as well use it.

"What should we do?" Thomas called to Daniel. "Should we alert someone?"

"Get the shovels, Thomas," Daniel said calmly, "and help me carry him into the woods."

Chapter 36

Jason got to the church just in time for the service. The road was thronged with carriages, a massive black hearse with black-plumed horses parked in front of the main entrance. Two undertakers, their top hats adorned with flowing black ribbons and white carnations in their buttonholes, were in the process of directing the pallbearers as they prepared to carry the flower-laden casket into the church. No graveside service for Tristan Carmichael. This was to be a sendoff fit for royalty.

The pews were full, dozens of black-clad mourners, mostly men, solemnly staring straight ahead. The vicar was already at the pulpit, ready to begin, and Tristan's family were all there in the front pew, Lance's face lined with grief while Cecily's was covered by a thick mourning veil. Two couples, presumably Tristan's sisters and their husbands, sat next to them, several subdued children seated between them.

Jason had no way to identify Michael O'Keefe, but he spotted Simcoe, Davy Brody, and the Plimptons. Moll sat between Bruce and her father-in-law, Limpy, her face blank. Jason wondered which silent mourner might be Victor Roy and if he was seated near Cecily Carmichael, but their possible involvement no longer mattered, at least not today.

Jason waited until the coffin was carried in, then slipped outside. He found Joe, who was waiting around the corner, and issued instructions before getting in.

It took close to an hour to get to Upper Harlow, but Moll and Bruce wouldn't be back for another hour at the very least, especially if there was to be a wake after the funeral. Jason thought Lance wouldn't pass up an opportunity to mourn his son and display his wealth and power at the same time. He had to put on a show of strength to remind everyone that he was still in charge and the Carmichael enterprise would continue uninterrupted.

The maidservant smiled when she opened the door to Jason. "I'm sorry, sir, but Mr. and Mrs. Plimpton are not at home just now."

"Are they not?" Jason asked, hoping he looked sufficiently put out. "I could have sworn Mrs. Plimpton told me she would be at home this afternoon."

"They went to Mr. Carmichael's funeral. Mrs. Plimpton didn't want to go, but Mr. Plimpton said they had to attend. 'Show their faces' were the words he used."

Agnes went silent, her cheeks turning pink as she probably realized she'd revealed too much and might get in trouble with her employers.

"Oh, of course. I must have forgotten that Mr. Carmichael was to be laid to rest today. I wasn't invited to the funeral," Jason confessed.

"Did you know him, sir?" Agnes asked, then went even redder when it must have dawned on her that she was chatting to a noble personage as if he were one of the neighbors.

"Yes, I did. In fact, our paths crossed several times. Have you ever met him? Agnes, was it?" Jason asked, smiling down at the girl.

Agnes nodded, clearly pleased that Jason had remembered her name. "Mr. Carmichael came to see Mrs. Plimpton."

"Really? I didn't know they were friends. I assumed he was an associate of Mr. Plimpton."

"He were, sir, but he seemed to know Mrs. Plimpton quite well."

"Did he stay long?" Jason asked.

"Not too long. I thought Mrs. Plimpton would call for refreshments, but they went out into the garden, and then Mr. Carmichael left. He seemed quite angry."

"Really? Why?" Jason asked, feigning innocent curiosity.

"They had quite the row."

"What could they possibly have to argue about?"

"I don't know. I tried not to listen," Agnes said as a deep blush crept up her pale neck once again. The poor girl wore her every emotion on her fair skin.

"You must have heard something," Jason suggested conspiratorially.

Agnes shook her head. "I didn't. I only heard Mr. Carmichael mention Lucas, and then Mrs. Plimpton started to cry. I don't know what he said to upset her so, but she looked shattered."

"New mothers tend to be emotional," Jason said.

"I wouldn't know, sir."

Agnes was growing visibly uncomfortable and was inching back into the house in the hope that Jason would finally leave. He had to hurry if he was going to ask his questions.

"Anges, was Mrs. Plimpton at home on Monday morning? It's only that I thought I saw her in Birch Hill."

"The mistress went to see Mr. Brody. She said he needed help with the accounts. She's good with numbers, and Mr. Brody relies on her."

"So, it was her," Jason said, smiling. "I wasn't sure. Was she wearing a cloak?"

"Yes. She prefers it when going on horseback." Agnes started when a baby's cry pierced the air. "That'll be Lucas. I must see to him, your lordship."

"Of course," Jason said. "I'm sorry to have taken up so much of your time."

"Not at all, sir."

Jason bid Agnes a good day and returned to the brougham.

"Where to, sir?" Joe asked.

"The Red Stag."

The tavern was sparsely filled with regulars, who called out to Jason deferentially when he walked in. Matty Locke stood behind the bar, filling tankards, and chatting up the patrons. Matty normally helped out at the livery, but Davy must have asked him to fill in while he was at the funeral and had yet to dismiss him. Jason could see Davy through the open door of his office. He was still dressed in his funeral best, but he was already working, an open ledger before him and a pen suspended in his hand. Jason walked past Matty and entered the office, then shut the door behind him.

"A word, Mr. Brody," he said.

"Something wrong, your lordship?" Davy set down the pen and leaned back in his chair, looking distinctly relaxed.

Jason didn't immediately respond. His gaze was fixed on the opposite wall, where a bow and a quiver of arrows hung from a hook.

"You like to hunt with a bow, Mr. Brody?"

Davy shrugged. "Sometimes. Why?" Understanding dawned, and Davy went a sickly white, shaking his head vehemently. "I didn't kill Tristan Carmichael, my lord. This was just a bit of sport. Evan Jones invited me to go hunting on Squire Talbot's land. We took down a doe."

"I need to speak to Moll. Privately."

"What about?"

"I have a few questions for her."

"And how am I supposed to arrange a private meeting?" Davy demanded. "She's a married woman now."

"Which is precisely why I must speak to her alone. I don't want her husband anywhere near."

"Ye're going to have to tell me a bit more than that, yer lordship."

"It's to do with the Romani camp in Bloody Mead."

Davy nodded. "I heard the Romani were back. So it were one of them that shot Carmichael? I reckon he tangled with one of their women and got what was coming to him."

"I didn't say that," Jason replied.

"Ye didn't have to. Every time they come, something awful happens." Davy's gaze was filled with decades-old pain. "I told Moll to stay away from them, I did," he said under his breath. "But she won't listen. Always running to Bloody Mead as soon as the caravans show up. She says they're her family. I'm her family," Davy exclaimed. "I'm the one who raised her, not the good-for-nothing Gypsy that ruined my sister's life. Moll has her own boy now. She has to look to his future."

Jason thought that was rich given Davy's unsavory connections, but an English swindler was never as threatening as a Gypsy swindler in some people's opinion, and Davy wanted to believe that his own dealings were well above board.

"You can warn someone and tell them to stay away, but in the end, they will do what they will," Jason replied noncommittally.

"Ye got that right," Davy answered morosely. "Lord preserve us from independent-minded women."

And foolish men, Jason thought, but kept that opinion to himself. "I expect to see Moll at Redmond Hall this evening. I don't care how you get her there."

242

Davy sighed heavily and nodded. "I'll do my best, my lord."

Jason left Davy to consider the most effective course of action and stepped outside. He had some time before he had to return to Redmond Hall, and he needed to speak to Daniel.

Chapter 37

Jason immediately sensed an atmosphere when he got to Harriet Elderman's house. Tilda started like a frightened rabbit when he asked to see Daniel, and Harriet hurried past him, her face tense, and her back rigid as she carried a tray up the stairs. The only two people upstairs had to be Charlotte and Annie, and Jason thought one of them might be ill, but neither Mrs. Elderman nor Tilda said as much or asked for his help.

"Is everything all right?" Jason asked as he handed his hat and coat to Tilda.

"I really shouldn't say," Tilda whispered. "Not my place."

Tilda's cryptic answer only added to Jason's trepidation, but he could see from her closed expression that he wasn't going to get much more out of her. She made a vague gesture toward the back door and rushed off. Normally, at this time of day, the aroma of cooking would waft from the kitchen, but Jason didn't smell anything edible. The house was strangely quiet, and he realized that Thomas hadn't come out to meet the carriage when Joe pulled up in front of the door, which was also unusual.

Jason found Daniel in the garden. He was sitting on Sarah's bench, his vacant gaze fixed on nothing in particular. Daniel's hands were dirty, his shirt was stained with what looked like blood, and two shovels leaned against the wall of the potting shed.

"Daniel, what happened?" Jason asked as he approached.

"Victor Roy tried to take Annie. I was sure he was going to kill her."

"Where's Annie now?"

"In her room. She became hysterical once it was all over, so Mrs. Elderman took her upstairs and gave a few drops of valerian to help her rest."

"And Roy?"

Daniel pointed to the garden gate. Instead of interrogating him, Jason walked toward the gate, opened it, and continued into the forest. He couldn't see anything at first, but then, about fifty yards on, he noticed that the ground had been recently disturbed. That explained Daniel's state and the presence of the shovels. Returning to the garden, Jason sat down next to Daniel.

"Did you kill him?"

Daniel shook his head. "I just stood there, helpless," he said furiously. "There was nothing I could do. Roy had a knife to her throat, and he was taunting me." Daniel looked up, his expression pained. "He threatened to take Charlotte and sell her to… to… men." His voice broke on the last word. "I don't think I should leave on my honeymoon, Jason. I can't leave Charlotte and Annie unprotected."

"Charlotte will be safe with us," Jason replied. "We will take her to London, and you can collect her when you and Flora return. And I will make sure Annie is safe. I promise you, all will be well." Jason's gaze strayed to the shovels. "If you didn't kill Roy, who did? Was it Thomas?"

Daniel shook his head. "It was Evan Jones. He appeared as if by magic, shot Roy full of arrows, and vanished again. He must have murdered Tristan Carmichael, and now I will have to arrest him after he saved Annie and safeguarded my daughter."

"Evan Jones didn't kill Tristan Carmichael," Jason said.

"How can you be sure?"

"Because I think I know who did."

Daniel made to rise, but Jason laid a gentle hand on his shoulder and pushed him back down.

"Daniel, tomorrow is your wedding day. I want you to go inside, have a hot bath, then enjoy a good meal and pour yourself a ridiculously large brandy. Doctor's orders."

"But—" Daniel began, but Jason didn't allow him to finish.

"Your part in this investigation is over. Leave the rest to me."

"Thank you, Jason."

"You never need to thank me."

Jason followed Daniel inside, asked Tilda to pack Charlotte a bag, and lifted her into his arms once Mrs. Elderman brought her downstairs. Harriet looked angry and sad to have to part with Charlotte sooner than she'd expected, but she understood Daniel's fear and didn't raise objections.

"Annie will be staying with me," Harriet said firmly. "The man who murdered her brother is gone, so no one has anything to gain by hurting her. And Annie needs a home."

"And you need someone to love," Jason concluded.

Harriet teared up. "With Sarah gone, and Charlotte to have a new mother, I will end my days alone. And now I won't have to. Annie needs a mother, and I need a daughter. And I will do my best for her."

"I don't doubt it for a moment," Jason replied. "Annie is lucky to have found you."

"And I feel blessed to have found her. This is not an ideal beginning, but we will face the future together."

"Will I see you tomorrow?"

"No. But I would like to see Charlotte before you leave for London, if I may."

"Of course. You can call on us anytime."

"Bye, Granny," Charlotte said, and by the way she clung to Jason, he could tell she was eager to leave. She had seen more than she should have and was understandably terrified.

Jason settled Charlotte next to him once they climbed into the brougham, and she leaned against him and took his hand. They rode the rest of the way in silence.

Chapter 38

By the time the children had their nursery supper and were put to bed, Jason was forced to admit that Moll might not be coming. He could understand her reasons for staying away, but now he would have to take the conversation to her, and that would complicate matters, especially if her husband happened to be at home. The meeting would also have to wait until next week, since tomorrow was about Flora and Daniel, and Jason would not neglect his duties as best man and prioritize Tristan Carmichael.

Jason had just settled in the drawing room with a pre-dinner drink while Katherine went up to dress when Dodson announced Moll and Davy Brody. Dodson seemed particularly dismayed and grumbled something about Jason's grandfather never allowing such riffraff in the house in his day. Jason was in no doubt that his grandfather was spinning in his grave, and had been since Jason had first taken up residence at Redmond Hall and had involved himself in a murder investigation. Jason briefly wondered what his own father would have made of Jason's sideline and hoped his dad was at peace and not having it out with his gruff sire somewhere in the afterlife.

"Please show them in," Jason said.

Dodson drew in a sharp breath and stiffened his spine, as if he were going into battle, then marched out into the foyer. How black and white life was for some people, Jason reflected as he waited for his visitors to come through. A moment later, Davy sauntered into the drawing room as if he were there to buy the place, but Moll hung back, her apprehension at odds with her normally boisterous personality. She wore a cloak of dark red velvet and a matching bonnet, but even the rich color couldn't disguise her pallor.

"Good evening, yer lordship," Davy said. "As requested." He pointed to Moll as if he'd just delivered a cow or a horse.

"Please, have a seat," Jason invited, and Moll reluctantly made her way toward the settee.

"Should I call for some refreshment, sir?" Dodson asked, his tone so snooty, even Jason felt unwelcome.

"Thank you, no, Dodson," Jason said. "But perhaps you can give Mr. Brody a tour of the cellar. I know how he likes wine stores."

Davy and Dodson wore identical expressions of astonishment and seemed all set to argue, so Jason said, "I need to speak to Moll privately."

"Now, look here, yer lordship. Moll is a married woman. Think what her husband will say when he finds out I left her alone with a man," Davy began, but Jason raised a hand to stop him.

"My interest in Moll is purely professional, and I think you know me well enough to trust that I won't try to molest her as soon as you walk through the door."

"It's all right, Uncle Davy," Moll said. "Go on. Ye won't get another chance to take a peek at the wine cellar, will ye?"

"Are ye sure, Molly? I can stay," Davy offered.

"I'll be fine," Moll said, and shot Jason an inquiring look.

"She will," Jason hurried to reassure both Davy and Moll. "Dodson, shut the door behind you."

Jason turned to Moll, who was perched on the edge of the settee, her gaze lowered to her clasped hands. Jason was certain she was watching him from beneath her lashes and desperately trying to appear calm.

"I think you know why I asked you here, Moll," Jason said.

"I'm sure I don't," Moll replied, but Jason could see the effort it took her to maintain her composure.

"Is Lucas Tristan Carmichael's son?"

Moll shook her head but wouldn't meet his gaze.

"I don't have proof that will stand up in court, but I think you shot Tristan Carmichael. And you used Luca's bow to do it. Why, Moll?"

"I will have yer word of honor that anything I tell ye stays in this room," Moll said, finally looking up.

"You have it."

She nodded and swallowed hard, her throat straining and her generous bosom heaving as she took a fortifying breath.

"When Tristan came back to Essex, 'e said it were because of the cholera outbreak, but that were only partly true. 'E needed to lie low for a while. There were some resentment about an underling 'e'd killed. Clarence Tipton. Tristan needed to make a show of strength, but that poor sod, Clarence, didn't deserve what 'appened to 'im. 'E'd been set up to take the blame for leaving the warehouse door unlocked."

"Who by?" Jason asked.

"Tristan didn't know for sure, but 'e thought it may 'ave been Michael O'Keefe."

"He was Tristan's second-in-command. Why would he do that?" Jason could guess, but he wanted to hear it from Moll.

"Because any time someone 'as power, someone else wants it for themselves. Tristan were afraid some of 'is men would turn on 'im if he pointed the finger at O'Keefe."

"But Clarence Tipton was an acceptable sacrifice?" Jason demanded.

"Clarence weren't popular with the other lads, and it bought Tristan time, but 'e knew 'e'd gone too far."

"That doesn't explain why you killed him. Surely you didn't do it to avenge Clarence Tipton?"

Moll fixed Jason with her dark gaze, and he could see the conflict raging within her soul. She wanted to tell him the truth, but she also knew what that would mean. An admission of guilt could be her undoing, even if Jason had promised not to reveal what he had learned.

Moll sighed heavily, her shoulders slumping with the weight of her burden. "The Tristan I knew would've felt genuine remorse for what 'e'd done. 'E would 'ave compensated the widow and 'er child and made sure they were safe, but Tristan had grown hard and cruel. 'E were making plans for when 'e went back to London."

"What sort of plans?"

"'E were going to take down O'Keefe, and 'e were going to do it publicly."

"Are you saying it was O'Keefe who shot Tristan Carmichael in the woods?"

Moll shook her head. "O'Keefe weren't going to do that, not on the sneak. If 'e wanted respect, 'e'd have to take it in full view of the men."

"Did Tristan tell you all that?" Jason asked.

"'E needed someone to talk to. 'E couldn't tell 'is father, and 'e didn't much like Cecily. 'E didn't trust 'er."

"But he trusted you."

"'E did. 'E said 'e loved me and should have stood up to 'is father and married me. I tell ye what, yer lordship, I'm glad 'e didn't. Uncle Davy were right when 'e said that a wolf cub might be sweet, but 'e'll still tear yer throat out when 'e grows up."

"Is that what happened? Did Tristan go for you, Moll?"

Moll nodded. "Tristan came to see me, but always while Bruce were out. 'E said 'e were just being sociable, but 'e wanted more. Much more."

"Did he hurt you?" Jason asked softly.

"Not in the way ye think. 'E said if I didn't come to 'im, 'e'd tell Bruce Lucas were not 'is but Tristan's. 'E'd ruin my life because 'is own existence 'ad become unbearable. 'E said everyone was out to get 'im."

"Did he ever mention Victor Roy?"

"Yes. 'E said Roy were a snake in the grass and one to watch out for. 'E even asked Lance to sack 'im, but Lance said Roy were a good lad. Loyal. Tristan said I were the only true friend 'e ever 'ad."

"He thought you'd make him happy?"

"'E wanted control over me and vengeance against Bruce," Moll said.

"Did Tristan hold a grudge against Bruce?"

"No, but 'e envied 'im. In 'is eyes, Bruce were a free man, but Tristan never 'ad a choice." Tears slid down Moll's cheeks and glittered in her eyelashes. "I didn't know what to do. Tristan were threatening me, and 'e weren't going to wait much longer. 'E were through playing games."

"What did you do?"

"I went to the Romani camp on Sunday. I wanted to confide in Zemphyra and ask Luca for 'elp, but when I got there, I changed my mind. The villagers don't trust the travelers and want them gone. If Zemphyra or Luca got involved, people would unleash violence on them. I couldn't let that 'appen, not again."

Jason remained quiet, sensing that he was about to learn what had really happened that fateful morning. Moll paused, her gaze going to the door, but the foyer beyond was quiet. Dodson and Davy were still in the cellar, and Katherine wouldn't be down until seven thirty.

"I asked Luca if I might borrow his bow. Just to practice my archery. 'E didn't want to give it to me. Said 'e planned to go hunting. So I promised to bring the bow back Monday morning. And I took some rope as well. I told Luca it was to tie down a target." The tears came faster now, and Moll spoke through the sobs. "I asked Tristan to meet me when 'e came to the Stag on Sunday. 'E'd taken to doing that since Bruce and I saw Davy on Sundays. 'E'd just sit there, watching me."

"And he agreed?"

"'E were 'appy. Said it'd be like old times when we used to meet in the woods. Secret lovers was what 'e'd called us. Except we weren't, cause now 'e were threatening me and my family. As soon as Bruce left on Monday, I told Agnes I 'ad to see Uncle Davy and made for Birch 'Ill, except I never set foot in the village. I'd 'idden the bow in an 'ollow tree, and I brought Bruce's cloak and top hat. I retrieved the bow, put on my disguise, and went to the meeting place. If anyone saw me, they'd think they'd seen a man walking through the woods, and they couldn't see the bow beneath the cloak. I waited for Tristan to show, and when 'e did, I shot 'im."

"Why did you tie him up?" Jason asked.

"I wanted to make sure 'e were found. No one would see 'im if he were lying down in the bracken. So once 'e were dead, I propped 'im up and tied him to the tree, then went back to the camp and gave Luca 'is bow." Moll's eyes were filled with fear. "Will ye turn me over to Inspector 'Aze, yer lordship?"

Jason reached out and laid his hand over Moll's wrist. "No."

"But it's yer duty to up'old the law."

"Yes, it is, but there's legal law and moral law, and I can't in good conscience send you to the gallows when all you did was protect yourself and your family. I know what Tristan was capable of, just as I know that the world is a safer place without him in it. Go home, Moll, and be happy. And if you can, work your charm on your husband and get him to leave that life behind."

"Bruce wants to go to America," Moll said. "'E says it's the land of opportunity."

"It is, but there are plenty of opportunities to fall in with men like the Carmichaels in America as well. You have to want to be better, Moll."

"I do. We do." Moll smiled, her hand going to her belly. "For our children."

"When are you due?" Jason asked.

"Not till April, but I hope to be away from 'ere by then."

"Then godspeed, Molly," Jason said. "Godspeed."

An indignant Dodson saw Moll and Davy out while Jason hurried upstairs to change for dinner. He now knew the truth and was ready to close the book on Tristan Carmichael for good. And as long as Lance Carmichael was made to believe Victor Roy was responsible for Tristan's death, which he would assume as soon as he heard that Victor Roy had vanished on the day of the funeral, neither Lance Carmichael nor the Brentwood Constabulary would need to look further afield. Lance would think Roy had run off to avoid retribution and spend the rest of his days hunting a ghost. And DI Peterson was as yet an unknown entity, and one Jason didn't need to worry about tonight.

And now they could finally turn their attention to more pleasant things.

Epilogue

Every pew in the church was filled to capacity when the Reverend Talbot took his place at the altar. He looked a little less gruff than usual, the benign expression he wore for baptisms and weddings on full display. Daniel felt a bit self-conscious with his face clean-shaven after years of hiding behind a beard, but he felt dapper in his morning suit and silk waistcoat and thought the white rose Katherine had pinned to his lapel looked decorative.

Jason looked effortlessly dashing, and after escorting Katherine to the front pew and making certain she was comfortably settled, he joined Daniel. Katherine Redmond was draped in a striped gown of green and burgundy satin and wore a matching bonnet decorated with stiffened burgundy flowers.

As the door swung open at the back, Daniel was surprised to note a late arrival. Ransome hurried into the church and slid into the last pew, his moustache waxed into stiff points for the occasion and his usual black waistcoat exchanged for a more festive affair in silver and mauve. Everyone was dressed in their Sunday best, including the children, but no one could match the loveliness of Charlotte and Lily. The girls walked down the aisle hand in hand, their shining faces framed by dark curls and white bonnets. They carried baskets of rose petals but quite forgot to sprinkle them in the path of the bride and looked confused once they reached the front, unsure what to do next until Katherine motioned to them to stand off to the side.

Daniel's breath hitched in his throat when Flora, radiant as the morning sun, appeared at the end of the nave. She wore a gown of lace-trimmed cream silk, and her hair was swept up and decorated with a modest tiara that held her veil in place. Daniel had never seen Flora in anything but prim, serviceable gowns and was struck by her elegant beauty and utterly humbled that such a magnificent woman would be willing to spend her life with him. Flora floated down the aisle on the arm of her father, who appeared resigned to having a policeman for a son-in-law and beamed at

Daniel and then at his wife, who dabbed at her eyes as happy tears slid down her plump cheeks.

Liam's tiny fingers held onto Katherine's hand as he watched his mother walk down the aisle behind Flora, Mary's flaming hair vivid in the light spilling through the stained-glass windows. She would arrange the bride's veil and train before stepping aside for the duration of the ceremony. Micah's eyes followed Mary, a wistful smile tugging at his lips as he no doubt remembered other happy occasions and other people, all of them now lost to him. Next to him, Tom Marin smiled at Mary as well, but his admiration was that of a boy on the cusp of manhood who had seen his friend's sister in a new light. And there was Moll, seated next to Davy Brody, her gaze fixed on Jason, her expression inscrutable.

Daniel forgot all about the guests as Flora took her place next to him and grinned in a way that was distinctly inappropriate to the occasion. Or maybe it was entirely appropriate because it highlighted her disregard for public opinion and reminded Daniel how much he loved her free spirit and ability to remain entirely herself in any situation. His eyes misted with tears, but he didn't look away in embarrassment as he normally would. He had been blessed, and he was so grateful.

And even if he and Jason had failed to solve the murder of Tristan Carmichael, there would be other investigations once he returned from his honeymoon and he and Flora were back in London. Lance Carmichael was welcome to conduct his own inquiry if he so wished, but Daniel didn't think he'd ever find the culprit.

Daniel held out his hand, and Flora grasped it, their attention focusing on the Reverend Talbot as he began to speak.

"Dearly beloved, we are gathered here in the sight of God and in the presence of family and friends to join together Daniel and Florence in holy matrimony."

Daniel barely heard the rest. All he saw was Flora's joyous smile as she said, "I do."

The End

Printed in Great Britain
by Amazon